THE
RELUCTANT
GOVERNESS

Author :   *Roger Kendall*

CONTENTS

CHAPTER 1

The youth climbing up the hill was oblivious to the two girls sitting on their horses under the spreading branches of the old Oak. The gnarled ancient tree had been a sapling when the land had become part of the family estate. Dappled sunlight played on the grass.

Hannah leaned forward along her mounts neck. 'Who's the boy?'

'James Thompson, son of the new steward, miss,' said Tom the groom.

'What do you mean new steward?'

'We'd best get Jacks up here with his ferrets before yer break your horses' legs,' he said head down, pushing some stones into a rabbit hole with his foot.

'Tom, why is there a new steward?'

'Don't you know?'

'Know what?' said Anne the younger sister, edging her pony closer.

'The estate's being seized by your father's creditors.'

'Don't be ridiculous, how can it be?' said Anne.

'Is this really true Tom?' said Hannah.

'Yes mam, we are all very sorry.'

'It isn't true, and he shouldn't be here. Father wouldn't let it happen. It's just gossip,' said Anne, tossing her head.

'Oh Anne, I'm sure it's only some misunderstanding,' said Hannah who always thought the best of everyone. The boy,

1

seeing them for the first time, smiled and gave a little wave.

'Impertinence,' said Anne, jerking her mounts head up and kicking its flanks. It broke into a canter.

'Careful,' cried Hannah, as she gently tapped a heel against her pony's ribs. Young Thompson turned and watched. The younger girl, her bonnet flapping around her neck exposing rebellious copper locks that danced in the sunlight, sat straight backed on her side saddle. She was at one with her mare but, while pretty with a small up turned nose and a scattering of freckles, it was Hannah, with golden curls beneath a wide feathered hat, that held his gaze. His expression softened. Neither girl looked back for Hannah rarely noticed the admiring glances that followed her.

When Anne clattered over the cobbles of the stable yard, the light stone walls of the great house beyond reflected the morning sunlight. The stables were busy. Men she didn't know, wandered around with pencil and notebook. She sat waiting for a groom to take her pony but as none emerged, she slid off, and tied its reins to the nearest ring. Glancing back at Hannah, still some way off with their groom running along behind, she walked around to the front of the house. Two waggons stood on the shingled drive, a place for fine carriages, not old carts. The front door stood ajar. Inside three men were trying to manoeuvre a pianoforte down the stairs.

'Simpson, what's going on?' The butler turned and bowed. He appeared hesitant, older.

'You'd best see your mother, Miss Anne.'

'Where is she?'

'In her sitting room.'

'At this time?' said Anne, glancing up at the great hall clock which revealed that it was near eleven. Her ladyship was normally in the south facing drawing room by this time, not still in her bedroom suite. Anne ran up the stairs, a behaviour always frowned on by her mother but equally ignored by Anne. A passing maid coming down looked away, but Anne glimpsed red-rimmed eyes. She burst into the room and stopped. Her mother sat at her desk toying with a silver pen. It was a fine room, a Gainsborough landscape, the best of several good oils and the view over the park a delight on a sunny day. A view Anne had known all her life.

'Mother what's happening?' Lady Osebury turned very slowly and regarded her second daughter. Annoyance, impatience but also pity appeared in her steady stare. Her normal mature beauty was strained, cheeks hollow. Anne was used to censure but never pity.

'I'm sorry Anne. I never expected it,' she said, looking down at the pen which she continued to twist.

'But what's going on?'

'The furnishings are being sold. Everything.'

'Why?'

'Oh, Anne it's the will, your uncle's will.'

Admiral Tellinworth was looked down on by her parents for his disreputable lifestyle but in the few times Anne had met him she had rather liked the roguish old seafarer.

'Oh no, has he died then?'

'Yes, nasty man. Cut your father out altogether. Wills cause so much unhappiness.'

'Mother! Poor old Admiral T and all you worry about is his money.'

'You'll see, what it means soon enough.'

'But father has his own money, hasn't he?'

'Which he speculated. Without the estates we are in trouble and every tradesman for a hundred miles knows it.'

'The house in Hampshire?'

'No dear, we can't go there. It's not ours.'

'The London house?'

'Rented, which we can't keep on.'

'What is going to happen then?'

'There's a castle in Cork.'

'Ireland!'

'But we will probably go and stay with your uncle, a Mr Rawlins in Herefordshire. He has a fine old house they say. We can use the East wing.'

'Who's Mr Rawlins?'

'I think he's your father's second cousin on his mother's side.'

'What share it, like some poor relation?'

'But that's what we are,' sighed Lady Osebury, 'That's what we are. Oh Anne, we must be very brave and – I think you will have to break it to your sisters. I can't, I just can't. Oh, I had such hopes of the London season. Hannah is so lovely but beauty with no money -.' She sniffed.

The glimpses in the misty rain of what looked a fine grey house through the undergrowth, had Anne leaning forward. The stumps of great oak trees long sold, edged the pot-holed drive. A few sheep moved out of their way. A drip from the canvas top fell on her neck. She shivered and shook her head.

'Why didn't we come in the new carriage?' she asked, but no one answered. 'There's no one waiting, and look the windows are like eyes, staring out of a skull on a gibbet.'

'Anne! How can you speak like that?' said her Ladyship, glancing at her husband who sat rigid as if frozen in anxiety.

'It does look very odd,' said Hannah, 'but you can't expect

the servants to be waiting in the rain.'

'Servants have umbrellas.'

'Do you think it's haunted?' said Grace the youngest sister, standing and squeezing past Anne. Fair hair, and fair skinned, her blue eyes wide with the excitement of a child of ten, she leaned out. 'It's as big as Longleat.'

'Sit down, Grace,' said her mother.

'I'm sure it's very nice inside,' said Hannah.

'No Hannah, even you won't find it very pleasant without glass in the windows,' said Anne, glancing at her mother. What were her parents thinking of, bringing them to a place like this? For a moment she wondered what her mother was feeling, how the loss of affluence had affected her, but the empathy was fleeting. Anne was only seventeen.

'It's only some of them and only on one wing,' said Hannah, straightening her bonnet.

'And the other wing has half the roof tiles missing,' said Anne.

'But you will soon get workmen in won't you father?' said Hannah, turning to Sir George, who remained staring ahead and saying nothing as the carriage rolled to a stop. The driver, straightening his back, limped round to open the carriage door. Jane, her ladyship's personal maid, who had been travelling on the box with the driver, followed to stand shivering beside him, her cloak dripping onto the weed clogged shingle.

Instead of letting their parents lead the way, the girls tumbled out. Anne and Grace scurrying up the marble steps. Although worn, with weeds in every crevice, they maintained a faded elegance as they curved around to a single wide door. Grace who had won the race, stopped, but Anne pushed past and tugged a rusty bellpull. They looked at each other. Dusk was beginning to fall but there was no glint of candlelight or footsteps. Anne turned the brass handle, green with age, and pushed. By using all her slender weight, the door, creaking its reluctance began to move. Gaining momentum, it crashed against the wall. The sound echoed around a marbled hallway as they stepped inside.

'What's all the noise,' said an old man emerging from the gloom sporting silver side whiskers, a silk scarf and thick jacket. 'Oh, you're here, are you?'

'Will you send someone down for the luggage,' said Anne.

'And whom be someone?' said the man.

'One of the servants.'

'Send who you please,' he replied swinging his arm around in a wide gesture to the empty hall. It was the right sort of hall for a line of servants, for great statues and suits of armour, but there was nothing, no one. It was completely bare except for the man with his twisted smile. 'Reckon your driver will manage.'

'Our rooms then?' said Anne, turning to her parents who had entered. 'There is no servant here to greet us, except this man here.'

'And what is your name my man?' said Lady Osebury.

'Peter Rawlins, your ladyship and welcome to my home.' He gave a slight bow, the twist of his mouth even more pronounced. 'Mrs Perkins is in the kitchen. Be a drop of soup and bread and meats after your journey in the dining room, when you're ready. Rooms on the second floor, right at the top, and keep going right,' he said pointing up the stairs. He started to shuffle away.

'Really,' exclaimed Lady Osebury to herself.

'Eh, what about the horses?' said her husband as if finally

awakening.

'There's plenty of stabling but the carriage needs to stay out till the morrow. Hinge broken on the door. No doubt Higgs can get it done in the daylight,' shouted their host over his shoulder as he made his way to the warmth of the kitchen.

'What shall I do ma'am?' said Jane. She stood swinging a large hat box but there was no reply. Her mistress stood rigid, her eyes travelling up the great stairs, the lighter squares where pictures had once hung, the cobwebs on the distant ceiling.

'We'd better find our rooms,' said Hannah, 'then Jane can help mother change.'

'What change for dinner! I don't think it's expected. We aren't going to stay here for long are we father?' said Anne.

'No, but I need a drink,' he muttered as he started across the hall in the direction of their host.

'Come on,' said Grace running up the stairs, her steps echoing off the bare walls. With a general sigh the others followed.

In the corridor a thread-bare runner and a few plaster statues on stands and side tables gave a suggestion of furnishing. Portraits, mostly dark with age, stared down at them as if annoyed at the invasion of their privacy.

'Right at the end,' Anne repeated, 'We should have brought a candle.' They turned down another corridor with a line of panelled doors to either side. The first, opened into a large room with a four poster and dark furniture. A tapestry hung on one wall but was so old, that, what must have once been a colourful scene, was now little more than brown sackcloth.

'Too dingy, it'd better be fathers,' said Anne and they went on to the next door. There were five rooms in all but on only three, had the dust sheets been removed. The shutters and glass were broken in the fourth and a pigeon flew out as the remains of a curtain fluttering in the wind. A cold damp smell of mould. The one at the end was locked, with a draught flowing through the keyhole and underneath. She shivered. 'I suppose, Mother better have the blue one and we'll all share the pink one, well I think it's pink. At least we might keep each other warm.' They turned back to it.

'Look Anne the fire's been laid. We just need someone to light it.'

'Perhaps we could do it ourselves, there's a tinderbox here,' said Anne going to the wide fireplace and picking up the box. How many times had one been lit in her presence, but she had never noticed exactly how, even when a servant had been struggling to start it and keep it burning? She took out the tinder, which was oily shavings and nestled them in among the straw under the pile of sticks. She struck the flint against the steel, but it didn't appear to produce any sparks. Again, and again she struck at different angles, until, with her fingers aching from the effort she managed to direct some sparks onto the tinder. It glowed briefly and went out.

'Should I blow on it?' said Grace. Several times they managed to light the tinder and even made some strands of straw glow briefly but each time it went out.

'Bother. We will just have to find a bedpan. We'd better find this Mrs. Perkins,'

'And I'm hungry,' said Grace getting up.

'So am I, but we must tell mother that this is our room. I hope the sheep don't keep us awake.'

In the dining room there was a long table on which stood two candelabras but as they each had only one candle alight, they gave little illumination. The shutters had been closed and there were few chairs. At one end sat Sir George, an empty plate and a dusty bottle before him. He was staring into his glass of red wine.

'It hasn't been laid,' said Anne. Grace however, passed her a plate from a pile on the side table, which sat beside a rolled joint of beef with an only a few slices carved, a loaf of bread and a large wedge of cheese.

'It's a sort of picnic,' said Grace hacking at the cheese. Pieces sprayed onto the oak floorboards.

Looking around as if from guilt at helping herself, Anne tried her hand at cutting a slice of bread. By the time she had hewn out a pile of untidy slices and dug a great slab of butter and chutney from their pots, her elder sister and mother had joined them.

'Nice cheese,' said Grace.

'Don't talk with your mouth full,' said her mother sitting down at the table.

'Why haven't they lit a fire in here?' said Hannah.

'We tried lighting a fire upstairs, but it wouldn't stay lit,' said Grace.

'Where is everyone?' said Anne, but then a door opened, and a large middle-aged woman entered in a bustle of skirts. She carried a blackened pot.

'Evening ma'am, sir, could you put a mat out ducks?' she said, nodding at Grace. They all stared at the woman as she stood swaying with the large container. 'Soup. Oxtail when you're ready but hurry up girl I can't hold this for ever; a mat.' With a glance at her family Grace reached for one of the woven mats that sat in a pile on the main table and brought it across to the side. 'There's bowls and spoons. Just help yourself like.'

No one spoke as she turned and went back to the kitchen.

'We need a warming pan,' said Anne as the door closed behind the cook.

'What a nerve,' exclaimed Lady Osebury.

'Would you like a bowl, mother?' said Grace on tiptoe, peering into the depths of the pot as she stirred it with the heavy ladle that protruded from it. 'It smells appetising.'

'I suppose so, but you better let Anne do it before you spill it everywhere. No Grace.' But it was too late, the big ladle caught on the edge of the pot and splashed hot soup on Grace, the floor and the table. She jumped back licking one hand and rubbing her forehead. 'Ouch, ahh.' Only Anne moved, grabbing her sister's arm, she dragged her in the direction of the kitchen.

'Mrs Perkins,' she shouted as she went through into a corridor. Where was the kitchen? The first door led to a servant's sitting room, the next however was the kitchen. As they pushed open the door, Mr Rawlins looked up from his paper and Mrs Perkins turned from the stove. 'Cold water please,' said Anne staring around.

'Whatever's the matter,' exclaimed the cook.

'Quick, Grace has scalded herself.'

'I've some ointment.' But Anne had seen a pump in the corner and pushing Grace to it, pumped some water into the sink below.

'Put your hand in and wash your forehead,' said Anne pumping away, water splashing up. Mrs Perkins came and hovered, holding a kitchen rag which Anne took and used to wipe away the last vestiges of the sticky soup. 'Does it hurt?'

'Just a little,' said Grace but her watery eyes suggested otherwise.

'Brave girl. Let's have a look. You could have blisters, but it isn't so bad, and it hasn't burnt you through your dress, has it?' said Anne beginning to wipe it down.

'Not with the number of petticoats mother made me wear.'

'We'll have to get them washed. Who does the laundry?' said Anne turning to Mrs Perkins.

'Well, reckon you or your maid could use the cellar. There's a copper and a tub there but it don't get used much, except when we does the spring clean.' Mr Rawlins had stood and closed the door, reminding Anne how warm the large kitchen was compared with the rest of the house. Large logs glowed in a wide fireplace, cum range, with its metal brackets, chains, and pots.

'Exactly how many servants do you have to run your estate,' said Anne turning to Mr Rawlins as he returned to his seat beside the large pine table which dominated the centre of the kitchen and picked up his paper. A small glass of port stood beside a plate with the remains of cheese and biscuits. He put down the paper and looked at her, one hand idly searching for the last elements of cheese. He scooped a morsel and put it in his mouth.

'Well, not sure; there's Martha that comes and does some heavy work, and sometimes she brings a girl from the village. There's Higgs who does the vegetables and odd repairs and the boy who looks after my mare. Four, plus Mrs Perkins.'

'But you can't run a great house like that.'

'Well, we live here quite happily, don't we Mrs Perkins?'

'And eat in the kitchen?'

'Why not, it's the warmest room in the house.' Anne looked from the cook to her employer. Did they really live like this? Employee and employed rubbing together as if equals, camping out in this vast house, not caring as it crumbled around their ears. Anne knew little of the details of maintaining and cleaning a grand property, but she had seen that it was an industry, with a strict hierarchy of management, systems, and exact ways of doing everything that had evolved over centuries.

'You brought a maid and I presume Sir George will keep on his coachman. You can hire more if you wish. There's enough folks in the village that would jump at a position, but they'd be more of a problem than they'd be worth.'

'Our rooms, we need to warm the beds. Can Mrs Perkins bring up a warming pan?'

'You be careful with them beds. There's plenty of embers. Come in when you've finished your supper and I'll fill a pan for you, but don't you singe them sheets,' said Mrs Perkins as her employer turned back to his paper.

'I'm hungry,' whispered Grace.

'Alright,' said Anne with a last rub of the dress. Back in the dining room she found it in silence. An atmosphere as cold as the air. No one asked after Grace's hurt, but she went to Hannah, and they hugged and whispered together. Anne served out two bowls and took them to the table. Looking around, she hesitated. The few chairs were around the wall. She would normally stand and wait for a footman to position her chair and tuck it in behind her. It was strange to pick one up and carry it over. How much had her life changed. What future would there be from this house? 'What neighbours will we have mother? What society is there here in this damp countryside?'

'I'm sure there will be many suitable families,'

'But you don't know?'

'Father will call on all the best people, won't you?' said Hannah.

'It all happened so suddenly. We believe Lord Duncan has a house in the county, although he may be in town now and there's the Fitzwarrens, they must live near here. Mr Rawlins can introduce us,' said Lady Osebury with a glance at her husband. He, realising his glass was empty, began to pour another.

'Mr Rawlins! An eccentric old man hiding in a collapsing ruin with his cook; I don't think so.'

'Anne, don't be rude.'

'And when will a new governess arrive?'

'We're not sure. We may wait a little.' Another glance at her husband, a worrying chew of her lip.

'I'm ten, I don't need a governess. Hannah can teach me,' said Grace taking a large spoonful of soup, some of which added to the stains on her dress.

'You would just do what you want. Hannah can't control you and I still need help with my French.'

'That's not fair. I don't mind teaching Grace.'

'But I will have to be there, or she won't do anything, she'll be off running wild.'

'I won't. Just because Hannah doesn't tell me off.'

'Anne, your drawing things came in your small trunk. You can do some sketching with Grace tomorrow.'

'What go and draw sheep? Father we must have a Governess. Their wages are very little.'

'It might be embarrassing until we've settled in. Just wait Anne, we'll have to talk to Mr Rawlins,' said Lady Osebury.

'But he's no gentleman.' Speaking rather loudly she hadn't heard the door open. The only noise was the scrape of branches against the window and an outflow of breath. She turned, saw the maligned person, gulped and ran out into the hall. She rushed up the stairs, stumbling in the gloom and threw herself onto the bed. Hot tears of shame. Disgust at herself, hatred for her parents, bitterness for not being tall or having Hannah's beauty or temperament, of not being the baby anymore. She slid under the covers, but even fully clothed they felt damp. She shivered. They had been going to warm the beds.

'Bother, there must be a back-stairs but without a candle I'll never find it,' she sighed. Rubbing her eyes, she crept back down the stairs. One lamp had been left alight in the hall, so she tip-toed over to it with her bedside candle in its holder and managed to light it. She realised that she could get to the kitchen without going into the dining room and found Mrs Perkins sitting at the table, a pint glass of ale before her. Her eyes were closed but opened as Anne quietly closed the door.

'Can I have the warming pan?'

'More fuss, I've only just sat down. There's one hanging over there. Plenty of warm embers, but don't use red hot ones.'

'Aren't you going to do it?'

'No, it's easy enough, don't you know nothing?'

Tentatively Anne used a pair of tongs.

'How many?'

'They'll be cold by the time you've done it; half full.' When she felt she had enough, Anne stood up holding the handle with both hands and stepped towards the door.

'You need one of your sisters to hold the candle and open the doors.'

'Can you, please.'

'Why don't you get your sister.'

'I've sort of been sent to bed early.'

'In trouble are you, well, alright then,' she said heaving her bulky frame from the chair. Anne followed her up the stairs after a worried glance at the dining room door. As soon as they reached the bedroom the older woman deposited the candle on the washstand and left. 'Night then and don't singe the sheets.' 'Thank-you Mrs Perkins.' Putting the pan on the hearth she threw back the covers. Running the pan over the bed she wondered at how long and should she put the top covers on while she did it? Why hadn't she been more observant? She'd have to start learning a lot of new skills, but she didn't want to. The bitterness returned. Being waited on, with all the boring, practical part of life being done by others, that was how it should be, how she expected it and how she wanted it. Being looked up to as part of an important family. Quickly, with one hand, she flicked the covers over the pan and ran it backwards and forwards. I suppose I'd better go and do the other beds.

She slid the pan into her mother's bed, but the sheets were so tightly tucked in, she had to let go of the handle to use both hands to tug them out. There was a smell of burning.

'Oh no, I'm in trouble now,' she said snatching it out. 'It's their fault for making me do it.' More carefully she applied the heat and then to her father's bed and then back to her own bedroom to give her bed a second session. Putting the pan on the grate she ran her hands back through the bed. It felt better. She had no desire to return to the kitchen in case Mr Rawlins was there. She heard footsteps along the landing. She wanted to hide but it was Hannah.

'Anne, I've brought you a sandwich. You really mustn't be so rude.'

'Was Mr Rawlins very upset?'

'No but mother was, it was very embarrassing. No one knew where to look. You can't stay up here for ever. Tomorrow you will have to apologise.'

It was a wide bed, but they were not used to sleeping together and while her sisters were soon asleep Anne struggled, trying not to disturb them as she tossed and turned, annoyed at their change of circumstances and her own failings. She awoke to find Hannah up and polishing the mirror.

'Where is Grace,' said Anne, luxuriating in spreading her legs across the bed.

'Outside somewhere.'

'I thought you were going to teach her some history?'

'Which is why she is in the park.'

She looked at the little carriage clock, 'It's nearly nine, we'd better go down.'

They found their mother in the dining room alone. She looked tired.

'How are you mother?' asked Hannah.

'Well enough. Where's Grace?'

'She had breakfast in the kitchen and went outside.'

'You will have to take her in hand, I can't do it anymore. There's coffee and tea.'

'Nothing else hot then,' said Hannah inspecting the remains of yesterday's joint, sliced ham, and a bowl of prunes. 'Is father up?'

'No, he has a bad head.'

'When then, will he call on our neighbours?' said Anne.

'Not today anyway so you need not stay in for callers. It's stopped raining so find Grace and do some drawing. Hannah can help Jane when the rest of the luggage arrives today.' But she was wrong, for when Anne arrived back for lunch, she found two gentlemen of the cloth sitting talking to Hannah and her mother.

'Aah Rector, this is my second daughter, Anne and that was Grace who ran upstairs. Anne this is our rector who has been kind enough to call and Mr Spenliff, his curate.' Anne, her fingers black with ink and pencil, stayed back and did a little bob. She was also aware that her boots and stockings were far from presentable.

'How do you do Miss Anne; I hope you will soon settle in.'

'Thank you, Rector.'

'Our coming was very sudden, so we have not yet had time to meet our neighbours. Sir George isn't feeling well this morning after our long journey,' said Lady Osebury.

'Can you tell us about the county families?' said Hannah.

'There are few of your standing, and several of those are presently in town.'

'But there's the MacDonald's, they have three daughters too, and the Simpsons, they are a large family, and the two older daughters are your age,' said the curate. Too many daughters, thought Anne. The older man was rather stout, with several warts on cheek and nose. A nose which sprouted black hairs to match the great bushes, that were his eyebrows. There was the usual parson's severity, in each formal word, but Anne suspected from the sparkle in his eyes, that back at the rectory, he would probably be laughing at his parishioner's foibles and pretensions.

'Do you have a large parish?' said Lady Osebury.

'In area yes but as it is mainly small farms it's hard for many to come to the main church here. There are several small churches, so my curates and I, are kept busy.'

'You have curates in plural?'

'Well, one other, a young gentleman from Newcastle,

whom half of my congregation cannot understand.'

'And where is your home Mr Spenliff?' said Hannah.

'I'm from Surrey.'

'What made you join the church?'

'Well, my father is the vicar in a small village and the way of life appeared to suit me. I like theology, study, and reflection but I also find the challenge of trying to apply it to the lives of ordinary people very satisfying, although I confess to often failing. My elder brother is in the navy but from his letters it appears a cruel service and now he is back on half pay, his prospects are not so good.'

A pleasant young man decided Anne. With an open, clean-shaven face, black curling hair and a dimple when he smiled, he appeared boyishly handsome. He was small of stature, and his brown face suggested he spent his time striding through the countryside visiting the sick and lonely. Leaning forward he added.

'A career, where your advancement relies on further wars, is not one I relish.'

Hannah smiled her agreement. Anne glanced at their mother, who didn't appear pleased at the young man's charms. Poverty-ridden curates were not welcome in her circle, especially around the beautiful Hannah.

'Mr Rawlins has a family pew, which he does occasionally use. May I presume you will continue to use that pew, or shall I have another one set aside for you?' said the Rector.

'I'm sure the present one will be acceptable,' said Lady Osebury, but her gaze had not left the curate. 'Your father holds the living, I presume, Mr Spenliff?'

'Yes, your ladyship?'

'But would it pass on to yourself?'

'It might happen, but it is only a small parish, and my father is in good health. Fortunately, it has a garden and paddock which helps him make ends meet.'

'Do you have ambition for something a little better?'

'Well one day perhaps but I am happy here at present.'

'Do you have any relatives who might assist you in obtaining a parish in due course?'

'I don't think so.'

'No Bishops in the family?' said Anne.

'I'm afraid not and my father's living is in the gift of Lord Onslow, whom I haven't even met.'

'Not good Mr Spenliff, too many curates and not enough livings,' said Anne.

'True,' he said sadly.

'Well, we have taken your time long enough. It has been a pleasure to welcome you to the parish, Lady Osebury, you and your delightful daughters. I do hope Sir George is soon feeling better.' said the Rector rising.

'Thank you for coming and your kind wishes,' said her ladyship. Hannah and Anne rose, and curtsied, the gentlemen bowed. 'Anne will see you out as we haven't arranged adequate staff yet. We were very surprised to find Mr Rawlins has so few servants.' As they exited the room the younger man turned and flashed an extra smile.

'This way Mr Spenliff,' said Anne but thinking, there's no hope for you there. When she returned to the drawing room, she found her mother and Hannah sitting as she had left them. Both had continued with the sewing on their laps.

'Really Anne your stockings are a disgrace. You will have to find a way to appear respectable in the drawing room.'

'It can't be helped if I am to traipse round the country with

Grace and don't have my own maid. Are we to have some luncheon?'

'They were good sort of gentlemen I suppose but it's a poor part of the country,' said her mother.

'I thought Mr Spenliff was very pleasant,' said Hannah.

'Yes, and he is already in love with you. I see you intend continuing to go through life breaking every poor boy's heart,' said Anne.

'I'm sure he's not.'

'Oh yes he is, but it's a peculiar name and he's as poor as a church mouse.'

'Forget the curates. I begin to despair of this situation,' said her ladyship as Sir George entered. He glanced around.

'There's nothing set out in the dining room. Where are we eating?'

'I have no idea, perhaps you'd better check with the kitchen.'

'Me! The household is your responsibility.'

'There is no household, nor have we seen Mr Rawlins.'

'How is your head, father?' said Hannah.

'You have just missed the local Rector who has paid us a visit,' said her ladyship. 'You need to be available for visiting.'

'That can wait. Have you seen Dickins?'

'Did you see him, Anne?' said Lady Osebury.

'He was cleaning out a stall and complaining that he was a coachman not a "muck-shoveller."'

'You'd better go and find the cook and see what we can eat.'

'Why me? Hannah can go.'

'Just go,' said her mother glancing at Sir George whose face was darkening with rage. Anne saw the look and went.

She found the cook sitting at the table reading a newspaper, a glass of ale before her, just as she had left her the night before. An old woman was on her knees scrubbing the floor.

'You can read, Mrs Perkins?'

'Good enough to see what a mess the fools are making of our country.'

'I must compliment you on your reading but when do servants comment on political matters.'

'And a woman too, is that what you think? The Luddites rove the cities, the cost of bread is rising and wages falling. Why shouldn't a woman understand what's what?'

'I'm not sure my parents would agree but what they would wish for is for some sustenance. A cold table with tea, would probably be acceptable.'

'I suppose they expect to eat in the dining room. I'll plate something up, but you will have to carry it through.'

'Me?'

'Of course, who else?'

'Why doesn't Mr Rawlins have more servants?'

'It is up to him. He cares for nothing except hunting and his books. It'll be rabbit pie again tonight,' she said nodding at two rabbits waiting to be skinned on a butcher-block table as she rose. 'We'll have to have more help; I told the master that last night. Follow me.' They went through to the dairy where the remains of the beef joint and ham from breakfast were on a stone self. The cook handed Anne a stack of platters. 'There you are and when you've taken this through, there's cheese over there and pickles and fresh rolls in the kitchen when you've done.' She left Anne, who watching her leave, sighed and after a glance at the various shelves, put the platters down and put the joint and the few slices of ham remaining onto the top one. When she arrived back at the dining room the others just sat and watched her carry the heavy plate to the table.

'Hannah, you need to come and help and mother, I really think you need to see Mrs Perkins.'

'Yes, see the woman and bring back some bottles of Burgundy,' growled Sir George, leaning his head on his hands, elbows on the table.

'It's Grace that should help,' said Hannah.

'I don't see why it should be me all the time,' said Anne.

'What do I say to the woman? Rawlins is your cousin,' said Lady Osebury.

'Come on Hannah,' said Anne.

'But I need to finish this stocking. I shouldn't be waiting on tables.'

'Hannah, just help Anne.'

'Alright, come on Grace,' said Hannah.

'Quiet! Go, just go, all of you,' shouted Sir George. The three girls quickly left, spending time searching the larders, dairy, and kitchen with the grumbling cook, however eventually a large pot of tea, bread, preserves, and meats were assembled. Anne was careful to take in a bottle of wine first.

They were just finishing lunch when Mrs Perkins entered wiping her hands on her apron. 'There's a wagon outside for you. Told them to take the stuff up the main stairs. Best you see to it.' She picked up a pile of plates. 'I'll leave you girls to bring the rest.'

'Oh, dear me, this is impossible George, we really can't stay here, you must do something.'

'Humph,' he said, then stood up, gripping the second wine bottle by its neck, and went out the door.

'George,' said Lady Osebury, rising to follow, 'You can't just walk away from it. What about the luggage.' A door slammed, further shouts.

'I suppose we'd better clear up. Don't pick at the beef Grace,' said Hannah looking round at the remains. 'How can five of us make such a mess?'

'Just the left-overs. Those rolls were nice,' said Grace.

'What about our baggage. We can clear this up later,' said Anne heading for the hall. They found the wagoner and a tall youth who they recognised as James the steward's son, standing in the hall staring around.

'Our parents are rather occupied,' said Anne, hoping the distant shouting couldn't be heard. 'Can you show me what you've brought, and we can decide where you can put it.'

'Begging your pardon miss but I need to be on the road sharp like. We'll put it here and your servants can store it how you like.'

'There's no hurry Bert,' said James. 'Where's the other sister?' He blushed as Hannah arrived in the hall.

'There's a slight lack of servants here,' said Anne. 'So, if you could carry some of it up, it would help. Hannah would be pleased to have all her dresses and bonnets up-stairs, wouldn't you?'

'Anne,' hissed Hannah.

'Of course,' mumbled James but he was still blushing, head down.

'It's not my job,' grumbled the wagoner but the heavy trunks were soon bought in. Dickens joined them from the stables.

'The little pianoforte can stay here with those boxes of books,' said Anne.

'I don't know why we brought it as it doesn't hold its tune, we should have kept the new one. This trunk is mine,' said Hannah. 'Would someone be kind enough to carry it upstairs?' James moved quickly and grabbed it. He struggled under the weight while Hannah swished by and up the stairs ahead of him.

'This is mine. Dickens would you be so kind. I'm in the same room as Hannah. And this,' said Anne, to the carter is one of mothers. If you like to follow me, I'll show you where it should go.' When James returned to the bedroom with a second box, Anne was unwrapping her art folder. She was already thinking of what she could hang on a bare wall.

'Whose are these,' said James stepping to the bed and picking up an oil painting of a foxhound. 'It's very good.'

'Thankyou.'

'What! you painted them?'

'Of course.'

'But they are nearly as good as I could do,' he said turning them over and intently looking at each one.

'Why shouldn't they be. Are you such an artist?'

'I intend to be somehow. But you're only a girl.'

'You presumptuous boy, I'll wager yours's aren't so wonderful.'

'Well, they are. I like this drawing of the old man; however, most girls just paint flowers and things.'

'I've plenty of those but I drew most of the servants at the house. I could have drawn you if we'd stayed, although I'm not sure if I could have caught your insolence quite right.' A shout from the hall.

'I'd better go but if you ever come back, I'll draw you and your sister, and we'll see who's best.'

'What are you doing with that one?' said Anne as she noticed a piece of paper was tucked under his jacket.

'Nothing, just wanted to show it to the carter.'

'You little thief. That's Hannah isn't it?' she said taking the drawing of her sister from him as he stood shame faced.

'It's only a little sketch.' There was another louder shout and the outside door slammed. 'Can't I keep it?'

'No and I hope you have to run after the wagon all the way to Hereford.' Reluctantly he turned and left.

'You could have given it to him Anne, you've plenty more of me,' said Hannah who had been emptying her trunk in the other corner of the room.

'What give a servant a picture of you? That would not be seemly.'

With the wagon having been fully unloaded, several portraits, boxes of books, a gun cupboard and various odd boxes remained in the hall. Everything else was in their rooms. The girls spent the rest of the afternoon emptying trunks, rediscovering old dresses, dolls, and samplers.

'When will it be dinner time,' said Grace, as she repositioned one of her many dolls on the dressing table.

'Soon but we have forgotten to clear the lunch things. We will be in trouble.' said Hannah.

'Well, we haven't. Someone else would have done it by now,' said Anne.

'Anne, I think you ought to go and check now. I need to let out this dress slightly. I can't see we are going to receive any new ones for a while.'

'But there must be money for a dress, my grey one is fit only for the garden and why should I go?'

'But at least it fits, my muslin is tight.'

'Yes, you're getting far too buxom. You will just have to eat less.'

'I suspect the food here is going to be very repetitive so that might be easy.'

'And mine doesn't reach my ankles,' said Grace.

They found the dining room as they had left it. The old table in the autumn dusk appeared depressing with its scattering of crumbs and plates, surrounded by an odd mixture of chairs strewn across the room.

'Anne, I thought you said someone would have cleared up,' said Hannah.

'It appears to be down to us. We'd better go and do battle with the cook.'

In the kitchen there was no Mrs Perkins, just a skinny child of about ten who was stirring a great pot with one hand and licking the fingers of the other. A dirt stained, frightened face, that looked away as she accelerated her mixing.

'Where's the scullery,' said Hannah, but the girl just lowered her eyes to stare into the pot, saying nothing.

'Hannah, I think it's through here,' When they emerged from the scullery, they found Mrs Perkins had returned and was decorating a large pie that she had baked in the bread oven. They breathed in the aroma of baked pastry and rich game. Even Sir George cheered up when he saw the pie. Mr Rawlins joined them briefly but appeared to prefer to eat in the kitchen. Even there he wore a muffler. Anne managed a not very fulsome apology, but he didn't appear offended. In the evening, the girls explored the main floors of the house, finding their way by candlelight. They managed to avoid the various buckets strategically placed to catch the many leaks. They also discovered the library where their father hid. They found him sitting at a desk, with some unfinished correspondence but two wine bottles and a glass appeared to have greater prominence. The library was untidy, but the shelves were full, and the room looked well used and valued. Cautiously they crept in, watching their father, expecting reproof, He just stared morosely at them as they inspected the books. They were all rather serious.

'Not much for you girls, although you might find something Anne,' he said, 'but keep out, and next time knock.'

The following morning, Anne, was engrossed in the painting of some late roses that were climbing up a redundant post in the walled garden when Jane found her.

'You are wanted in the drawing room Miss Anne.'

'Bother. Oh, all right. Do we have visitors?'

'Yes, three ladies.'

'I'll come. Thankyou Jane. I suppose you don't know if I'm to change.'

'Lady Osebury didn't say.' And with a little bob Jane left.

'Grace, I have to go in. See if you can read some more of your book before lunch and can you bring my easel back and make sure you wear your hat?'

With a last glance around the garden, Anne emptied the water from the pot, collected her paints and the nearly complete picture. She was pleased with her work although she was never entirely satisfied. The garden was very pleasant, most of it had run wild, with brambles predominating but there were a few apple trees and cultivated plants that struggled through the choking weeds. One corner however was neatly dug with lines of onions and cabbages still in the ground. Lots of picturesque settings to paint she thought as she left.

In the drawing room, she was introduced to a Mrs Simpson, and her daughters Charlotte, and Emily, as they rose and curtsied. The daughters giggled, appearing to find this particularly amusing. Anne glanced at Hannah; whose good manners prevented even a raised eyebrow.

'Anne has a good eye. She paints wonderfully well, don't you? Perhaps you could show Mrs Simpson what you have been doing this morning,' said her mother.

'Yes of course but it's unfinished,' said Anne retreating to the side table where she had deposited the thick watercolour paper. It was greeted with oohs and ahs, and more giggles.

'I haven't quite caught the drops of dew right. Do you paint?' said Anne. There was a shaking of heads.

'No but Charlotte embroiders very well,' said Mrs Simpson.

'I love the shade of your dress,' said Hannah.

'Yes, and it has the lower waistline. It's the coming fashion,' said Charlotte.

'But the lace isn't very good,' said Emily. 'It's not genuine Belgium lace.'

'I fear we will all have to have new dresses,' said Mrs Simpson.

'Tell us about the other families that we ought to know,' said Hannah.

'Well, there's the MacDonalds but their daughters are very plain,' said Mrs Simpson. There's Mr Edwards the member of Parliament, he's an elderly widower although he's still rides with the hunt and two other bachelor gentlemen, but they are both in their forties, Mr Langley and Sir John Siddley. The two Miss Lulworthes are very gentile but only have £100 each a year to live on and the Jenkins are an old family. Their children are very young, and they appear to have considerable trouble finding good nannies.

'Sometimes the Denfords give a ball,' said Charlotte.

'Yes, Lady and Lord Denford are usually in town but come down for occasional shooting parties and at least once a year they bring more friends and have a ball,' said Mrs Simpson.

'There's the rector and Mr Spenliff,' said Emily with a giggle and a glance at Charlotte.

'No young men, beside the poor curates?' said Anne. Charlotte blushed and joined Emily in a giggle.

'No but Sir George must call on the Denfords when they are here.'

After more pleasantries, the visitors rose and took their leave. Jane saw them out.

'Oh dear,' said Hannah.

'The society here appears very limited however a ball might be an opportunity for Hannah,' said Lady Osebury.

'What silly girls. I cannot imagine their conversation goes beyond, fashion and future husbands,' said Anne.

'Which is the way it should be. Marie Therese was not a good influence. We were advised not to employ a French governess.'

'But Marie Therese was lovely. We really miss her and anyway we often learnt more of the world from Father's books and newspapers.'

'Well, she's back in France and happily married.'

'I know,' sighed Anne, remembering both their times of fun but also the deep discussions. 'I have left a letter out to be sent, will anyone arrange for it to go to the post?'

'Letters are expensive.'

'Mother, are we really that poor?'

'At the moment, however it may get better, but what is heart-breaking is that we will not have anything to settle on you when you marry.' Lady Osebury gave a little sniff.

'Don't we receive something when we are twenty-five?' said Hannah.

'Yes £150 per year and no creditor can touch it but it is nothing.'

'It's more than the Miss Lulworths,' said Anne with a smile.

'Yes, and they are poor spinsters living in a cottage.'

'I'm not sure that would be so unpleasant.'

'Oh Anne, you must marry. It is the only way to any sort of future. Hannah must find a rich man to lift us back into the society we belong, and hopefully one of his friends might accept you.'

'Might accept me!' Anne leapt to her feet. 'Is that what you think of me, a booby prize.'

'I'm sorry but it must be said. You haven't your sisters height, looks or temperament which are difficulties enough but unless you curb your opinions you will be shunned.'

'Anne is really very pretty although she doesn't protect her complexion properly,' said Hannah.

'Just because Father lost his money and you fell out with Admiral Tellinworth.'

'How dare you be so rude Anne?'

'Me! Constantly harping on about Hannah's beauty as if she is some princess, and me the unloved toad. That's not rudeness I suppose?'

'I'm just trying to warn you that without a suitable husband, life is very limited. You are nearly eighteen. You must think of the future.'

'Why should you put such responsibility on Hannah. You will judge all her suitors on their purse and give no thought for Hannah's feelings. Her own happiness shouldn't be mortgaged off for yours.'

'Because God has given her the gifts for just that.'

'What, to gain riches from her looks. That is ungodly.'

'It is not money, it's society, our standing in the community, being someone, being a lady. We need to have our rightful place with superior gentry. Hannah's grace and breeding would be welcome anywhere.'

'We don't seem to have any money, but the Rector and the Simpsons kindly called on us,' said Hannah.

'Yes, but they may be laughing at us behind their closed doors,' said Anne. 'Look at these shabby chairs, and the curtain over there is in danger of coming down completely.' They all looked around. At first glance the room was adequately furnished, with stylish wallpaper but the wall-corners were worn back to plaster in places. There were light squares where pictures had once hung and the curtains were indeed ragged at the bottom, besides threatening to slide off the broken rail. It also lacked homely knick-knacks, comfortable cushions, or any personal items.

'Yes, but it is a stylish room and with a few little touches it could be very elegant,' said her Ladyship.

'But it's income, without it we can do little, yet money isn't a polite subject for conversation.'

'No Anne, it isn't. There are many subjects that you might have discussed with Marie Therese that are not suitable for the drawing room.'

31

'But what is going to happen? Are we to carry on living in this shabby place with no servants and Dickens says the coach is unusable; it needs new traces and a spring. When we visit our neighbours are we supposed to walk? Or is father going to do something?'

'Anne, go to your room, now! You are not to question your father.'

'But -.'

'Go!'

Anne picked up her painting and went back to the garden. There was no sign of Grace so leaving her watercolour on its easel she went in search of her. The undulating fields were all down to grass and sheep, except for the milk cow that Mr Rawlins kept for home use. An occasional oak not lost to the demand for timber during the Napoleonic wars still stood. It was a wide panoramic landscape with the Welsh mountains in the distance. She breathed in the crisp moist air knowing she ought to be appreciating the beauty of the scene, but it wasn't adequate to overcome the bitterness of rejection. She continued through a gate and across another field where she shouted for her sister. In the distance she heard the trumpet of the hunt and the baying of hounds. She felt as trapped as a fox that had been forced to earth. How could they spend a whole winter in the dreary house and empty countryside? She wanted elegance, bright chandeliers reflecting the sparkle of jewels and witty companions dressed in silks and lace.

Where was the girl? 'I suppose she'll come when she's hungry,' she muttered to herself. Crossing another field back to the house she heard a cry and tracing its direction she found a tall sycamore and looking up into the higher branches saw her sister waving.

'Grace! Be careful. Can you get down?'

'Of course, but it's a wonderful view,' was the reply, as in a flurry of petticoats Grace descended. They collected the painting equipment and books and found Hannah in the dining room still sewing.

'What's happening about lunch?' said Anne.

'I'm not sure. Mother is discussing something with father,' said Hannah. Was there distant shouting? Anne decided she didn't want to hear.

'Why aren't you doing something?'

'Me, what should I do?' said Hannah.

'See Mrs Perkins and set out lunch.'

'But you're better at that than me.'

'Exactly so it's about time you learnt. When I'm not here you will have to do it.'

'But Anne there is nowhere else you can go.'

'Perhaps I will go and stay with Marie Therese.'

'Really; mother wouldn't let you.'

'Or become a governess. I have a little money of my own.'

'What money?'

'Just savings from the allowance we used to receive. I didn't spend all mine on ribbons and lace. Enough for a journey to France. Are we going to live all winter in this depressing place counting the cost of every candle?'

'Do you think there will be fresh rolls again,' said Grace.

'Come on let's see.' They had set out the usual fare of cold meat, cheese and conserves, when Lady Osebury joined them.

'Perhaps Anne, you'd better plate up something for your father and take him a bottle of burgundy, but just one.'

'It's always me,' she said, but then she had once been her father's favourite, before Grace had taken her place. She found him slumped in an easy chair, a newspaper on his lap. His bloodshot eyes opened, and he warily watched her. Putting the tray on the side table she picked up an empty bottle but put it down and wondered over to one of the bookcases. She heard the suck of the cork coming from the new bottle and the flow of wine into a glass behind her. She turned, braced her shoulders, and gulped. Her head fuzzy with fear.

'Don't you think you are drinking too much sir?' The end of the sentence rather soft. Sir Osebury stared, leaning forward trying to decipher the hardly audible sounds, the unbelievable question.

'What! How dare you, what do you know? Have you had to deal with swindlers and fools? Get out. Try making your own way and we will see what becomes of you. Out.' He drained his glass and held as if to throw it. She backed out. Returning to the dining room her mother glared at her.

'I should have sent Grace. Have you offended your father again?'

'He'll kill himself with his drinking unless you do something.'

'If you have goaded him with your audacity, you will only make matters worse. You're no help at all.'

'Me, I'm to look after Grace, set out the meals and ignore my father becoming a drunk.'

'You go too far young woman. Where are the genteel manners of your sister? I have never known such rudeness.'

'Well, if I'm not wanted here, I will go to France or take a governess position.'

'You will do neither.'

'But I must, Father has told me to make my own way. What else can I do?'

'You cannot demean yourself in such a role?'

'Why not, Marie Therese's life with us appeared more pleasant than waiting on tables.'

'But a governess, it cannot be countenanced.' Anne turned to the side table and began to serve herself. She didn't feel hungry, but she wasn't going to leave the dining room again unfed. 'Do you hear me you will not lower yourself.' But Anne said nothing.

The stilted conversation at the evening meal did nothing to improve the atmosphere so Hannah was happy to take Grace into the music room and try to improve on her playing, however it wasn't the sort of noise to encourage others to join them. Anne sought the warmth of the kitchen. Mr Rawlins and the cook were playing cribbage.

'May I join you, and could I have a look at your paper Mr Rawlins?'

'Yes, however I have not read it in entirety, as Sir George has been reading it so, please do not take it away.'

'Thank you,' said Anne. On a scrap of paper, she began to write down addresses and forms of expression.

'And what are you looking for Miss Anne?' said Mr Rawlins looking up from his cards.

'I was thinking to advertise for a position as a governess.'

'I'm not sure, that you would find such a role would suit you.'

'Why not? At least I will meet others of my station.'

'But you will not be of their station. It is a lonely position. You are not one with the servants, nor one with your employer's guests.'

'Mr Rawlins, I am sorry I was rude the other evening, and

I hope you will not find me impertinent now, but can you explain why you prefer the companionship of the kitchen to the drawing room.' Mrs Perkins glance was enough to silence her, but she wasn't put off. 'I know nothing of your background.'

'It is not for you to question your kind host who has taken you all in.'

'That's all right, Mrs Perkins. I was brought up here, but my brother was due to inherit the estate from our father and I as the younger son was entered into the navy as a midshipman. From a shielded background at thirteen I was not ready for the bullying and belligerent life of the crowded wardroom on a triple decker. However, I eventually managed to become a lieutenant and was even at the battle of the Nile. My father died from a fall when hunting and the estate passed in good order to my brother, although heavily mortgaged.'

Glancing at a card, he laid one and for a few minutes he concentrated on the game. 'But when my brother drunk himself to death, I resigned my commission and returned to run the estate. I was shocked to find the debts considerable. In desperation I sold off pictures, furniture, in fact anything saleable and even some land. The house will stay up long enough to shelter me for my lifetime. To escape the "dog eat dog," world of advancement in the service, to go out each day with my gun and to chat in the market square with farmers and small landowners is contentment. To see the acreage I have left, properly managed and cared for is enough. It is the land that I value, not the house. Tomorrow we will enjoy venison. Lord Denford's deer often wander in my hills. If I become bored with shooting, there are carp in the big pond and trout in the stream.'

'You do not ride with the hunt?'

'I used to but after my mount refused a hedge and left me

in some brambles with a broken arm, I decided it was time to be sensible.'

'You do not visit your fellow landowners or enjoy the pleasures of drawing room conversation.'

'No, flattery and woman's gossip are not for me, nor can I abide hours dressing, or complicated cravats. Do you know, men are now wearing girdles, just like a woman's corset?'

She laughed. 'Really, then they are just as vain as us ladies.'

Mr Rawlins returned to his cards and Anne to the paper which she continued to read. She was beginning to think that the old man was not so eccentric as she had first thought.

'I saw in your stables that you have a fine mare.'

'She is old now, but she is of excellent stock and as I do not maintain a carriage, I continue to need a good horse.'

'Do the sheep belong to you?'

'No most of the estate I still own is let to small farmers and shepherds.'

'So, you receive rents?'

'For a young woman you have an inquisitive interest in matters that are not the usual concern of your class.'

'My governess was a woman of wide interests. She was from Brittany, but her family fled to England in 1795.'

'They were aristocrats?'

'No, but her father was the trusted steward of one and fled with him. They returned when Napoleon was overthrown in 1815, Marie Therese stayed and only left two months ago, when she married a merchant from Vannes. I think her wider family were apothecaries, and doctors but they all owned a field or two. She was always interested in farming.'

'In answer to your earlier question I do receive rents which cover the mortgage. When I save enough capital, I buy back another field that once was ours.'

'Would it not be a better investment to mend the roof?'

'The house is too big. I have always thought I would end up taking down one wing and selling off the stone.'

'Or you could decorate the main rooms so visitors could be greeted in some style.'

'Perhaps your father could manage that.'

'I'm not sure he's ready. We appear to be very short of money and he's taken it badly.'

'I'm not surprised, I hear he was so seriously taken in, that he then persuaded all his friends to invest their money. Not only did he lose his own, but his friends also lost theirs too. Never have financial dealings with friends, it quickly destroys any relationship. Would your parents allow you to become a governess?'

'Probably not, but I think I will advertise anyway.'

'And if you receive a suitable reply?'

'Then I will have to persuade them,' said Anne with a smile. She'd lived through a few arguments before, and she could do it again. 'If it didn't work out, I could just come home or get another place.'

'But you would need a testimonial for your next position. Servants, governesses, whatever, need recommendation. Without it, people end up in the street. If you left without a good reference, it might be difficult to obtain employment again. Isn't that right Mrs Perkins?'

'Yes, word gets about, and you'll never get another situation. Hunger and the workhouse tis the lot of ordinary folks without a good reference. Different I suppose for you as you could come back here.'

'Really?' sighed Anne, 'that's terrible.'

'Them's that have and them's that don't, tis a world apart.'

'Three months ago, father was bringing people to stay, visitors every day. We had balls and glittering parties. Only Hannah was out and allowed to dance, so Grace and I spent most of our time on the stairs watching but it was still fun. We didn't realise how happy we should have been. Now, you say if I become a governess and don't do what I'm told and couldn't get a reference I'd have trouble getting a second position?'

'Not used to being submissive, are you?' said Mr Rawlins.

'No,' she laughed, 'perhaps I'm not.'

'So, when your family had a party, where was the governess?'

'Sometimes she was with us on the stairs, but she was more often in the party and meeting people.'

'Unusual.'

'If I were to write an advert would someone take it to the post? I have money for the paper and the letter.'

'Best to take it yourself if it's to be a secret. The village is only a mile away.'

'Thankyou Mr Rawlins,' she said rising, the conversation having helped her make up her mind.

'Before you go, I need to talk to you about a singed sheet,' said Mrs Perkins but Anne was out of the door before she had finished.

Back in her bedroom she wandered up and down, moments of indecision fluttered in her heart. The small fire that Jane had lit had reduced to a smoulder. The aroma of coal smoke mingled with the damp smell of mildew. She ought to poke and blow it into life, but she hadn't the energy. In the cold room, her confidence at disobeying her parents began to evaporate.

Taught to honour parents, to ignore the vanity of fine clothes and position had often been the subject of sermons at the many Sunday services she had attended, and it weighed heavily.

Glancing at the fire, she was reminded of all she missed. She pulled a shawl from her trunk and cuddled it around her. She didn't want to work, didn't like the idea at all. To gallop her pony hard, till her legs ached and her back was stiff, was a pleasure, to stride gracefully on a long walk with her sisters was no chore and to dance all night until she was exhausted was fine but to bend down and stoke the fire back to life that was too much like physical effort. And her poor pony that she had taken for granted; how she missed her. How she missed the chance of fine new clothes, of guests and their admiration, of the old mansion, of her paintings. Vanity, all was vanity, but she couldn't become a rustic spinster, she had to go, and no one was going to stop her. She sat down and began to compose her advert and work out the cost.

She awoke at 4am worrying about the enormity of her decision and only went back to sleep after reminding herself that she could always delay in sending it or not send it at all. However, the following afternoon, the three girls walked to the village. Beyond a scattering of cottages, a general grocer, a smithy and a haberdasher, there was little else.

'We'd better enquire at the haberdasher,' said Hannah. As they looked over a poor stock of cloth, ribbons, buttons and knick-knacks, Anne turned to the old woman who stood anxiously watching.

'Excuse me but we were wondering how to send a letter. Is there a post office?'

'No madam but Mr Maddocks the grocer, he sends any post

down to Pontrilas in the wagon that comes up once a week, and the post collect it from there.'

At the grocers they had to step around the buckets, balls of rope, and implements to reach the counter where a bowing, bobbing, smiling sort of man insisted on being of service. After considerable discussions over means of travel, safety of the coins in the packet and costs, Anne paid over the agreed amount for the two items. Grace bought a piece of cord to make a skipping rope and they began to walk home. They hadn't left the hamlet before Hannah turned to Anne,

'Who was the packet for?'

'It was just a letter.'

'But it had money in it.' Anne didn't reply as she feared Grace hearing and letting out any secret.

'I'll tell you when we are home,' said Anne eventually as she began to walk faster. Hannah although taller struggled to keep up. As Grace was trying to skip her way home, she was gradually left behind. After a quick glance behind at her younger sister, Anne whispered.

'Please don't tell mother but the money was to pay for an advertisement; for a governess position.'

'What! Anne, you can't, father wouldn't let you,' said Hannah stopping abruptly. The burble of the stream running beside the lane masked her words.

'Why not, there doesn't seem to be much happening here. One ball a year, no London season. Let's keep walking.'

'But you can't leave me on my own.'

'I know, that is something I will regret and have on my conscience. I'm sorry Hannah and I will miss you too, but it will be an adventure.' They carried on walking, Anne with head down.

'You can handle Grace better than I.'

'You will just have to be stricter.'

'A governess situation will be very wearing. And you will have to take instruction, something you might find difficult.'

'Of course, and I might only last a week, but I might meet some rich young duke.'

'You always said you weren't worried about marriage.'

'I wasn't until we came here. I think as mother says, "Without a suitable husband, life is very limited." Here I realise how restricted it can be without the position a husband gives you, especially a wealthy one.'

'It's not like you to be so materialistic.

'I know. If I were a man I could go to Paris and study great paintings and might become a famous painter but as women, our lives are so restricted.'

'Having children isn't limiting, it must be wonderful.'

'Of course, with a good man in comfortable surroundings, but first you have to find that gentleman. The fishing pool around here is very small.'

'So where is my rich duke?'

'I'll leave you Mr Spenliff.'

'Huh, that would give mother a heart attack, but he is very nice. It's a pity we can't just marry for love.'

'We can and must. The trick is to only fall in love with someone rich.'

'But don't the gentlemen have the same wish?'

'I think Hannah you have hit the nail on the head. However, you are enchanting enough to have an advantage over me. When a young man of suitable fortune meets you, their own mercenary disadvantage is immediately forgotten.'

Back at the house life slipped into a routine. Anne's par-

42

ents arguing, Sir George retreating to the library whenever possible, to drink, not read. Grace enjoying the countryside and discovering a badger sett and fishing with Mr Rawlins. Anne practiced her teaching skills on her sister, painting and escaping to the kitchen to check for her advert, which ten days later she had the nervous pleasure of reading. It was a further week before her father called her in from the garden.

'Anne what is this, I have just paid for an express post. It is not from France so who is writing to you?' Anne reached for the letter, but he held it higher.

'I don't know sir until I have opened it.' He handed it to her and stood waiting, expectant.

'Well?'

'It's from a Mrs Percival.'

'We know no Percivals.'

'No sir but she wishes to offer me the position of governess, at £35 per year.'

'What! How did you come by such a suggestion?'

'She appears to be an elegant lady by her hand and the address given sounds very fine.'

'You have avoided my question young lady.' Anne raised her gaze until she was staring into her father's bloodshot eyes.

'Yes sir. You told me I would have to make my own way, so I advertised for a position.'

'Without permission. How dare you? No daughter of mine would sink so low.'

'What am I to do. There is no society here. I have received no allowance for three months, I need paints, paper and canvas and a new day dress yet mother can give me nothing. I'm told, even in Hereford the tradesmen will give us no credit. As soon as our finances are suitable, I can return, but until then I must earn my own living.'

'That's ridiculous, your mother will not allow it and I can find money for some paper.'

'I must answer Mrs Percival and we are so far from the post that a letter takes ages.'

'You can answer in the negative.'

'When I do go, Dickson would have to take me, perhaps as far as Hereford before I can catch the post coach.'

'You are being very presumptive, nor could you travel alone on a public coach.'

'Mrs Percival says she will send a maid to meet me in Shrewsbury.'

'Let me read her letter.' Hesitatingly, she handed it over. Could she remember the address if she were to defy her parents? 'Arleston Manor does have a good ring to it. Shropshire is not so far, perhaps Mr Rawlins may know this part of the family. The Percival's used to rule the English borders keeping the marauding Scots at bay. Not as it matters as your mother will not allow you to go.' Anne held out her hand for the letter. For a long moment he glared at his daughter as she stood statuesque, resolute.

'You aren't going and if you did you would be back in five minutes. You are not used to real work, and you'd soon fall out with the family.' He continued to hold the letter before eventually placed the offending missive in her hand.

'Thankyou father,' said Anne, turning on her heel. Should she wait for her father to discuss it with her mother or go straight to her? Much as she feared what her mother might say, she breathed in, pulled herself up and strode into the drawing room. Her mother and Hannah were sewing.

'We may have visitors today. I think you would be better

staying here and improving your embroidering rather than be-ing with Grace,' said her mother, before Anne could speak.

'We are studying the Tudors and for once I have her in-terest. I don't want to lose her attention while I have it, but I do have something serious to discuss with you now. I have received a letter from a Mrs Percival, a gracious lady living in Shropshire who has offered me a position as governess. I wish to take it without delay.'

'Governess!' said Lady Osebury sitting up sharply.'

'It will give me an opportunity to mix again in society. I will only be doing what I do here but with a small income and a chance to meet people,' continued Anne quickly.

'It is not seemly. I cannot tolerate it. How did you come by such an offer?'

'I advertised in the Post.' Anne glanced at Hannah who appeared as shocked as her parent. Anne stared at her sister, willing her support.

'Without permission, in secret, you wicked girl. Do you not know you are descended from two great families? To degrade us by putting an announcement in a paper, a public newspaper. It cannot be countenanced.'

'But what can I do? I need to find a role befitting my fami-ly,' said Anne beginning to pace up and down the room.

'It is not fitting. Sitting in the kitchen looking at Mr Raw-lins's newspaper has put ridiculous ideas in your head and to surreptitiously contact a newspaper - - -.'

'Hannah knew and until I had an offer of somewhere re-spectable it was hypothetical anyway.'

'You knew?' said Lady Osebury, turning her ire on Hannah. For a moment Anne felt the guilt of telling on Hannah, yet Anne knew that somehow, she had to force her sister's hand.

'Well, yes and we thought you might not approve.'

'Not approve, you are correct there. So, you conspired together?'

'No mother that is unfair. We have both felt our position difficult and while I remain unsure of Anne becoming a governess, I think it not unreasonable and worthy of consideration. If it isn't successful, no harm is done.'

Anne wanted to reach across and embrace her sister. Never had she loved her more.

'Your own position would be immediately undermined if it was known. Your own chances of a good marriage.'

'And who are these rich young men, who will be turned away? Where are they?'

'Oh Hannah, I know.'

'Where are our friends? Who can we go and stay with?'

'I really don't know. I have written to many of them, but replies are few and invites none. I had hoped you could stay with the Jenkins in town or Lord Howle but none of them have offered.'

'Mother, I'm afraid they will not have forgiven father for his enthusiastic recommendation of the investment company; so many people lost money,' said Anne walking to stand behind Hannah.

'I fear you are right, but I still hope to obtain an invite for you,' said Mrs Lady Osebury, with a long sigh.

'In the meantime, let me make my own way. If matters improve, I can return or join Hannah.'

'You are too young, and we need you here.'

'You can manage, and it will do me good to widen my acquaintances, rather than vegetate here.'

'I'm sorry, it just cannot be.'

'Why not, you must realise I have to do something. Don't we have to accept our situation, to try to start again?'

'But your wonderful paintings. Aren't you happy here, looking after Grace, free to paint, to read?'

'Yes I am, but as you said, without a good husband, life is very limited. I think I would like the adventure of travelling to a new home, to meet new people and to discover for myself what it is like to earn my own living.'

'It would be much harder than you think but it is not to be so. Just forget the idea.'

'I will let you think on it, mother. I need to go, please read Mrs Percival's letter. I am sure it will be a suitable position,' said Anne passing it over. He mother took it as if it were some unclean rag found in a ditch. 'I'm in the garden with Grace and a book, acting as governess!'

CHAPTER 2

At breakfast the following day, nothing was said. No conversation, no warm smiles from her Ladyship. Hannah and Grace quickly left the dining room.

'Mother I have to write today as letters take so long. It was my only reply.'

'I don't like it and your father will definitely not allow it.'

'But I have to. You know I must try to enlarge my acquaintances. When father's affairs have settled, I can return. In the meantime, my upkeep will be at another's expense, I can widen my experience, see the latest fashions and meet some fine people.'

'You would never last. Your character isn't suitable. You'll be back in a week.'

'Hardly, from Shropshire. I'll reply but Mrs Percival may have already filled the post by the time it reaches her.'

'Sir George won't let you. I'm warning you Anne.'

Back in the bedroom Anne started writing, hoping that the slowness of the post wouldn't upset the offer. She realised that she couldn't complete the letter however until she had made further enquiries of the post coach times from the village shop. She toyed with her pen a simple quill. Could she really defy her parents? This wasn't about deportment or what she chose to draw or how she addressed the servants, this was about leaving home. No well-bred daughter went against her families wishes but in the mildewed house, with the strange

Mr Rawlins and his casual attitude to those of the lower orders everything had changed. The bitterness in her heart at their fall from status and the challenge to make her own way back to society were both very strong. As for disobeying her father who had caused their downfall, she felt no guilt.

The letter was completed the following morning while leaning on a barrel, with her little bottle of ink and a pen. Was it a lie, to say our coachman will bring me to Hereford, when they would just be riding horses?

Ten days later a letter arrived confirming the position. Avoiding her parents, she made arrangements about travel with Dickens and Rawlins and beyond dark looks, her family made no attempt to stop her. When the time came to leave the next morning, neither parent had yet given permission, or had offered any blessing. They stood on the weed dominated drive, with the maid and cook, watching Dickens strap a large trunk either side of one of the coach horses. Anne sat on the other, for Dickens would ride Mr Rawlins borrowed hunter. Anne glanced at her parents, fearful of further argument yet knowing it was too late. She had won but she wanted to leave on a conciliatory note. Perhaps forcing her will on them and then expecting kind words was asking too much.

'Have you enough money for the inn,' said Lady Osebury at last.

'Yes, father has given me some,' Although not as much as she had hoped.

'Come back if you hate it,' said Hannah.

'She will, in about a week. She's no idea,' said Sir George shaking his head and walking back up the steps to join Mr Rawlins.

'Goodbye and good luck,' shouted Mr Rawlins followed by a general muttering of good wishes. Hannah stepped forward, to touch Anne's knee.

'You must write I'll be lost without you and Mother will miss you.' They both looked at her Ladyship who stood, arms folded, stern and sombre.

'Well, you'd better start writing today as I won't get it for a week.'

Dickens mounted up and gave a jerk to the leading rein of the packhorse.

They were saddle sore by the time they trotted into the county town and Anne was happy to eat a light supper in her room at the inn and sleep in the strange bed. She had a purse full of pennies for the porters in the morning, but it needed a larger coin for the coachman to accept the trunks. Even then they muttered at every change of coach. The excitement of travel with ordinary people, the effort to keep her skirts and petticoats clean, and her attempts to avoid the physical contact of fellow passengers as the coach rolled and bounced along the poorly maintained roads left her even more exhausted. A lady should sit straight, alert, head high but she found herself nodding. Determined to stay upright and awake she was mortified when she was jerked out of her sleep to find she had dozed off, with her head resting on the shoulder of the overweight parson beside her. At the Shrewsbury inn, she couldn't sleep and awoke late. She was still eating her breakfast of ham, bread roll and drinking chocolate when a maid entered.

'There's a man for you madam.' A big man holding a battered top hat, his head bent to avoid the low beams followed the maid in. He nodded nervously to her.

'Excuse me ma'am but I'm from Mrs Percival. When you're ready.'

'And your name?'

'Bert Miss. You be young to be a governess.'

'You girl, can you show this man where my trunks are while I finish my breakfast,' said Anne. The man followed the maid upstairs as Anne sipped the hot sweet drink.

'I wasn't told like, that you'd got luggage,' he said, coming back into the dining room, leaning back to balance the weight. 'I only brought the governess cart seeing how you might like to see it.'

'What a little tub-like gig?'

'Yes ma'am.'

'That's unfortunate, isn't it? she said. After finishing her drink and handing a coin to the maid, she followed the man out to the gig. With two sideways facing seats, designed for one lady and small children she marvelled at the servant's choice. A small black horse, head down, waited patiently.

'Did Mrs Percival tell you to bring it?'

'The housekeeper just said use a gig.'

'Well, I can drive it. The trunks can, I suppose, be on the floor on top of each other, and if you sit on the rear edge of the floor holding the door open with your legs hanging out, we will all get in.'

'You don't want me to drive?'

'No there wouldn't be room would there. Please collect the other trunk.'

'Do you know the way?'

'No but you can tell me can't you,' said Anne her patience running low.

It was a two-hour journey through pleasant, farming countryside. Little was said at first, but Anne shifting her legs that were cramped in the small space, decided she shouldn't waste the opportunity. Initially, she just asked about the large houses and farms they passed, then.

'Well Bert, what is Arleston Manor like?

'Very grand.'

'How many servants?'

'I don't rightly know. There's fifteen of us in the grounds.'

'So, you are a gardener Bert, not a coachman?'

'Yes, the mistress is visiting today and using the big coach.'

'What about the children?'

'Well now,' he said turning his head round and peering past a trunk with a look of concern, 'They cause us a mite of work sometimes.'

'In the garden?'

'Yes, running amok through the vegetables and leaving the hot house door open.'

'Please tell me about them, I don't even know how many charges I will have, or their ages.'

'Well, I suppose you be looking after the three boys and the little girl. I know she's five and the boys are older. I don't reckon you be teaching the Miss Percivals, do you?'

'I don't know; how old are they?'

'Miss Abigail is sixteen and Miss Eleanor be about two years more.'

Three boys would be difficult enough, without older girls the same age as herself. Perhaps she could be friends with the older girls. The companionship with well-bred young ladies of her own age would be excellent. She hadn't much experience of boys and hadn't thought it likely to have to teach them. Didn't boys normally get sent away to school?

When they reached the estate and its village, Bert began to point out who lived where and what they did. The few people in the street turned and stared at Bert sitting with his long legs hanging out of the back of the gig, his feet brushing the ground. They turned into a long curving drive and the horse suddenly sped up at the hope of release from its burden. As they neared the house with its grand façade Anne reined in the horse and turned to Bert.

'Where should I stop?'

'You'd best go round the back to the tradesman's entrance.'

'Wouldn't it be easier to take the trunks up the main staircase? Do you know which will be my rooms?'

'I dunno, Mrs Carpenter the housekeeper will show you. I've never been up the stairs. You'd best move over,' he said as a large coach, its black paintwork and brass lamps gleaming, clattered out of the attached stable yard and pulled up in front of the main entrance. Two magnificent black stallions, complete with feathered head gear, stopped, to stand with nervous anticipation. Healthy creatures, full of untapped energy, rattling their traces, ready for action. The driver stayed in position but a second coachman who had been standing on the boot at the rear, leapt down and ran up the marble steps.

The door was opened by a footman who stood to one side as a large lady in layers of satin followed by a much younger version sailed out. The coachman by the entrance, ran back down to hold the carriage door open. As Mrs Percival descended, she spied the little governess cart and Anne trying to extract her feet from where they had been squashed into the few square inches of space left by her trunks.

'Bert, can you take my trunk in?' said Anne. With a nervous glance at his employer, he dragged one out, and began to totter towards the steps, keeping to the furthest edge from Mrs Percival.

'Good afternoon, Mrs Percival I presume,' said Anne climbing over the other one, Anne Osebury at your service.' She gave a little curtsey when she reached the ground and endeavoured to straighten her bonnet.

'You appear to have a great deal of luggage,' said Mrs Percival coming closer.

'Just a few dresses, paintings, books and things.'

'Mm, well they ought to have gone up the back stairs. See Mrs Carpenter, who will show you where you will reside and introduce you to your charges. If you come to the drawing room before dinner, we will discuss your duties, but I expect you to have met the children and be settled in by then.' She turned and stepped towards her carriage. The coach footman bowed as she ascended, followed by her daughter who didn't look at Anne. They sat back, the door was closed, a gloved hand waved, and the great coach clattered out, the second coachman neatly leaping on to the rear step.

'Thank you for your kind welcome,' muttered Anne. In the hall there was nobody but the footman, who opened the door.

'Where do I find Mrs Carpenter or perhaps the Butler?'

'I don't know but Agnes will take you to her,' A young woman, with slightly dishevelled hair escaping from under her cap entered the hall. 'Agnes this lady needs to see the housekeeper.'

'Best follow me ma'am, I think she's in her sitting room.' Bert came in and deposited the second trunk inside the door but quickly left. They found the housekeeper, sitting at her desk, writing up accounts from a pile of bills. The room was close to the kitchen from where the aroma of roasted meats assailed their senses. Looking up for a moment, the middle aged, rather gaunt woman stared, her face screwing up in annoyance at the disturbance. A small fire was the only thing of cheer in the room. Recognition brought an imperceptible smile although perhaps one tinged with pity.

'Are you the new governess?'

'Yes, I am, and Mrs Percival said you would be kind enough to show me to my rooms.'

'Well, you are very young, I hope you can cope, the lack of governesses has been troublesome. I'd better show you to the nursery,' she said with sigh. Leading up a back staircase they ascended towards the third floor.

'My trunks have been left in the hall, could you have them sent up,' said Anne as she followed.

'If you cannot collect them yourself, but they need to come up these stairs.'

'As you wish, but I would like to change after a bath, so hot water too.'

'A bath!'

'Of course, travel can be very wearying and leaves one feeling rather dirty.'

'You expect me to send maids up to your room with a bath and jugs of hot water in the middle of the day?'

'A cup of tea or coffee would be appreciated too.'

'My orders were to introduce you to the children without delay. Nothing about baths.'

'I'm sure good manners and hospitality would make such orders unnecessary. You cannot expect me to be introduced to my charges with the dust of the road still on my brow.'

'Oh alright, I'll see what can be done; you want to go to your room first?'

'Yes please.' It was an attic room, but of reasonable size with its own sitting room. The furniture was sparse and the bed soft, but it would do, except there was no wardrobe and the fire had not been lit in either room. 'Mrs Carpenter I am sorry to add to your work but there is no wardrobe, nor has the fire been lit. Perhaps I can live out of my trunks for a day or two, but it is freezing. Can a maid light a fire please?' The housekeeper turned and looked Anne straight in the eye. 'Is there anything else your ladyship will require?'

'No that will be all, perhaps a piece of cake with my tea?' It wasn't till she had stood and looked out at the wonderful views of a wide park for some moments, that she wondered if the housekeeper had been facetious. A large curving lake, small-rounded hills, great individual trees and the occasional wood, the careful design of a master landscaper. Capability Brown's work for sure and beautifully done. Well, she had arrived, but was it all a terrible mistake? She sat on the bed and waited but no trunks arrived or bath. She stood up, walked along the corridor, looked into a storeroom but didn't open any closed doors, heard children in the distance and returned to her room. She sat again and waited. Should she go and find someone? Where was her cup of tea? Finally, the floorboards creaked outside, - and a footman stumbled in, putting a trunk down with a bang.

'Careful, there's china inside,' said Anne. But the man turned and went without a word. Should she tip another member of the household?

There was a small chest of drawers which would store some under garments, and she could set up her easel to display an unfinished painting in her sitting room. A framed self portrait of when she was younger, and a pencil sketch of her horse on the side table. With her toiletries, hairbrush, and hand mirror on the chest it started to look like home, if a bare one, however it didn't feel like it.

There was the sudden noise of children shouting and three boys burst into her sitting room. She met them at the door of her bedroom.

'Are you our new governess?' said the tallest.

'Yes, and you shouldn't be coming in here without knocking. What are your names?'

'We can go where we like; - it's our house. You can't,' he said.

'Your name, young man, and age.'

'I'm master Robert and I'm twelve.' He was tall for his age, dark curly hair, looking strong and fit. He strutted over to the side table and picked up the horse drawing.

'And I'm Alfred and I'm nearly eight.' Shorter, a more open face, trusting even, a little nervous. Freckles and fair. She turned to the last boy who was also dark haired.

'I'm Edmund and I'm nine and I don't like Latin. Father says I don't have to learn it.' A woman of about thirty entered, looking flustered.

'Sorry Miss, but I couldn't stop them.' A small girl peered round her ample skirts. 'I'm Jenny MacAllister their nanny.'

'How long have you come for?' said Alfred.

'As long as I'm wanted.'

'Miss Robinson only stayed a month,' said Edmund.

'We don't need a governess anyway,' said Robert. 'Who drew this?'

'Your mother says you do, and I drew it.'

'It's only a pony,' said Robert putting it back carelessly so it fell over.

'So, tell me, what has Miss Robinson taught you and what books have you been reading?' They all looked blank. 'What is your favourite adventure story?'

'There was one about Robin Hood,' said Alfred.

'What about King Arthur or Robinson Crusoe?'

'They're all silly,' said Robert.

'Well, if you go back to the school room, I'll bring a book and you can show me how well you read.'

'We have to go outside and see to the hounds,' said Robert.

'I don't think so. Your mother will expect me to tell her how well you are doing, so go.' They all shuffled out except the little girl who stayed and stood watching her as she hunted for a book in the depths of her trunk. 'What's your name?'

'Camilla,'

'Ah, found it. Well, Camilla, do you know your letters, your ABC?'

'A is for apple,' she began to recite.

'Well done, keep going and as you do, you can show me to where your brothers are.' When they reached the slightly ajar door, Anne hesitated. It had suddenly become very quiet. Anne pushed the door with her foot and stepped back as a heavy bible thudded to the floor. Stepping over it she tried to look severely at the two smaller boys. Edmund giggled but Alfred looked worried. Looking around she saw that the room was otherwise empty.

'Where are Robert and your Nanny?'

'He's gone to see the hunt come back,' said Alfred, 'and Nanny went to get Edmund an apple.'

'He's going to miss out. Pick up the Bible, Edmund, and then sit here beside me. I will read a portion and then you will each read a paragraph. Camilla can listen.' Alfred read well but Edmund although older couldn't manage any of the longer words. A maid interrupted them, to tell Anne that she had brought up a hip bath. She didn't appear pleased to hear that Anne would use it later. She spent the rest of the afternoon with the two boys, making them copy a knight in armour from the book. Robert came back and she cajoled him into joining in. She found some teaching materials in a desk and finally managed to get them to copy some copperplate writing. Only Alfred showed any aptitude. When they complained that it was getting close to their dinnertime, she gave up and Jenny began to organise their meal.

After a lecture on good manners when eating, Anne retreated to her rooms where she was cheered to find a fire had been lit, even if it was threatening to go out. She was soon on her hands and knees blowing it back to life. She rang the bell and asked for hot water and a cup of tea to be brought. It wasn't enough for a proper bath and the tea never came but when she found her way to the main stairs, she felt presentable. As she descended to the lower floors, a young woman dressed in the fashion of the day was coming up.

'And who are you?' said the woman stopping, to stand regal and severe. Anne wanted to laugh at such a thin young person endeavouring to look down her nose.

'How do you do, I'm Anne Osebury the new governess.'

'You should use the back stairs unless you have your charges with you.'

'These are more suitable as I need to go to the drawing room,' said Anne stepping up one stair to be at a similar level to the woman whom she realised was only about sixteen.

'You can reach the drawing room by the back stairs just as easily, I believe.'

'Will I be tutoring yourself?'

'I shouldn't think so.'

'Well, I must be on my way,' said Anne, continuing down the stairs.

'Excuse me, I haven't finished.'

'Sorry but I am late to see Mrs Percival.'

In the drawing room Mrs Percival was busy chatting to an older lady.

'Ahh, Mrs Exton this is Miss Osebury, our new governess. I understand you have already started teaching?'

'With some difficulty. They appear to be unused to -.'

'No excuses now, they are good boys and will do what you want if you are kind.' Wasn't Mrs Percival going to ask her to take a chair?

'May I sit?' said Anne looking around, choosing her seat.

'No, you were late down; we are just going into dinner. I'm sure you will manage.'

'But Mrs Percival, the boys must be a long way behind. Are they going to be sent to a boarding school? If so, they are far from ready.'

'No, my husband is against it. His school days were very unpleasant.'

'What about your older daughters?'

'I think some French conversation would be excellent and you said you were fluent.'

'I would be happy to instruct them,' said Anne, dreaming of using French grammar to take the girl she had met on the stairs down a peg. 'But Robert is too old for a governess, he either needs a male tutor or school.'

'That is for me to decide, but in the mean-time I want you to ensure they receive a suitable education.'

'I will do my best, but can you tell me what they have been studying, and what hours you expect me to work?'

'Whenever you are needed. Nanny can't cope on her own.'

'Where will I dine.'

'With the children of course.'

'The children have already eaten.'

'I'm in no doubt the kitchen can send something up.' Anne on the verge of expressing her frustration and comment on the rudeness of the house bit her lip. 'That will do. Thank you for coming, and now, Mrs Exton, we can go into dinner,' said Mrs Percival rising. Anne was left standing in the middle of the room. Fuming she walked about the room and then her confidence suddenly disappeared.

Back upstairs she hesitated to use the bell. She heard a commotion, sighed and walked down to the nursery and bedrooms beyond. Jenny was alternately shouting and pleading with Edmund and Alfred to get into bed. Robert was cleaning what looked like a real musket, if a scaled down one. They didn't immediately notice Anne.

'If Nanny tells you to get into bed, you get into bed!' she said as loudly and sternly as she could. The two younger boys scrambled into bed. Robert looked up from his gun and squinted along the sight at a picture on the wall rather close to her. 'Don't ever point a gun at anyone even if you know it to be unloaded.'

'I know that.'

'Good; I hope you don't keep any gun powder up here.'

'No, I'm not allowed. I shot two pigeons yesterday and a crow.'

'May I look?'

'I suppose so, but women don't like guns,' he said. As she

stood holding her hand out, he reluctantly passed it over.

'It's beautifully made. You are very fortunate,' she said, turning it over and examining the detail, and fine etching. She cocked it and then released the hammer gently back in the correct manner before Robert could complain.

'It's just a smaller bore than father's.'

'Who goes with you?'

'Sidney, one of the grooms mostly.'

'Are you allowed to go on your own?' He shuffled his feet and started putting his cleaning things away. 'You mustn't, Robert. Accidents happen. When do you go to bed?'

'Not till eight.'

'Good; then you can read to me before you do.'

'What, now?'

'Yes, now. We can go to your room and leave nanny with your brothers to say their prayers. I will get a book.' Robert's reading was poor for his age, but she thought he would eventually enjoy the story. She left him to say his own prayers and stood indecisive in the corridor. Finally, she found her way down the stairs, exploring as she went. In the servants' dining room, all was cleared away. A maid quickly stepped into another room. Three footmen were playing cards at one end of the table. They looked up but didn't speak.

'The kitchen?' she asked.

'Through there. You be the governess I suppose, had Bert dragging his feet all the way back from Shrewsbury.'

'Yes, it's not a big cart. Thankyou.'

Entering the kitchen, she looked around. Several women turned and stared. 'Excuse me who's in charge?'

'Me, but we'll not have your haughty ways here,' said an older woman.

'Perhaps common courtesy might produce some refreshment. I haven't been offered a hot drink or piece of bread and butter since I arrived.'

The woman shrugged. 'Maude, get the lady a piece of pie and will you take small ale?'

'I'd rather have tea or chocolate.'

'Would you!'

'May I eat in your dining room?'

'The mistress might think that familiar. I'll plate up something on a tray and you can eat it in your rooms.'

The pie with an apple and a piece of cheese washed down with hot chocolate should have been enjoyable but sitting alone in her room the ache of loneliness made it stick in her throat. What had her father said? She wouldn't last a week.

CHAPTER 3

The following days were an increasing struggle with homesickness, just when she needed every ounce of confidence in dealing with three feral children and their conceited older sisters, but little Camilla was her shadow and delight. There was some satisfaction in bending the boys wills to learning something. Jenny, their nanny, was always pleasant but in awe of Anne. The other servants generally ignored her, neither giving her the respect due her class or the friendship of theirs. She feared her letters home would become an expense eating up her wages. She was desperate to write but she hesitated. How could she disguise her melancholy and the shock of her treatment? Sitting, huddled close to the fire, she knew she had to begin, as it might be a fortnight before she had a reply.

Dear Hannah, How I miss you all. It is a fine house, with many guests and servants, but however wonderful the grounds it is lonely. The elder daughters are haughty, miserable creatures whom I hope to humble a little when I teach them French. Abigail is pale and thin but rather elegant, Eleanor voluptuous, although she isn't as pretty as she thinks she is. Please feel free to let mother read this letter, for I am prepared to admit she was right about the conditions of my employment, but I will survive and much more than a week. I have three boys to teach and a little girl who is very sweet. I have never thought the use of the cane was a good thing but here, I think, it might be put to great use. It is a shame it's not allowed. The house has a coldness, not literally, although it can be freezing but something is lacking, perhaps respect for the family, perhaps kindness by the family. It is all very interesting to see how others live.

The fire was dying, and the scuttle was empty. Why hadn't the maid topped it up? Perhaps she could find another place to sit, nearer to other people, rather than alone in her room. The house had a main drawing room which was in constant use but there was a second one that faced west which was a pleasant place to sit at dusk. There was also a small one that faced east which was sometimes used in the morning. No one would be there. She crept down the stairs with a candle and on reaching the pink room as it was called, lit the small central chandelier. A fire had been laid but not lit. She soon had it blazing and with the door closed, the room began to warm up. The flickering flames, and candlelight, reflected off the pictures, with their gold frames, and the vases and decorations of the ornate room. Dipping her pen, she continued.

I have the free use of a governess's cart so, when the weather is fine, I will take them for a drive. The journey here was exciting but long, with so many changes of coach. The family wear the latest fashions and have some wonderful gowns which I will endeavour to illustrate below rather than try to describe. Have you met any more neighbours? Have you called on the silly Simpsons yet, if so tell me how they live?

What else could she say without revealing her despondence? She sucked the top of her pen. She had never known how much her family meant. She began to describe more of the journey, trying to portray an amusing picture of Bert, with his feet dragging on the ground as he sat on the floor of the cart. As she wrote she began to feel in touch with her sisters again and in the pleasant setting of the fine room her mood began to lift.

The door opened.

'What are you doing here? This is not your place,' roared Mrs Percival. For a moment Anne was too shocked to speak. 'Well, explain yourself.'

'I had letters to write and as the room was empty - .'

'You have a sitting room. What more do you expect? Do you know what candles cost!'

'I suppose I expect to be able to mix with my equals and perhaps even with a little society.'

'But you are just a governess. Your place is in the nursery, not here. Leave and go to your room, and don't let me find you abusing our hospitality again.'

Teaching French to Abigail and Eleanor was tedious and hopeless. Neither teacher nor pupils were interested but it was Anne's only chance to sit again in a drawing room. Abigail, would sit rigid, condescending, as if French were below her. Eleanor, hardly listened, often practicing alluring smiles in her hand mirror, making the same mistakes in her grammar, asking the same questions, never learning. Anne thought that if she didn't have the most beautiful dresses, she would have looked like a buxom milkmaid but in the layers of satin and the latest puffed sleeves that Anne coveted, she had to admit she appeared attractive. Only once did Eleanor take any interest in French, which was when Anne spoke about words for love and romance. Those expressions and their sultry intonations, Eleanor was thrilled to practice, repeating them until she had caught their seductive accent.

When the afternoons were fine, Anne took the younger three for a drive in her cart around the estate and to the village or dragged them on long walks in the countryside. On her tenth day, after the children were in bed, she descended to the main rooms, creeping past the music room where there was a gathering of local gentry listening to a quartet. She gently knocked on the door of the library expecting to find it empty, but a voice called her to enter.

'Ahh, our pretty governess,' said Mr Percival from behind a cloud of cigar smoke, to the gentlemen beside him. 'Miss Osebury isn't it; this is Doctor Hadlow, Sir James Corwell and Mr. Tiverton. Gentlemen, the keeper of my wife's little terrors.'

'Very pleased to meet you sirs but I hadn't wanted to disturb you. I expected you to be in the music room with your other guests.'

'So, you admit you were up to no good.'

'Oh no, sir. I had no wish to disturb anyone. All I wanted was to see what volumes you had, that either the children or myself would find enjoyable or enlightening. Is there anything you would recommend?'

'Ha, it is no good asking Percival, he never even takes them down to look at the plates and as for reading them!' said the doctor.

'You are wrong sir, only a week ago I looked up a guide to horse doctoring. I would recommend James White's Veterinary Medicine to anyone. An excellent read.'

'That probably wasn't quite what I had in mind.'

'What did you want, some romantic nonsense. That's all my wife reads,' said Sir James.

'Do you ride, Miss Osebury?' said the Mr Tiverton. He

was sitting further back, in the shadows, away from the candlelight. He was younger than the others and lounged on his chair, one leg casually draped over the other, giving a sense of bored apathy.

'I did sir, when we lived in Hertfordshire and as for reading, I do enjoy quite a wide range of books.'

'She rides around in a governess's gig filled with children. A very pretty picture,' said Mr Percival.

'Do you prefer that?' said the doctor.

'No, but neither Camilla nor Alfred have a pony. Also, I doubt that I could control the children on separate mounts.' She hesitated, 'perhaps I ought to come back at a more convenient time.'

'Of course, whenever you like.'

'Thank you, but may I ask if Robert is going to school soon? He is old to be taught by a governess.'

'There are no plans, boarding schools can be a ghastly place for a young mind,' said Mr Percival, with a flick of his head, as if trying to release horrible memories.

'Do him good, toughen him up,' said Sir James.

'Yes, Percival you must send him,' said the doctor lighting yet another cigar. Tiverton coughed.

'No, the day I left, I swore no descendant of mine would be incarcerated in such a system.'

'Best days of my life. Don't you agree, doctor?'

'I wouldn't go that far. I remember weeping for the first 24 hours, but I eventually overcame it. What about the grammar school in Shrewsbury? He could lodge locally with a suitable family and come home on the weekends. Did you board Tiverton?'

'No, I had a tutor. My brother and I used to play him up

horribly. You have my sympathy, Miss Osebury. I cannot think of a worse position.'

'And what did he teach you?' said Anne, staring through the smoke, trying to make out his features.

'Not enough, Oxford was a shock.'

'You see sir,' turning back to her employer, 'school would be best for Robert. He is wayward. He needs a strong hand.'

'Not easy, I suppose for a slip of a girl like yourself to manage. I will give it some thought.'

Anne always used the main stairs when she had children in tow but was also inclined to use them at other times, partly because she forgot, partly, because she thought it her right. Again, Miss Abigail commented and Mrs Percival while not saying anything to her face, scowled, and made it quite clear by standing watching her, that this was not her place. The days were long, the lesson onerous but by about 8.30pm she was free, so it became her habit to slip into the entrance hall, still in her grey, day dress. A fire was usually lit beside two easy chairs, tucked in one corner. She would find a book or the day's newspaper and sit and read it by the light of a candle, the main candelabra not being adequate for the poor print. She was deep in her reading one evening when she felt the presence of Mrs Percival standing watching.

'Are you comfortable Miss Osebury?' Anne sat up straight from her languid position.

'Yes, thankyou Mrs Percival.'

'You can look at the paper tomorrow when the gentlemen have finished with it.'

'But the news will be stale by then. I am quite happy to read here, thank you.'

'My guests will be perturbed to find a strange young woman lounging here.'

'I am sure they will not think me a ghost or give them any cause for thought.'

'No, but they may wonder.'

'Tucked away in this corner I cannot be of consequence to any visitors.' But the light from opening doors was shining out as guests emerged from the music room.

'I suggest you go to your room.'

'I will Mrs Percival in a moment, but if you could be generous enough to allow me to finish this article.'

'Just this once take the paper with you.'

'That is very kind, but I am nearly finished.'

'Ah, the governess, what are you reading now?' said a male voice. Looking up she saw a tall slim gentleman with the strong features of a Roman nose and cleft chin.

'About the bread riots Mr Tiverton.'

'So, will that be part of tomorrow's lessons?'

'No just writing and reading, plus perhaps a little learning about the great lakes.' She couldn't decide if he was good looking, nor how old. Probably in his late twenties or even over thirty. He had a confident air. Mrs Percival had a decidedly displeased expression. She held a closed fan which clicked as she flicked it against her thigh in annoyance.

'And what will you tell them about the Great Lakes. Learning their names, is I suppose, a good exercise for memory.'

'Well, can you imagine, they are so very cold in winter, that they completely freeze, allowing people to travel for many miles across them a long way from the shore. The Indian tribes have such wonderful names, and they bring pelts down the rivers by canoe, traversing great rapids, beaver to make hats for you gentlemen, and silver fox for us ladies. The war of 1812 is interesting too. Do you know it is called the carpenter's war?'

'Is it?'

'Mr Tiverton, I was going to introduce you to Lord Belletine and I see he is free, come now,' said Mrs Percival, her hand gripping the young man's arm and practically dragging him around. He glanced back over his shoulder.

'Sorry, you will have to tell me another time.'

'If my employer allows it,' muttered Anne to herself. The guests flowed out in a bustle of conversation and loud goodbyes. None of them took any notice of the girl in the corner as she pulled her shawl around her shoulders to counteract the draught from the opening door. The fire beside her flickered and flared. When the footman closed the door for the last time Anne glanced up, in case she was due further censure from Mrs Percival, but it was her husband who walked over.

'So, this is where our little grey mouse escapes her charges?' said Mr Percival.

'Yes sir, it is a good spot for reading the paper or a book and warm enough. You don't mind me sitting here?'

'No, you are very welcome. Always good to see a pretty face.'

On the next evening, she was again in the hall but after a short perusal of the paper she started a pencil drawing in her sketch book, copying a George Stubbs painting on the stairs. She had to squat on one knee to hold the pad. A candle in a tall candlestick beside her gave a shadowy light. She saw Abigail coming down and because the steps were wide enough for her to pass, Anne didn't move. She was waiting for the haughty girl to comment and so continued to ignore her spectator. For some minutes nothing was said, and Anne began to wonder at what her audience was thinking, standing quietly behind her. Only the scratch of the pencil on paper, her own breath and the occasional, distant, laughter from the kitchens broke the silence.

'You draw very well,' said Abigail.

'Thank you, you're very kind,' replied Anne very nearly saying, that's the first pleasant word I've heard from you. 'Do you draw?'

'I used to, but Mother thought I ought to concentrate on my embroidery.'

'You could find time to draw if you wanted.'

'Mother says gentlemen are not interested in whether a lady can paint.'

'Does that matter?'

'Of course, it's very important to be considered as having the correct accomplishments.'

'I'm sure a future husband would want to see all that his wife might enjoy doing.'

'We must always be seen at our best. Governesses don't get married, do they?' said Abigail as she stepped past.

'Ha, I'm sure they do,' said Anne. Of course they do, but then how can you meet eligible men if you're not allowed to mingle in society. She stood, all interest in her sketching gone.

On the following day, when she was speaking French to Abigail in the drawing room, Mrs Percival joined them.

'Anne we will be visiting my brother in Shipley next week, leaving on Monday. The children will be going too. Please endeavour to pack suitable attire for the children, for at least two weeks, possibly three. We will travel in two coaches. You and Nanny with the young ones in the Landau, myself and the rest of the family in the Barouche.'

'Will I need an evening gown?'

'Err no, of course not.'

'Thank you, I will discuss with nanny what to take.'

'Good. Now I have visitors at any moment so perhaps you can end your French conversation lesson and leave the drawing room. Abigail you can stay.' As Anne made her way upstairs, she was surprised to hear a cry from one of the main bedrooms.

'No, please, not here,' A woman's voice and then a giggle and one of the younger maids appeared in the doorway, her face flushed. She took one look at Anne and scuttled away. What was going on? The servants shouldn't be carrying on in a family bedroom. It wasn't her concern, but they could get into trouble. Perhaps she ought to warn whoever was behind it. No footman should be in this part of the house. A man strode out wearing a wide grin, but it was no servant, it was Mr Percival himself. He glanced at her but said nothing as he stepped past. Anne stood there, shocked, did he actually wink at her? He was down the stairs and out of sight before she moved. As she did, she noticed the housekeeper standing, watching, in the shadow of a far doorway. Anne walked towards her, but Mrs Carpenter stepped into the room. Anne found her in the bedroom supervising two new maids who were stripping the bed.

'What's going on here, Mrs Carpenter?'

'Nothing to speak about, just be careful yourself. Don't pull the sheet like that, you'll tear it,' said the housekeeper turning to her young apprentices.

'Is that why Agnes is leaving?'

'I'll not comment but we do sometimes have trouble keeping maids.' It was a thoughtful Anne who made her way to the noisy nursery.

Trying to interest the children in the scenery, as the two coaches clattered through the countryside for long hours spoiled Anne's enjoyment of what should have been an interesting journey. The autumn colours were at their best but in the crowded coach with the hood up, with boys fighting and a little girl wanting to be on Jenny's lap one minute and Anne's the next, it was easy to miss the best views. They reached Iron Bridge just before three in the afternoon as Mr Percival had chosen to lengthen their drive to visit the famous town. The surrounding area breathed smoke and noise, great tall chimneys and brick kilns emerged from the haze. Everywhere resounded to the rumble of wagon wheels and the ring of hooves on the cobbles from the constant flow of commerce. Glowing furnaces could be seen between the houses and for a moment, as they passed, they felt its heat.

The two coaches drew into the Tontine Hotel. The owner rushed out into the courtyard, opening the door of the first carriage with bows and compliments. He handed down Mr and Mrs Percival and then escorted them and their daughters to their quarters, leaving Anne and Jenny to stretch their tired limbs and try to keep the children from under the horses' hooves as they stood waiting. Barmen went to-and-fro as the horses were taken from their traces and another coach arrived, jamming the yard with activity. Stepping inside the busy foyer Anne and her charges were ignored until the owner returned.

'Right ladies, if you will come this way. I have found you a room close to Mr and Mrs Percival.'

'I'm not sure they will want us to be next door.'

'I'm sorry we are very busy. Please follow me.'

After they had settled into their rooms, which for Anne, Jenny and Camilla meant sharing a bed, they all walked to the famous bridge, where other ladies in fine dresses and gentlemen in morning dress strolled, admiring the bridge and each other. They then walked up to the beginning of the canal where the area was busy with working men and women, loading and unloading to a background roar of furnaces and human hubbub. The air had the smell and grit of industry.

'Well, Robert, have you seen anything like this before?' said Mr Percival, coming to stand by his son. 'This is the future; iron and steam, the 1820's will be an exciting age. Now there is peace, Britain will lead the world. Once, our seamen sought treasures from around the globe, now instead, they ship our products to buyers, desperate to purchase our cloth, our ceramics and metal manufacture; treasures made here. Miss Osebury, don't you feel proud of your country?'

'Yes sir, it is very exciting, I never expected it to be like this.'

They wandered on with Mr Percival, a different man, talking and sharing with his eldest, with an enthusiasm that Anne had not seen before. She and nanny each tightly gripped a child's hands amongst the bustle and dangers that surrounded them.

'Hello,' said a voice at her elbow, 'It's Anne Osebury isn't it, how come you're here?' Anne turned to find James Thompson.

'We are staying at the Tontine, but do you work here?' said Anne, her surprise and slight disdain clear as she looked the young man up and down. His brown cotton, workers coat, with its splashes of glaze, fine white dust in his hair and dirty hands marking him as an artisan.

'Ha, for us artists it is difficult to stay clean,' he said, smiling confidently.

'An artist! What sort of artist?'

'At a china works. An apprentice. Most of the factory uses transfers but on the fine vases there is much free hand work. A chance to make a name for myself.'

'What are you doing Anne? Who is this young man?' said Mrs Percival approaching, having noticed that Anne had stopped.

'This is Master James Thompson whose father became the steward at our old house in Hertfordshire after we left. Mrs Percival my Employer.'

'Well keep up; this is not a safe place to dawdle.'

'Sorry,' whispered Anne, as her employer walked away. 'I'm acting as governess to the family. But you are far from Hertfordshire.'

'Yes, my parents are still there. I reside with an aunt who has a fine house here.'

'You didn't want to follow your father's career?' said Anne and then glancing at her mistress added, 'keep walking.'

'Oh no, collecting rents and worrying about drainage and rooves is not for me. And how is your sister?'

'Still as beautiful as ever.' James blushed and turned to look at a group of men struggling to unload a heavy boiler from a barge.

'When are we going to have dinner?' said Alfred.

'Soon, but first your father wants to show us the sights.'

'With your art you could work here too. Better than looking

after difficult children,' he said glancing at Edmund, who was twisting his hand, desperate to escape Anne's strong grip.

'No Edmund!'

'I want to be with Robert.'

'No, you must stay safe.'

'I must go, or I will in trouble. Perhaps I will call at the hotel later,' said James hurrying away.

'If you do, come after the children are in bed. After eight,' she called. She had never had much time for the confident conceited boy, but it was a relief to meet him again. Someone who recognised her family yet spoke naturally.

She couldn't escape her charges until nearly nine but when she reached the foyer he hadn't arrived. She stood feeling out of place. Everyone was male, generally dressed in dark tail-coats. They didn't appear the type of gentry who would have visited her home or the Percival's, but men of business and the talk was of business. Or she wondered, correcting her first impression, were some of them from her class but acting differently in a different setting? Occasionally someone would glance at her, and the waiters appeared particularly disturbed by her presence, but no one spoke their concern, they were all too busy. She shouldn't be there, and needed to return to her room, but she was fascinated by the conversations around her.

Her nearest neighbour was describing the raising of fresh equity for a new canal. It was a different world and one of which she had little knowledge. She turned for the stairs knowing a servant would be sent for her if James arrived.

'Anne.' Came a shout and turning she saw James who swept in, plonked his top hat on a table and called for a glass of ale. He was dressed like the others, smart and business like.

'Well Anne, please sit down, may I call you Anne, what a surprise finding you far from the landed gentry's estates. I understand the Percival's have quite a pile in the country.'

'Yes, it's a grand house but not much of a home. Tell me about what happens in your works?'

'Well, most of the output is in standard porcelain, made individually on moulds by workers. When they have been air-dried, they are taken to the kiln. Hundreds, if not thousands are gradually stacked inside until it is full and then the kiln is fired. Days later when it has reached temperature and then cooled again, they are removed, and most are decorated by transfers.' The waiter put a glass of ale on the table and glanced at Anne.

'Sorry, would you like some refreshment?' asked James.

'No thank you. Please go on.'

'Lines of women sit applying the transfers, while others paint the gold or coloured edge on the plates or cups. Some pieces may have further hand painted extras. Again, the decorated pieces are stacked in the kiln and given a second firing. Any pieces that survive both firings will be sent to the cities to be sold or to customers around the world.'

'That's all very interesting but what do you actually do?'

'Well, each works will also make hand thrown pieces, special vases and plates, sculptures and anniversary plaques. They have to be decorated by hand, with beautiful scenes, or with faces and figures. There are only a few top artists who do the individual pieces and four apprentices like me who are learning.'

'Are you allowed to paint finished items?'

'It's best I show you. Come and meet my aunt and you can see some pieces that didn't survive the kiln.' With a glance around in case Mr Percival was in the room she rose. It felt strange, exciting, to step out into the dark street, alone with James. No chaperone, no one to ask permission from. She was her own person, but her euphoria dissipated as a drunk zigzagged towards them and a beggar sitting on the ground on the other side of the street held out his hand.

'You must be cold?' said James.

'I'm fine.'

'It's not far. My Aunt Agnes has a good fire and will be pleased to meet you,' he said, increasing the speed of his walk. He increased it again when he discovered Anne could keep up. They were in the main street, walking beside the Severn River with a mixture of houses, on the other side. He stopped and they crossed the road. She followed up the steps of a white house with three storeys. Opening the door with a key, he gestured her to lead the way into a standard hall. After taking her shawl, he opened the first door on the right into a snug sitting room. A lamp on the table illuminated a lady knitting in an easy chair beside a coal fire which glowed brightly in the grate.

'Aunt, this is Anne, her father is Sir George Osebury. Anne, my Aunt Mrs Turnbull. I had mentioned that I had assisted a carter taking their luggage almost to Wales.' With a questioning glance at her nephew, she gestured to a second chair.

'Draw up the chair for her James. You must be cold. Would you like a glass of sherry to warm you?'

'Perhaps just a little one, thank you,' said Anne as she sat and leant forward to warm herself.

'Anne is acting as governess to a wealthy family who are staying overnight at the Tontine, but she ought to be an artist, so I wanted to show her some of my pieces.'

'What are you making?' asked Anne.

'Just some winter stockings; it is the only thing I can do in the reduced light in the evenings. Can you pour the sherry James? Elsie has gone out. I only have the one servant now, but James is a good boy and doesn't mind doing little things.' Anne could feel his embarrassment which he did his best to hide by leaving the room. He returned with several large plates, which he put at her feet, before exiting again. She picked up the top plate which had a deep crack, but the central picture of a gypsy girl was skilfully painted. The second plate had a river scene with boats and the third pastoral. They were large and made to be displayed on a wall. James came back with a glass of sherry and a vase. The vase had a harbour scene on both sides.

'Did you want me to get you anything Aunt?'

'No thank you but would Anne like a piece of seed cake?'

'I've eaten already thank you, but James did you paint these?'

'Only in part,' he said leaning over her and running his finger around the rim. 'You see the decoration round the edge and the background, I did all of it but not the figure; that was done by Miss Quantrel, our best artist. That's her initials on the back.'

'A woman! With her signature on it?'

'Well, just initials, but the real collectors know, and her signed pieces are sought after.'

'I had no idea that a woman could earn her living from her art.'

'Oh yes,' he said, picking up another plate. 'This next work is only a transfer, with the rim decorations again done by me. The transfers were designed by her. In the third,' he said, squatting down. 'I again painted the background and Bill, the figures but he's not so good as Elizabeth Quantrell. The vase, if it hadn't been damaged in the kiln, is one of the best pieces our works produce and is very expensive. I'm not allowed to work on them.'

'And how long is your apprenticeship?' said Anne, tracing her finger along the design. How satisfying it would be to produce such a beautiful creation.

'Five years,' he sighed, 'but I'm doing much more freehand work than I should, seeing that I've only been there such a short time. Several painters have left.'

'Are you paid?'

'The first year is only £12 per year and that was only because my father knew one of the directors.'

'No one can live on that,' said Anne continuing to turn the plate over.

'No but a top artist can name his salary.'

'These leaves and flowers along the rim. Did you really do them?'

'Of course; you haven't seen any of my other work, have you?' he said leaping up and hurrying out of the room. He came back, his arms loaded with sheets and canvasses, a pile that was in danger of cascading onto the floor. The first sketch was of his aunt in her armchair, knitting. Anne glanced at her. The pencil work had caught the cosy scene of a contented lady by her fireside.

'He's good isn't he. Not very flattering though,' said the aunt.

'You look very charming,' said Anne with a smile, but her smile disappeared at the next drawing. 'You naughty boy, this is Hannah, isn't it?'

'Yes, and just from memory so it's not very good, don't look at it.' He knelt on the floor to hand each one to her. There were still life paintings, of guns and dead birds, dogs, plus landscapes and portraits. Anne had to admit that he had talent, no wonder they were letting him get ahead.

'I don't see any pictures of flowers or leaves.'

'No,' he laughed. 'It isn't exactly my style, but I can copy them, so it hasn't been too difficult to learn decorative patterns. You could do well, as I'm sure you often paint flowers. In fact, I know you can, remember, I saw some of your work and was surprised how skilled you were. You could become a top artist too.'

'I'm not that good,' she said smiling, 'and I'm only acting as a governess until we have a chance to stay with some of my parent's friends or until Father's finances improve. Even in my present employment I receive three times your salary.'

'Yes, but in a few years, I will have different companies bidding for my talents.'

'James, an elegant young lady like Anne will marry a fine gentleman. She can't be spending her days coarsening her skin with the clay or glazes.'

'You don't want to paint portraits or go to Paris?' said Anne.

'I'd love too if I had someone to sponsor me or if I had a private income, but ceramics are very special. An oil on canvas will only last, at the most, 800 years, glazes rarely fade, and china lasts forever.'

'Unless you drop it.'

'And the factories are such an exciting place. Everyone striving to produce something beautiful or useful and you never know if it will survive the firing.'

'Do you have many children to teach, Anne?' asked Aunt

Agnes.

'Four, and three of them are rather spoilt boys but I'm managing, just.' James sprang up again to collect some more drawings while Anne continued to chat to his aunt. On his return their conversation widened. The enthusiastic young man and his kindly aunt found much to talk about. Anne began to feel drowsy, but she was loath to leave the cosy fireside and their friendship. Finally, she stood.

'I have taken your time long enough but thank you for a very pleasant evening.'

'You must escort her back to her lodgings James.'

'Of course, but there is no rush to leave.'

'I must,' said Anne, yawning as if on cue, 'It's been a very tiring day but thankyou again for your kind hospitality.'

Outside it had grown colder so there was little breath for conversation as they hurried along the empty street. Once inside the hotel foyer James took her hand.

'Thank you for coming. I know my aunt really enjoyed meeting you.'

'And me her,' said Anne, looking around, wishing to avoid the Percivals.'

'Now Anne, if ever you wish to become an artist, you could stay with us, and I guarantee I could obtain you a position.'

'As an apprentice!'

'No, the daughter of Sir George and Lady Osebury would have to start higher than that. It would be easily possible to find you a special place. The wages might not be very much to start with, but you wouldn't be treated as an apprentice and of course your place in our home would be with the utmost propriety and at my aunt's expense.'

'I couldn't presume on her hospitality like that.'

'She would be delighted to have you. I know your society and companionship would bring her great pleasure. It's a big house, four bedrooms besides the servants' attic rooms. Not big like yours of course.' He laughed, 'but big for ordinary folk.'

'Well, it's good to know there is something else I could do if I were desperate, but work in a pottery, I don't think so.'

'You really could do well, and we'd be a happy family.'

'I'd probably be happier in your aunt's house, too, but it is not to be. Please thank her again for this evening and James, I must wish you goodnight.'

She found Jenny sitting on the floor outside their room.

'Ssh, Camilla had a nightmare and has only just gone off again.'

'I need my bed too,' said Anne with another yawn.

'Please, just wait or we'll be kept up all night and Mrs Percival will be very cross.' Anne sat on the floor, folding her legs in as another guest came along the landing. How had life come down to sitting on the floor of an inn?

CHAPTER 4

T he journey, the following day, brought them to a fine old house built of sandstone which had once been part of an abbey. As they drove into the courtyard, a maid ran inside, and soon there was a line of servants and family to greet them. The Percivals alighted and were greeted by Sir Harold and Lady Brockham, with their two daughters in their late teens, and their son, in his midshipman uniform. Jenny and Anne stepped out of the coach, quickly grasping the children's hands to stop them rushing forward. They stood and waited. Finally, Mrs Percival turned, and Anne let go of Robert's hand so he could be received but he was suddenly shy. She pushed his back lightly and under his father's stern gaze he went and greeted his cousins. The other children went forward, and the addresses continued with many "hasn't he grown, isn't Camilla's dress delightful, last time we saw you, you were in your mother's arms comments."

Eventually, the Percivals were introduced to the butler and the housekeeper and followed them in. Anne and Jenny walked behind the group. No one had thought to include them in the introductions, and they hesitated as they stood in the impressive hallway.

'Do we go with the children?' whispered Jenny.

'Just admire the pictures, they will call us when they want us. I think that's a Rubens,' said Anne, walking over to stare up at an old master, 'Magnificent. No, actually, I think it's good copy.' She continued up the stairs inspecting the art, enjoying the fine paintings. At least fifteen minutes had elapsed before the butler arrived back in the hall with a maid.

'If you can collect the children from the drawing room, Rose will show you where they will sleep,' he said, indicating the young maid.

In the drawing room Mrs Percival was as blunt as usual. 'Ahh Anne, my governess, and nanny. Please take the children to their rooms and arrange their dinner; they must be hungry.' The children were glad to escape, and they all followed Rose to the set of rooms set aside for their stay. A stay that might be reasonably pleasant, thought Anne. She was neither servant nor family but there were new grounds to explore, and the challenge of imparting knowledge would be at a reduced level as the children were expecting to treat it as a holiday. She was disappointed to discover there was no governess with whom she could share her frustrations or success.

The suite of rooms that had been the nursery, had not been used since the girls were younger, so the Percival children enjoyed exploring and finding old toys, long forgotten. Leaving Jenny in charge, Anne descended the main stairs in search of refreshment. The kitchen quickly supplied tea, and a maid offered to help carry a second tray with glasses of milk for the children. The maid followed Anne, who was carefully balancing the teapot to prevent it overflowing, when she sensed that another had joined them. As they entered the nursery, a long room with dormer windows, she turned and found that the midshipman had followed them in.

'Hello boys, finding all my old things?' he said. Turning to Anne he offered her his hand. 'Welcome, I'm Geoffrey Brockham.'

'How do you do, I'm Anne Osebury,' she said feeling slightly confused at the informality of the introduction. 'Are you on leave from your ship?' He was tall, suntanned, his long fair hair tied in a ponytail. Good looking in a boyish way.

'I'm on half pay like many in the navy. Not enough ships at the moment, but I'm sure I will get a place soon. Captains often have to wait but not the lower ranks.'

'When can we go hunting?' said Robert.

'Soon, perhaps, but it depends on your governess.'

'That's all he thinks about, he would have brought his gun if it had been allowed.'

'If he wishes he can join us in a fox hunt on Friday.'

'And me,' said Edmund from where he was sitting on the floor with a model ship, his lips producing the swishing sound of waves as he rode the ship over an imaginary sea.

'Edmund, you are much too young.' She turned back to Geoffrey, 'How do you like the navy?'

'Very much.'

'And have you been anywhere exciting?'

'Oh yes, both the Mediterranean and the Caribbean. There is absolutely nothing like it, climbing the rigging amongst the acres of white sail as the ship sways, looking down on the everlasting green waves and nothing on the horizon but sea and sky; wonderful.'

'Very poetical.'

'Thank you. The trouble is father expects me to resign my commission when he is older and manage the estates but it's not for me. To be master of my own ship is my one ambition. Don't say anything will you,' he whispered. Anne glanced round at the children and wondered how this secret would ever be kept.

'Now what sort of ship is this, Edmund?' said Geoffrey squatting down beside the boy.

'It's a sailing ship, or is it a schooner?'

'No, it's a brig because the -.'

Two maids arrived, carrying a tureen, and piles of bread and butter. One immediately began opening up cupboards and started laying the table, while the other returned to the kitchen for further dishes. The meaty aroma reminded Anne how hungry she was.

'Will you be joining us at dinner, Anne?' said Geoffrey.

'I will probably remain here and assist Nanny,' she said, with a little hesitation, visualising Mrs Percival's expression if she arrived at the main table.

'I will leave you then. I expect it will be fine tomorrow, although cold, so we could take the boys up to my father's folly. I have a key and it's a wonderful view from the top of the tower.' As the maid returned with a second casserole, he bowed, smiled, and wished them good evening.

'There's a polite young man,' said Anne.

'Yes miss, very handsome.'

The morning arrived frosty and fine, the winter sun in an ice-blue sky giving little warmth. A servant called when the children were eating lunch to announce that the coach would be at the front entrance at one o'clock. When they emerged on to the shingled drive, Geoffrey was waiting for them on the steps. A footman opened the coach door.

'Right, all children facing backwards, adults facing forward,' said Geoffrey. The hood was down and as if discerning Anne's thoughts he added. 'We wouldn't be able to see anything with the hood up.' He handed Anne in, with a bow and an exaggerated flourish and then leapt in behind her, leaving Jenny to follow, so that he was sitting between them. It was a tight squeeze for three. 'You ladies will see the view better if I'm in the middle.'

'Sit down boys,' said Anne.

'Want to sit on Nanny's lap,' said Camilla, as the footman leaned in and arranged a thick blanket over their legs.

'No, you will be fine beside Edmund,' said Jenny but as the coach started the little girl pushed across and lifting the blanket squirreled onto her lap. Jenny tucked the blanket around her. Anne was very aware of her physical proximity to the young man. She tried to wriggle herself further away into the cushioned upholstery. Even through her thick skirt and petticoats she could feel his hip pressing against hers. She was embarrassed, wondered at his audacity and what her mother would say if she knew. Perhaps he wasn't aware. As they moved off, the cold air made her shiver.

'I hope you will be warm enough, Anne,' said Geoffrey. 'Being squashed together should enable us to remain comfortable.'

'We are rather close, aren't we,' she said, mindful of her body, it felt off putting yet exciting too. A fearful tingle ran through her.

'Yes, my apologies, but on a day like today being snug is very pleasant.' He began to point out some remaining ruins of the abbey, and minor landmarks. As he chatted on, she considered how different he was to some of the gentry she knew, natural, unassuming, unpretentious; she was beginning to like him. The lane wound through woodland and then began to climb a hill, the two horses blowing steadily. They could see a stone tower on its summit.

'We could have walked here,' said Anne.

'Really, my sisters would have never even considered it. I thought after we have climbed the tower we might go on to the church in the village; it has a fine screen and some interesting inscriptions. You can have your exercise going up the tower's ninety-nine steps.' As they drew to a stop at the top of the hill, Geoffrey was leaping out and holding the door and handing out the ladies before the coachman had dismounted. The simple stone turret projected skyward above them. He bought out a large rusty key which after some manipulating clicked the lock, and he was able to swing the door open.

'Follow me,' he said, 'but be careful at the top.'

'Now Camilla, let's count the steps, shall we?' said Anne taking the little girl's hand. 'One, two -.' The spiral staircase had several glassless windows but trying to keep up with the boys and count gave little opportunity to look. It really was ninety-nine and everyone except their guide was breathless when they reached the top and gazed out to the distant horizon. A kaleidoscope of colours, green and brown fields, with patches of woods in autumnal reds and yellows and the occasional dwelling or curl of smoke from houses hidden behind trees. The landscape appeared to go on for ever.

'What a wonderful view. It's beautiful.' said Anne leaning over the parapet.

'Yes, but perhaps a little flat, just minor hills, with no great mountains or wild peaks. I understand your home is in the Welsh Marches.'

'We can see distant mountains and the countryside is more rugged and mainly suitable for pasture, unlike your rich arable fields here, but this is beautiful. I would be content to enjoy this prospect every day.'

'You would be happy to live here?'

'Certainly.'

'Well next we must show you the Saxon church. They say it is very special; come on.'

'We don't want to see an old church,' said Robert.

'Oh yes you will, and I'll give a shilling to the child who finds a poking tongue. No not a real one,' he said as Robert poked his out, 'but one carved in stone.'

The little church, which was again not far and hardly worth taking the coach for, was in fine condition, with the scent of beeswax from the polished pews.

'Now who's going to win?' They searched the carvings on the screen and then on the pew ends and while the carvers had taken liberties in their sculpture, with strange animals, devils and ugly faces, there was none with extended tongue. Outside they scrutinised the gravestones but looking up, it was Edmund who cried out.

'There, look,' they turned to stare up at a gutter outlet, cum gargoyle, whose large mouth and extended tongue was the rain exit for the roof.

'Well done. Here's your shilling. Now let's go and see if there are any ducks on the pond.'

'But I haven't bought my gun,' said Robert.

'You'll have all your hunting on Friday. Come we must hurry, the weather may change, in fact tomorrow it may rain. What shall we do then Anne?'

'Perhaps we could read a play together. Would your sisters like to join us?'

'What a splendid idea, a play it is.'

As they rode on Anne turned to her host. 'How long do you remain a midshipman before you gain promotion?'

91

'When I go back, I hope to be appointed as a lieutenant. I passed the exam last August and as I'm nineteen, I have high hopes of a suitable posting.'

'You didn't want to include Abigail and Eleanor on this outing?'

'No, they wouldn't have come, and I see enough of them in the evenings. Their conversation is of fashions and dancing. They are nice enough, in a "can't be bothered to talk to you now cousin," sort of way.'

'Really, doesn't Eleanor try out her charms on you?'

'If she does, they are easily ignored. Being outside with you is much more fun than drawing room conversations. Ah here is the pond and wild geese too. Now some bread to feed them with.' Pulling a paper-bag out from under the seat he handed it to Jenny.

After the pond, they continued their country tour until his sudden realisation that they were all cold. With great concern, he had the coachman put the top up and they turned for home. At the house he bowed, took Anne's hand, remarked that he had really enjoyed the day but looking at the sky which had a certain redness, suggested that after all, they might enjoy the outdoors again on the morrow. He skipped away, leaving Anne and Jenny to bundle the children upstairs. When the children had finally been settled, she began to think of a play they might perform. What could they do that could use three boys and a little girl?

As she ran through various possibilities her pen poised and page empty, her thoughts kept drifting off to the enjoyable day that Geoffrey had organised. The informality of it all had been unusual. An attentive young man, good with the boys, charming, handsome, and sitting so close. Her initial shock at the physical contact, and guilt from it, had settled to a pleasant acceptance. It had given her feelings she wasn't prepared to acknowledge or consider but the warm glow remained. She knew that marriage would be her best route out of the poverty that had engulfed her family, but it had been considered as a distant goal, not something to come on her so suddenly. Was she ready, could her affection for him grow to the passion of marriage? Could she, out of need for financial stability accept the first man to show any interest in her? Marrying well was supposed to be Hannah's role as not only was she far more attractive, she was also the eldest but if it fell to Anne, she would have to do her duty. A duty that might be quite agreeable, she thought smiling to herself.

He really was very likeable and as much as she might have preferred someone older, perhaps more sophisticated, his family was wealthy, he the only son. It was an opportunity that she just had to take. A chance for Hannah, for her family. Was it so mercantile to think in such a way? As she thought of him, she knew she could grow to love him, and wouldn't her mother be pleased? She would have achieved what Hannah's beauty had not, but what would Mrs Percival say? She imagined her employer's annoyance. A brief outline of a modified Cinderella story was all that she managed before she retired to bed.

She went to sleep wondering if she could love him and awoke feeling she was in love.

At breakfast, the message came that Geoffrey would be ready for more outdoor activities at one o'clock, so she endeavoured to do some reading and writing with the children, much to their chagrin in the morning, with no concerns about the unwritten play. At 12.30 he appeared in the school room, carrying two bows and a large handful of arrows. She felt the colour rise up her neck and a strange shyness, that had her looking at the floor. A reserve she hadn't felt the day before.

'Archery practice this afternoon,' he announced, 'as soon as you have finished eating.'

'We have, just. Edmund, eat up your custard and then we can go outside.' With a scraping of chairs, the children were up and scurrying out the door.

'Coats, it's still cold outside,' shouted Anne, with a glance through the window at the leaden sky.

'Snow tomorrow they reckon. Perhaps we'll all be snowed in, and you'll have to stay all winter. Would you like that?' said Geoffrey.

'If your family wouldn't mind,' replied Anne head down.

'No, they would love you to stay. Not so much noise boys going down the stairs.'

Outside they found a target butt that had been set up in the walled garden.

'Well Robert, first let's see how you do with the little bow,' said Geoffrey. 'Now, you know how to aim?'

'Of course,' said Robert pulling back hard. His three arrows all hit the target but around the edge. 'My old bow at home is better.'

'We'll let you try the big one later. Now Edmund you try.' After all the children, including Camilla with help from their host, had fired their three arrows, they stepped further away, and he leaned back and shot an arrow close to the bullseye with the long bow.

'Good shooting,' exclaimed Anne.

'Thank you and it will be your turn soon but Jenny first,' said Geoffrey.

She shook her head backing away. 'No come on, if Camilla can, you can.' After further persuasion she allowed him to hand her the bow. She placed the niche of the arrow end into the string. 'Now aim and pull.' The arrow landed in the ground in front of the target.

'Try again.' None of them hit the target. She just wasn't strong enough. 'We will let Anne have a go and then later Nanny can try again. He stepped close to Anne. She took the bow.

'I have tried before but I'm not very good,' she said, setting the arrow. He put one hand on her shoulder and squinted down the arrow as she lifted and started to pull. She was aware of how close his face was, his breath warming her cheek.

'Aim a little high.' It was a hard to draw and her arm shook with the effort. The arrow soared over the target.

'Missed,' said Robert. This time Geoffrey put his left arm right round her, and breathing down her neck, endeavoured to squint along the arrow and pull with her.

'Missed again,' She laughed, accepted another arrow, and tried to pull but released it and relaxed her arm. Again, he was very close.

'You could try the small one,' said Geoffrey. His intimate contact was emotionally disturbing besides making it difficult to freely move.

'No, I'll be fine, but perhaps if you give me a little more space,' she said, lifting the bow, drawing the arrow, aiming, and letting fly in one movement. The arrow thudded into the target close to Geoffrey's.

'Well done. Try another.' The fourth arrow again hit the target but on the edge.

'My turn,' said Robert reaching out for the bow. He struggled to pull it but managed to hit the bottom of the target. They continued to take turns, gradually improving as the afternoon wore on, with even Jenny hitting the outside ring.

'Perhaps we can practice again tomorrow but it looks like rain soon and I wanted to show you the new hunter that has just arrived. My father often sells our horses or buys replacements,' said their host, starting to collect the arrows.

At the stables, the horse was brought out of its box and paraded over the cobbles. The chestnut coat of the great beast shone, and it appeared very large in the yard as the groom tried to hold it. It felt as though its iron shoes should produce sparks from the cobbles which rang as it kicked and practically danced with untapped energy. Jenny and Camilla stepped back but the boys both wanted to touch it, so the groom brought it to a stop and held it steady so they could reach up to it. It jerked its large head a few times, but finally allowed them to stroke the velvet hair of its nose.

After they had marvelled at it, they returned to the house and Anne took them to a corridor where there was a good picture of a horse and left them looking at it. She quickly collected her sketch pad and returned with pencils and charcoal.

'Right boys, the artist has painted well but you have just seen a wonderful live creature. Has the artist caught the energy and power of the animal we have just seen? Can we do as well or even better. Let's see how you can remember it,' she said handing out pieces of paper to the children. 'And you too Geoffrey.'

'Me?'

'Why not?'

'I could never draw very well.'

'What no drawings of the exciting harbours you have visited? Come on, let's see you try.' With a wry grin he took a sheet. Soon they were all sitting quietly scratching away. The corridor, being on the top floor had a sky-light, so they were able to continue for some time.

'While the children have enjoyed your sport, I'm surprised your sisters haven't joined us.'

'They are too busy gossiping and talking muslin and bonnets with Eleanor and Abigail.'

'Will they want to watch us when we perform the play?'

'No, I don't think so,' he said, screwing up his paper.

'Come on, let me look,' said Anne, her hand reaching out. He put it behind him. She tried to reach around him, but he deftly turned. 'It can't be that bad.' She followed around his back and went to grab his hand, but he lifted the paper aloft. Playfully she jumped to try and catch it, but he side-stepped. The children had stopped sketching and were watching. His hand came down as if to offer the torn drawing. She grabbed his fingers, but he was stronger and pulled his hand away, and her to him. Small pieces of paper fluttered onto the floor as she nearly fell into his arms. She steadied herself and stood erect. They smiled at each other.

'Tomorrow then, I'm looking forward to it, so I'll come after lunch, and we can walk the boards together.' He swept out with an imaginary-hat-waving bow.

'I'd better work something out,' she muttered. 'Right suppertime, yes Alfred, you can finish it tomorrow.'

The play was Cinderella, with Robert and Edmund as the ugly sisters, Geoffrey as the handsome prince, Camilla as Cinderella, Alfred as buttons, Anne the fairy godmother and the older boys also the mice pulling the coach. Jenny helped with the dressing up but refused to do other than watch and applaud. It was great fun.

Geoffrey played his part well. Dancing with Camilla, sobbing for his lost love over the remaining slipper, exclaiming his disgust at the ugly sisters' ugliness. It was a delight for Anne to watch him with the children but all too soon, the afternoon was over and the promise for the following day was the hunt. Anne with borrowed coat was to ride on what Geoffrey described as a very steady mount. It was difficult to get the boys to sleep, for Robert, who was also going to ride, was excited and Edmund, was in a rage, from being told he was to be left behind with Nanny.

Anne was thrilled to be taking part, although she had no great desire to see a fox torn to pieces. As a child however she had seen what foxes could do. She had been walking past a tenant's farm early in the morning when she had heard a terrible cry and then sobbing. The curiosity of a ten-year old had prompted her to enter the farmers yard and on to a large shed beyond. In the doorway the farmer's wife, her body shaking with unhappiness, was leaning on her husband's shoulder, her tears streaming down, while he muttered words that should not have been heard by a small girl. Feathers like snowflakes in a storm were eddying around their feet. Beyond the door, Anne saw the torn bodies, which included a scattering of yellow chicks. The picture had been difficult to erase from her memory. It seemed months since she had enjoyed a canter in the countryside which before their move had been her daily exercise, whenever the weather had been kind.

At the stable yard, Anne left Geoffrey to supervise Robert and found that the mount selected for her was a solid cob. The young groom was having trouble fitting the side saddle on its wide back.

'Haven't you anything else?' she asked, 'I'm not ploughing a field.'

'Well miss, Master Geoffrey said you was to have the safest mount in the stables.'

'Not that safe; I was riding before I could walk.'

'Most everything be taken.'

'Come on, there must be something better. A hunt is all about galloping and jumping.'

'Are you sure miss? Suppose you could have Penny. She ain't down to anybody. Sir Harry, he be riding Prince today.'

'So, Sir Harold normally rides her?'

'Yes, and she is steady enough for him, well most of the time. The mistress has ridden her too, so she'll accept a side saddle but she's a bit lively.'

'Lead on then and let me see her.' The mare was a very different beast, small for a hunter but decidedly energetic, shaking its head and moving around the box as the groom tried to saddle up.

'I think I ought to see the master, or I be in trouble,' he said, scratching his head.

'No, don't bother him, she will be fine,' said Anne, smiling as she caught and stroked Penny's head. 'Yes, you'll give me a good ride, won't you.' As soon as the saddle was on, Penny was led outside, and Anne mounted with difficulty as it was a long way up. With girth and stirrups adjusted she tried to walk the horse to where the hunt was gathering. The horse was not keen with such a slow pace, fighting its bit, kicking its heels, wanting to be away. Anne reined in hard.

'Hello girl, you riding today?' said Mr Percival sidling a great hunter towards her. 'She looks frisky enough. Think you can handle her? Hey Brockham, this filly of yours won't break my governess's neck, will she? Mrs Percival will be upset if we lost our governess.'

'Eh no, but not my first choice for a guest. She was to be left in the stable. You ridden much, miss eh -?'

'Osebury, sir.'

'Ah yes. Hey Geoffrey, why did you give Miss Osebury my favourite mare?'

'Oh no sir, I said she was to use the cob,' said Geoffrey walking over, leading his own mount, and Robert astride a shaggy pony.

'You didn't see the cob?' said Sir Harold.

'I saw him, but as I wasn't ploughing or pulling a cart, I thought Penny might be more fun.' The older men roared with laughter, but Geoffrey continued to look worried.

'Good for you but don't blame me if you end up in a hedge; she likes to jump,' said Sir Harold still grinning. 'Geoffrey, you won't be able to keep up.'

They walked out and then went into a trot. Penny was keen to overtake the others in the party. Anne had to work hard, continuing to rein her back, trying to keep towards the rear of about thirty riders. The hounds circled around, sniffing for a scent, going from covert to covert, from one field to another. The air was crisp, the grass covered in a light frost. Anne shivered in the slow pace as they regularly stopped, the hounds circling around unsure and then suddenly they were off. A horn was blown, and Penny leapt forward following the baying dogs. Anne had ridden many horses in her young life but even she was surprised by the sheer speed of the beast. She was passing others in a flurry of flying mud. On they went, Anne holding on a little desperately but enjoying every moment.

100

A hedge and she was setting herself up for a jump or last second instant refusal, but Penny effortlessly cleared the brushwork. Glancing back, Anne saw a jumble of riders, reining back the other side of the fence, milling around as one man dismounted to open a gate to let them through. Another hedge but she steered Penny towards the gate at the end. She steadied and straightened the mare, but Penny was leaping for the gate unbidden. Up and over and on, in a tremendous rush.

She passed another rider and then another. The hounds streaming out before her. What a horse. Just three riders were ahead. One of them turned.

'Wahey there. How's she doing?' cried Sir Harold as she passed.

'Wonderful sir, she flies.' She spat a piece of mud out from her mouth. It wasn't wise to grin.

'She does with me and I'm twice your weight. We'll be at the kill,' he shouted after her.

They were going uphill, but Penny did not slow and then along a ridge, the country spread out on either side. Then they were rushing hell-bent down the hill and over a ploughed field. Staying on was everything and at the bottom, the hounds disappeared into a thicket. The gallop was over, horses and riders stopping, chests heaving. The breaths heavy and moist, puffs of smoke in the chill air. Other riders were struggling up. Anne wiped some spots of mud from her face; she didn't feel cold anymore. Country gentlemen glanced at the stranger in their midst.

'Still in the saddle my girl, well done,' said Mr Percival cantering up.

'Yes sir, but what a ride.' Finally, Geoffrey and Robert rode up. The boy was all grins.

'Did they catch it?' he cried.

'I don't know Robert, it's gone to earth I think, but did you have a gallop?' said Anne.

'Yes, she was quite fast, but you were miles in front.'

'Robert rode well but Anne, were you alright? Not terrified?' said Geoffrey.

'I think she could jump over a barn if she had to.' They circled around for a while and then the hounds were drawn off and they continued to seek further sport, but no other foxes were flushed out and they had a mainly gentle ride back until the last fields when Anne challenged Geoffrey and Robert to a race. She tried to rein Penny in to give the others a chance, but the mare wasn't having it and they galloped up to the stables minutes ahead. Jenny and the children were waiting. Edmund was riding around the yard on a fat pony.

'Lift me on,' demanded Camilla and with some effort Anne and Nanny pulled her on. Anne did a circle of the immediate parkland. When she trotted back, some of the hunt had dismounted and were being handed punch and chunks of fruit cake. Others remained mounted, eating and drinking as they talked, some with one leg draped casually over the saddle. The children's interest was suddenly in cake, so she left them to find the young groom. He was very busy but immediately tied the horse he was leading to the nearest ring and took her reins. His white face stared up at her.

'You alright, miss? Master Geoffrey gave me a right telling off.'

'Sir Harold didn't mind, I'm sure,'

'Thank Gawd for that.'

'A wonderful ride, she's a fantastic mare,' said Anne, sliding off, giving Penny a hug and then limping away, her legs stiff and uncooperative. She stopped to watch, enjoying the scene of the gentry milling around and socialising. Just two other woman riders. A maid wound between them, topping up glasses with the steaming punch, a footman nose in the air, following, carrying a silver platter with more cake. Mrs Percival wrapped in a heavy coat was also standing surveying the scene when Edmund and Robert ran through the group, and each seized a piece of cake before running off. Their mother directed her gaze at Anne, who shrugged and went after the boys.

The next day Geoffrey took them to the nearest market town, where he bought them all sweets and a green ribbon for Anne's hair. As they travelled in the coach, Anne couldn't help but glance at him, trying to decide what her true feelings were. Was her warm regard, real love, or something less? She had decided that her affection was strong enough and his character decent enough, that if he offered her marriage, she had to take it and was happy to do so. However, it was still galling that in an obligation to her family, she had little choice but to marry for security, rather than her own desire. She felt resentment that it fell on her to bring the financial stability that they so desperately needed. It was supposed to be her parents' responsibility or Hannah's. Why should it rest on the eighteen-year-old middle child? It was fortunate that in Geoffrey her affection and the family needs could be pleasantly aligned.

He turned to her. 'Tomorrow night my parents have hired a musical group to play for some dancing. Many of our neighbours are coming so we are having a ball. Will you dance with me?'

'I'd be delighted, but I haven't brought a suitable gown.'

'It isn't really a formal ball, I'm sure it won't matter. You will look very pretty as you are,' he said, his face glowing with sincerity. That's not what others will think she thought, but it was always pleasant to receive a compliment. Overcoming the shame of her dress however was going to be a challenge. She pictured herself entering the room in her day dress, with everyone looking at her. The thought made her grow body hot with embarrassment, even in the draughty coach. She would have liked to have found friendship with Geoffrey's sisters, but this would just give them one more opportunity to look down on her.

She really missed the friendship of girls of her own age and being with her own sisters. There had been several close friends in Hertfordshire, whom she would have liked to have written to, but the cost of the post remained prohibitive. Geoffrey's naivety over her dress was quite sweet but it wasn't very realistic.

'Won't your mother mind if the governess turns up in her old frock. I have gowns at the Percivals'. but I was told they weren't needed.'

'No, my mother will be delighted for you to join us. I'm sure you will enjoy it. Your beauty will overcome any need of fashion.'

'Huh, I thank you for your compliment, but I am neither beautiful nor able to outshine your sisters and visitors in their fine regalia. But if I can be allowed to come, and perhaps stay on the edge and have the occasional dance, I should hope to be content,' she said her mind busy with thoughts of how to improve her dress with ribbons and accessories from the children's dressing up box.

In the evening she picked up a pen to write a quick letter.

Dear Hannah, Tomorrow night they are having a ball here and Geoffrey the only son, who is just a year older than myself has invited me. It's his home so Mrs Percival can't keep me locked up in the school room. Unfortunately, my gowns are left at her home but needs must. He is a delightful young man, really good with the boys, taking us all over the county and we have become firm friends. It may be another fortnight before we return to Arleston Manor but I think it best you write there, as letters are so slow. We went on a fox hunt yesterday and I had the most marvellous hunter to ride, she wanted to be at the front all the time and soared over the hedges.

On our journey here we passed through Ironbridge and stayed at an Inn there. It is a fascinating town, full of industrial activity but what was amazing, was that I bumped into that boy James Thompson. He is studying to be a ceramic painter at a great factory called the Severn Pottery. He invited me to visit his aunt, a delightful old lady and he showed me some of his paintings and the plates he had been decorating. He is more sensible than we thought when you get to know him a little. Perhaps I will have more information on the changing fashions when I write next. Looking forward to hearing all your news. Love Anne.

She folded it up, wrote the address on the outside and sealed it with a candle. How upbeat the missive had sounded; it would be good for them to hear how life had improved.

The following afternoon they read parts in a story and did more drawing. Geoffrey joined in and even showed his own efforts, but bedtime was early for Camilla and Alfred, the other two being allowed to join the dance or at least watch. Anne brought them into the music room at eight. Geoffrey was already there and rose to meet them. His two sisters came over and without a glance at Anne led the boys on to the floor. There was a scattering of visitors around the room, but few lined up for the first dance. Geoffrey bowed.

'It's only a country dance but there will be a quadrille and even a waltz later.' He took her hand and led her on to the dance floor. It was an old-fashioned slow dance, of crossing and following, flowing, elegant and easy. It also gave time for snatches of conversation. There was a second similar dance, just a little faster but still not much more than a promenade. People were crowding in. Geoffrey pointed out some of the newcomers as they circled but didn't offer any introductions.

'Ah that is Elizabeth Temple one of our neighbours I will be expected to dance with her later,' he whispered, 'but I ought to dance with my cousins now.' Anne was left to dance with Robert and then Edmund, while Geoffrey went off dancing with several young women, including Eleanor and Abigail. Anne had just persuaded Edmund to dance with his sister when Sir Harold approached. He bowed.

'A dance with our daring horsewoman if I may,' he said. She curtsied. It was a quadrille, and her partner had the practiced elegance of years on a dance floor.

'A lovely occasion and you lead very well.'

'Thankyou my girl. The delight of a pretty partner always brings out one's style, the same handsome girl who I will always picture charging up the hill behind the hounds.' She blushed and became fearful that the portly gentleman would claim the next dance. Geoffrey came to her rescue, and she lied to his father that she had reserved the next dance with his son. It was another quadrille which as they ended the first phase, circling hand in hand, he led her in the conventional

106

way, but the second time, he spun her twice as quickly as the music.

They laughed as she struggled to keep up, ignoring the condemning looks of the assembly. He then went off to dance with Abigail, but Anne noticed he didn't dare to spin her. She went to stand out for the next dance, leaning against the wall as all the chairs were taken, the room now being full. She could observe the fashions and how everyone displayed themselves, until Mr Percival asked for the next quadrille, he bowed low with an exaggerated flourish. They were in the same square as Geoffrey and Eleanor.

Mr Percival danced capably but he hung on to her hand at every point and in the gentle spin pulled her close when she should have been at arms-length.

When they passed back-to-back with the other corner, Anne and Geoffrey exchanged conspiratorial smiles. Geoffrey also tried to spin Eleanor, but she couldn't keep up and nearly fell.

'Come Anne, let's sit this one out and have a rest,' he said when the dance ended.

'Tired already; when the evening is still so young?'

'Catching Eleanor hurt my back.' They both laughed.

'You cannot dance so many times with me, or everyone will talk,' she whispered.

'Let them talk, I don't mind. Why shouldn't I dance with the most attractive girl in the room? My only concern is that you are enjoying yourself; which you are, aren't you?'

'Stop flattering me but yes, it's lovely to be dancing again.'

'See, not having a ball gown doesn't matter. You look wonderful as you are.'

'Thank you, but don't remind me about this dress. When

I'm concentrating on the dance, I can forget the pitying stares.'

'But you dance so well it doesn't matter, look at those two.' A middle-aged couple had gone the wrong way down the set and were too confused to know where to go. Other dancers turned them and pointed them in the right direction. Geoffrey and Anne giggled

'Another quadrille. I suppose I'd better dance with Abigail as she's not danced the last two, and I haven't danced with my sisters yet.' He rose and bowed to Abigail whose face lit up at his approach. Anne was happy to continue to watch and then a supper was served. Geoffrey appeared at her side, collected a glass of wine for her and tried to make suggestions about the various dishes on the buffet.

'Have you ever danced a waltz?' he asked as they wandered into the corridor in search of a seat. A footman brought two chairs to a gilt side table on which sat such a large bust that they had to have their plates on their laps.

'No but I have practiced it with my sister. At the last dance I attended in Hertfordshire it wasn't thought seemly.'

'Well, you will have your opportunity soon,' They continued to talk as others came and went, until the music resumed.

'The waltz,' he said rising and taking her hand. There were only a few couples on the floor as the music started and Geoffrey hesitatingly led her round. People were still eating but all were looking on. Gradually as they repeated the steps and entered into the rhythm, it became easier and natural. He held her loosely as was the fashion and they flowed on together, in a series of in graceful rotations.

People were watching them, admiring even. Geoffrey could certainly lead and as well as any man in the room. It was pleasant to be, if not at the centre of attention, certainly one of the more accomplished couples on the floor. His sisters, who had not said one word to her since she had arrived, were watching, and whispered together. Abigail joined them. Perhaps they might be more friendly in future.

There were several waltzes and three more quadrilles before the evening ended. By the time they had danced the last one, Anne felt not only that she had mastered the steps, but that she was being held and loved by her future husband. He held her hand at the door, bowed, kissed the tips of her fingers, and said he would see her on the morrow.

'Today,' she said as it was gone midnight. They both laughed, exchanged loving looks and Anne felt she was floating up the stairs. She went to sleep imagining herself in his arms.

When Jenny knocked at eight o'clock, Anne struggled into wakefulness. A quick breakfast, and a morning attempting to teach the younger two some arithmetic and deal with two older boys who also hadn't had enough sleep. Lunch came and went and then the housekeeper arrived.

'Sorry to disturb you, but Mrs Percival says to tell you, that you will be going home tomorrow. She says to have the children packed and ready by nine.'

'Tomorrow! I thought we were staying till next Thursday at the earliest,' said Anne.

'I dunno but that's the message I was given. Nine o'clock sharp,' she said.

'It was supposed to have been a fortnight,' said Jenny.

'Perhaps there's snow coming, but it's strange. Excuse me,' said Anne starting up and running after the housekeeper. 'Do you know where I might find Master Geoffrey?'

'I don't know miss. Heard he was going visiting with his mother this afternoon.'

'Visiting?'

'He was going to take me to the gun room,' said Robert.

'He was, wasn't he? I'm sure he will come later.' Might their sudden departure, force him to voice his attentions, to make a proposal? An exciting thought but it was also strange and worrying. Every day he had been enthusiastically entertaining them but on what had become their last day he had disappeared. No doubt he would call later in the afternoon. However, he didn't come, and after they had eaten dinner, Anne summoned up the courage to try to find him. A footman stood at the door of the drawing room.

'Excuse me, but has the family eaten?'

'Yes mam, they are all in the drawing room. Whom did you want to see?'

'Master Geoffrey.'

'Wait here, I'll see if he's available.' She stood waiting, as the seconds ticked by. She began to walk up and down, but no one came, and nothing happened. What was going on? Finally, the footman emerged and looking into the far distance, announced.

'Master Geoffrey is not in.'

'Of course he is; why can't he come?'

'He is not in,' repeated the servant. She stared at him.

'That's ridiculous,' but the stony-faced man continued to stare at the wall. She turned and started back up the stairs, her steps dragging as her hopes were left behind.

CHAPTER 5

The muffs were positioned, the china hot water bottles in place, the carriages packed and ready in the crisp morning air. The horse's breath in misty clouds. Geoffrey stood behind his family as they came out, but as he was half a head taller it was difficult for him to hide his face. She saw his attention was on the shingled drive. He did not look up, acknowledge her or even wave at the children as the coach pulled away. Only at the last moment was there a guarded glance, shame, regret, it was difficult to tell as the wheels crunched over the shingle, taking them apart.

'Coward.' Anne spat the words into the back of her hand as she waved at the others. She hadn't been ready for marriage; wasn't sure she had loved him, but it was crushing to be cast away so completely. Even Camilla climbing onto her lap, didn't soften her mood. Had the visit been cut short because of her? The talk had been of staying for three weeks but it had been eight days. Why, oh why?

'Tell us a story miss, please,' said Alfred as the miles ticked by. Anne grimaced and shook her head, looking out at the trees with their dusting of silver frost but neither the beauty, nor the children gave her any comfort. Her heart wasn't broken, but it was hurt, and her pride was badly dented. Her eyes threatened her further embarrassment, the cold air stinging them sharply to encourage the tears. She pulled her scarf higher. He would have been a perfect answer, so agreeable, so pleasant, and financially secure but a coward, perhaps it was better that the relationship didn't come to anything but oh it was so aggravating.

Had her poverty destroyed the chance of happiness, his parents pressurising him to give her up because of her status as a poverty-stricken governess? She supposed, seeing them dancing together, had revealed their growing affection. Why hadn't she seen the danger of being observed and if she could cope with defying her own parents to go away and be a governess, why couldn't he defy his? How could he become a captain of a ship, fighting slave traders and pirates, if he couldn't combat his parents' prejudices, or even apologise, and Sir Harold had been both friendly and kind. She exhaled her frustrations.

'We want a story,' repeated Alfred.

'Just watch the scenery Alfred, your governess isn't feeling well,' said Jenny.

'What's the matter,' said Edmund.

'Nothing you need worry about,' said Jenny.

'She's just sad because Master Geoffrey didn't say goodbye,' said Robert. Anne twisted around, surprised at his discernment. Was everyone aware? Had every servant and family member, knowledge of their friendship and the forced ending of it and did that include Abigail and Eleanor? Would the servants at the Percival's home soon learn of it? The warmth of her shame rose inside her layers of clothing.

Over the next week she struggled to settle back into being, just the governess, but it was hard to shake off her black mood. Gradually she found enjoyment in her own learning as she sought to teach her charges. She resumed her reading of the paper in the hall, except when it was Jenny's night off and occasionally Mr Percival or one of his smoking friends would exchange a word, but she kept away from the younger element who visited for the many dinners and dances that were central to the hospitality of the house.

She was at her usual place when the Doctor entered. 'You aren't joining the dancing tonight?' he said as he passed.

'I'm afraid I'm not invited.'

'No, I suppose you wouldn't be, less competition,' he muttered as he carried on into the music room. It was a large room, quite adequate in size for about forty guests to dance, with space for seats around the edge for onlookers. There was a raised dais in one corner, for a grand piano and other musicians when they came. Anne only went to the room when she delivered Camilla for piano lessons with Mrs Exton. She tried to read her book, but eventually as the guests came and went, the sound of laughter and music and the clinking of glasses, of society enjoying itself, became too much and she left them to their entertainment. Even back in her living room the book had lost its charm. She sighed.

When there was a fine winter day, ten days later, she decided a drive would be good for them all. She was supervising the groom rigging her governess's gig, when she spotted looking out of one of the stalls, a horse that wasn't normally there. She walked towards it.

'Hey Jenkins, is this a new arrival. What's its name?' she said running her hand over its neck.

'Penny mam.'

'I thought so. Has Mr Percival bought her?'

'Oh no, Mr Tiverton rode in on her, but I've not seen her before.'

'Really!'

After the children were in bed, she was down in the hall earlier than usual, waiting. As he came down-stairs she jumped up. 'Mr Tiverton, excuse me, but I couldn't help admiring your lovely mare Penny. Can I ask how you come to be riding her?

'Because I bought her.'

'We are just going into dinner,' said Eleanor, taking Mr Tiverton's arm.

'From Sir Harold?'

He stared at her. 'Of course.' He burst out laughing, 'I should have known.' He shook his head and disentangled himself from Eleanor. 'I had arranged to buy her months ago but when I went to collect her, he said he didn't want to sell her after all, although he needed the money. He said some chit of a girl, rode her without permission, jumping each hedge and passing every other rider, including the master of the hunt so now he wanted to keep her as my price was too low. Said the penniless girl nearly broke his sons heart too. Was that you?' He looked sternly at her, but his eyes twinkled.

'It could have been.' He leant close to her.

'Bad luck, the son has to marry money; they've run out.' he whispered before walking on. Anne wanted to enthuse about Penny's attributes, but her owner was disappearing into the dining room with Eleanor back on his arm. So, Geoffrey's affection had been genuine? Mr Percival pushed past with a sideways look and then turned and came back.

'Anne, it has been decided that Robert can join the shoot tomorrow and Mrs Percival wishes for you to be there to keep an eye on him. There are some important guests coming.'

'I will make arrangements with Nanny. What exactly would you like me to do, as I presume, I won't be shooting?'

'No, I'm afraid not, just make sure he enjoys himself but keep him safe and out of the way of our guests. It will be nice to have a pretty face amongst my shooting friends. One o'clock by the stables.'

'Yes sir,' said Anne wondering how Robert would like her hovering at his elbow. However, in his excitement as he ate lunch, he appeared to have little concern. When they arrived, groups of gentlemen were standing around in the stable yard. Two carriages were being used to shuttle groups up to an area of woodland. There were about a dozen guests and several members of staff with dogs. Men from the village who were going to be beaters were walking up and Anne decided to walk with them rather than wait. When they reached the woods, they found all the guests assembling in a line. Anne made sure she and Robert were at the end. Three of the guests each had a personal valet who would load for them.

'Hello Robert,' said the nearest guest, a young man whom Anne decided must be in his early twenties, 'and you, young lady, are the governess I believe. I'm Morley.' He gave the slightest bow and smiled.

'Yes, how do you do. Anne Osebury at your service.'

'Are you going to shoot?'

'No, I'm just here to keep Robert company.'

'Well, you could have a go later if you wish, unless you think it's un-lady like?'

'That's very kind. I've fired a small bore shot gun but not twelve gauge.'

'Yes, it might be hard on a lady's shoulder. What about the boy's gun?'

They began to walk forward; the smaller spaniels being sent into the undergrowth. When the first pheasant rose with a clatter of wings and a warning screech, guns were jerked to shoulder height.

'Not your turn yet,' said Anne as the doctor who was at the far left, aimed, and fired. The man beside him, whom Anne didn't know, fired immediately afterwards when it was apparent the doctor had missed. The bird fell like a stone and a larger dog was released into the wood to retrieve the pheasant. The line moved forward, and two more birds took flight. The next two guns fired and down they went. Another bird rose straight up, and a fifth gun fired. Everyone was busy reloading, except those who had an assistant who were just handed a second loaded gun. Only a few of the guns were double barrelled. The next bird flew low and managed to escape several shots. 'You're next but one; ready?'

Two pheasants broke cover together. Robert and Mr Morley fired simultaneously but only one bird fell. Anne had her hands over her ears. Thick smoke drifted across.

'I think I missed,' said Robert. He began to pour black powder down the muzzle of his gun.

'Better luck next time, Master Robert, smooth follow through with a small lead,' said Morley. 'Keep moving forward.'

Keeping the line straight, reloading, and moving was tricky but they continued into the undergrowth without disturbing more birds. At the end of the wood, a group took to the wing, the male's iridescent plumage a flash of colour in the winter sun. Guns banged away. They walked on to a second wood. The trees were well spaced and there was a plantation of coppiced hazel. The birds rose singly or in small groups, the sportsmen often out of turn depending on whether they had reloaded. Most of the guns were flintlocks and there were the occasional misfires. Robert was quite quick in loading and took his share of shots.

'Alright, Morley?' said Mr Percival coming over. Have you got one yet Robert?'

'Yes sir.'

'Well done. Had you had a second gun Miss Osebury could have loaded for you. Sorry to drag you out here girl but Mrs Percival insisted.'

'I said she could have a go,' said Morley.

'Well, if her shooting is as good as her riding, she'll show you up. How's the new gun?'

'Excellent.'

'Have you seen it Robert, it doesn't have a flint but uses little copper caps?' They all peered at the weapon as Morley held it out for them to inspect. The mahogany stock shone, and the metal work was beautifully engraved with scenes of hunting, a real rich man's toy. This young man had to be seriously wealthy to own such a gun thought Anne. She looked at him more closely. He still had the pimples of youth and while his blond hair and blue eyes had great charm, a lack of substance to his chin rather diminished his appearance.

'If you want to try it, then your governess can try yours,' he said with an engaging smile. Robert passed his to Anne. He took the gun, weighing it, feeling the balance. It looked heavy for him.

'It's loaded but needs a percussion cap.' said Morley, cocking the hammers and slipping on two caps as Robert held it.

'Is that all it needs? No extra gunpowder?'

'No that's it, quick and clean. Must be your turn soon. Lot of birds amongst the hazel,' said his father. Anne was assessing the feel of the single-barrelled twenty gauge. It was well balanced. She squinted along the barrel following a bird that had just flown. Somebody else was shooting. Robert's turn came, bang, he missed but Anne fired just after, and the bird fell.

'I told you so. She shoots as well as she rides.'

'Just a lucky shot, but it's an easy gun to use,' she said, standing the gun's butt on the ground and rubbing her right shoulder with her left hand. 'Didn't the recoil hurt you, Robert?'

'No, it was nothing,' he said proudly but the strained expression suggested otherwise. They continued in their line and Anne had a second shot and Robert several more with Morley's gun. When they exited the hazel, the shoot was over, and they walked back to the coaches which were taking them to the house. The important guests were the first to go. As they milled around waiting for it to return, Mr Percival came over and clapped Robert on the shoulder.

'Did you have a good day boy?'

'Yes, great, thanks.' He was carrying a brace of pheasants. He was the only one wanting to carry his birds, the rest were piled in a small cart.

'And you, girl?'

'Yes sir, always good to be outside in decent weather.'

'The black smut on your nose is very becoming.' She blushed. 'You must have a glass of punch when we reach the house.'

'Thank you,' she said, but she knew that Mrs Percival wouldn't want her mixing with their guests. Why were the men always so much friendlier than the women?

Late in the evening, she was sitting trimming the wick on

the Argand lamp in her sitting room, when she felt a draught. With the children in bed, she had been enjoying a quiet read. The door of her sitting room which had been left slightly ajar in case the children cried, was opening. The master of the house looked in. An odour of stale wine preceded him. He closed the door behind him. She relit the lamp from a candle and blew out the candle, wondering why he was there.

'At peace then, all nicely tucked up in bed?'

'Yes sir, all asleep but when it's Jenny's night off, I always stay listening for a while, just in case. With the door open, please.' The little room had two easy chairs with wooden arms beside a small table.

'What are you reading?' he said coming to stand beside the chair, leaning over. What was he doing here? She felt threatened. It wasn't the place. How could he think of visiting her when she was alone?

'Robinson Crusoe, probably for the fourth time.'

'Ah, one of my favourites too. Now Miss Osebury, Anne, how would you have liked to have been cast-away on a desert island, with handsome pirates chasing you; all wanting to get their hands on you? Exciting, and romantic, eh.' His hand gripped her shoulder. She shuddered and twisted but the hand remained. 'They'd have all fallen in love with you. You are lovely you know?' She froze, unable to think, it felt as if something like rigor mortis was setting in, her throat tight and unmovable. He pressed himself against the back of the chair as he began to gently caress her shoulder, running his hand up under her hair and onto her neck. His other hand reached down for her breast. All her training in polite, well-mannered conversation finally came to her rescue.

'Mr Percival, that was not a suitable comment, nor is this

the appropriate place to make it, please leave.'

'You are really very pretty. All alone up here we could give each other a little comfort. No one can see, no one would know.' His left hand retreated from her bosom, but his right held firmly to her neck as he bent down close, his alcoholic fumes wafting around her face. 'We are of one mind, you and I, so alike. Seeing you ride, joining in on the shoot, I saw how you love adventure and excitement, as I do.'

She sprang up, brushing his hand off. He lurched at her; she was around the table pushing it between them. It fell, the lamp splashing oil over the rug as it went out. The room was suddenly dark, the fire giving the only light. He nearly tripped over the table and stood breathing hard. 'Come now Anne we can be friends, I'm sure you are just as lonely as I am. You are such a sweet little mouse.'

'Please leave,' she shouted.

'There's no one in earshot. At this moment, nanny and the only servants who live in this wing are downstairs. I mean you no harm; we really ought to share a little affection. I can help you get on.'

'Leave,' she shouted louder. He stood swaying but then there was a little cry. Camilla!

'Someone heard,' she said pushing past. As she comforted the child, a door slammed. 'Who's there?' she called.

'It's me; Mrs Carpenter. What is it?' said the housekeeper peering around the door.

'Mr Percival was in my room; has he gone?'

'Yes dear, I passed him on the landing. Has he been troubling you?'

'Please don't say anything but I don't know what to do.'

'What happened?'

120

'He came in when I was alone and shut the door behind him,' said Anne as she cuddled Camilla, 'Shush, it's alright little one.' The child continued to whimper but remained half asleep.

'I did warn you. Did anything happen?'

'He wouldn't take his hand off my shoulder, but my shout woke Camilla.'

'You did well to cry out. You must lock your door.'

'I haven't a key. Oh, I can't stay here.'

'Why not? You don't think you are the only one he troubles do you?'

'No, but I must go, and tomorrow.'

'Even with all your airs and graces, you have done better with the children than your predecessors.'

'What do I say to Mrs Percival?'

'She knows what he is like.'

'And she doesn't do anything!'

'What can she do? He controls all their wealth, both his and hers.'

'Wouldn't her family support her in a divorce?'

'No, they wouldn't wish for the shame and scandal and it's near impossible for a woman to obtain one anyway. Most women just have to live with it,' said Mrs Carpenter with a shrug of her shoulders. 'She has her position, the children and a fine house.'

'That's terrible. Could you please tell Mrs Percival what happened?' said Anne carefully easing the infant into her cot. A sleeping child so sweetly innocent of the adult world.

'Alright, but she won't be happy.'

After spending time barricading her room, she slept fitfully.

121

As soon as breakfast was over, she found Mrs Percival in the drawing room with Mrs Exton.

'Could I speak with you alone please?' she said, glancing at the old lady who was darning a stocking, her fingers slowing as if she was readying to listen.

'I'm sure anything you have to say can be said in front of my aunt,' said Mrs Percival but looking at Anne's resolute expression, she added, 'but perhaps if you could be so good as to leave us, Mrs Exton.' They waited as the old lady gathered her belongings. Mrs Percival folded her arms.

'I am afraid I must give my notice and leave immediately,' said Anne as the door closed.

'That would be impossible.'

'But I can't stay here after what happened.'

'Some older men, if a young woman makes eyes at them, become very silly, but it means nothing.'

'Make eyes at him! I can assure you; that your husband's unwanted attentions were not encouraged by me in any way.'

'Why then did you join the men at the shoot?'

'Because Mr Percival said you wanted me to support Robert.'

'That is a lie. Robert was quite able to look after himself. ' Anne stood speechless. The tick of a clock was the only sound.

'It is not. You have my word as the daughter of a gentleman that I only went as a direct request from your husband. If that is what you think of me, it only confirms that my decision to leave is the right one. I am prepared to stay until the weekend, but I must make some conditions. The first is a lock on my door, the second is, you write a testimonial for me, now!'

'I'm sure that is unnecessary. Have you any further demands?'

'Yes, - actually there are.' Her treatment, the hours, the spoilt children and now, somehow, she was being blamed for her husband's philandering. Mrs Percival sat rigid; her face set hard. Anne knew she should not express her opinion and that she ought to give sympathy, but it was beyond her.

'My employment ends now, this moment. I expect no wages from today, I stay only as a favour to you, and not as a governess. I will remain as your guest, but I expect to be treated as such. I will carry out all my previous duties, but please note, in my own way with a free hand. I will eat at your table, be introduced to your guests as the gentlewoman that I am, otherwise I will be on tomorrow's post.'

'This is most aggravating. You are a governess and that is your place. I will arrange for new locks to be fitted, although I cannot believe it is necessary. I will write you a testimonial but as for the rest, it is not fitting.'

'Then I will start packing.' She stood up and turned towards the door. 'I hope you can find someone soon, as the boys need a strong hand.'

'Come back, I have not finished.'

'Mrs Percival, I don't think there is anything else to say.'

'This is blackmail.'

'No, it is justice. I have been treated appallingly here. Growing up in my home, our governess was treated with civility, and while she might have been on the edge of our social circle she was treated as a friend. She was not banished to the nursery and was always introduced to visitors. My father is a knight of the realm, yet you even suggested I didn't use the main stairs! As for Mr Percival, well, perhaps I will not say more but you have my commiseration. I will collect my wages such as they are, in the morning and the testimonial. I hope I can rely on a servant to escort me to Shrewsbury.' For a moment Anne thought by Mrs Percival's stony-faced expression that her wish might be denied, but a sigh and a nod suggested that transport and escort would be provided.

Back in her bedroom as she began to pack, her anger evaporated, and as the hurt pride and shame took its place, the tears began to splash on her garments as she mechanically folded them neatly into the trunk. It might make the clothes damp, but she was beyond caring. What could she do? Would she be able to catch a coach, what if they were all full, and the inn in Shrewsbury? Had she enough savings to pay her way? How was she going to face her parents? And worst of all, admit they were right! Perhaps Mrs Percival would apologise. Perhaps she would beg her to stay but it appeared unlikely, and the tears continued to dampen the contents.

In the morning she wanted to creep away, but Jenny and the children were there to see her off. A surprising hug from Nanny with Alfred and Camilla clinging tightly. Edmund just stood looking sad, but Robert stepped forward and held out his hand.

'Goodbye, Miss Osebury, have a good journey.'

'Thank you, Robert, I don't know what will happen, but your father has a good library, so search the books and read as many as you can. Goodbye.' She glanced up at the windows, where there appeared a general movement behind several. They would all be watching, servant and mistress, another failure leaving. Bert quickly loaded her trunks into a spacious gig, and they were off. She was determined not to cry but once out of sight, tears streamed down her cheeks. When after some time she was able to dry her eyes, she tried a little conversation with her driver, who made an effort to respond, but it quickly died, and a dull silence descended. When they reached Shrewsbury, she found a room and started making further enquiries over coaches for the following day. Ironbridge was closer than Herefordshire. An idea began to form, a crazy idea. Could she take up James' offer; did his aunt really want her to stay?

It was raining again on the second day, only increasing her depression and her growing fear of rejection, of being seen to be so stupid. By the time she had engaged a porter to carry her trunks to the house it was three o'clock, and the rain had finally stopped, having washed away the smoke and grime, leaving the air crisp and clean. Winter sunshine was glinting from behind the feathery clouds but if the black clouds had blown away, her own cloud of despondency had not. She stood, trying to summon the courage to ring the bell, the great trunks at her feet. Oh, why had she chosen to bring so much luggage? What use ball gowns and fancy objects? How could she be just dropping in with so much? With a last glance at the people going by, she jerked at the rope. The distant ringing confirmed it worked. She waited; perhaps they were out, and she could somehow meet James first, but the door opened, and his aunt looked up at her.

'Anne! What are you doing here?'

'I'm so sorry. I just had to get away and James said you might put me up for a few days.'

'Of course, come in, but is all this luggage yours? Elsie is out; perhaps we can drag it into the hall together.'

Anne had intended to keep her reasons for sudden flight secret but sitting in the cosy parlour with a cup of tea and the kind old lady, the reasons gushed out.

'Please do not tell James what made me come.'

'Of course not dear. He was very keen for you to work at the factory, but I fear you may find it hard and difficult. I will be delighted for you to stay but I really think you ought to re-join your parents.'

Anne was in the kitchen when James returned. She was trying to help Elsie prepare dinner, although she was very aware, she was more hindrance than help. Yet she knew, she had to be seen to try.

'What are those great trunks in the hall,' they heard him ask his aunt.

'A friend of yours, come to visit. Try the kitchen.' Bursting into the kitchen he exclaimed, 'Anne, this is wonderful; are you really going to become an artist?'

'Yes, if they'll have me. If not, I need to stay long enough to write home and receive a reply.'

'I'm sure they will. Do you have some of your paintings in the trunks?'

'Yes, several.'

'Then tomorrow we will take you to the factory or Elsie can, as I have to be there early.'

A reasonable dinner, pleasant conversation around the fire, and James's constant enthusiasm, put her mind at rest, and she slept well until four in the morning when she awoke to worry that her ability would not be enough, and she would be quickly rejected, or she would find herself doing hard menial work beyond her strength and patience. Painting could be frustrating but to be able to improve her skills would be worthwhile, yet to work in a factory, what was she thinking?

How could she lower herself? Yet she had discovered that without money you were destitute? Before her father's financial collapse, she had never even thought of it. She had carried a purse when shopping in town, but for most purchases the tradesmen simply said, "Yes madam we'll put it on the account," and that had been that. The inward debate caused her to become hot and then cold, to toss one way and then the other, backwards and forwards, unable to settle. She eventually slept again and woke with a thick head.

A large breakfast was presented to her as if her host wished to build up her strength. James had long gone and just before ten, she went with Elsie, a package of pictures and sketches under her arm. At the factory it was explained that she had come to see Miss Quantrell. A man in brown overalls escorted her past lines of women and children of all ages, who were sitting attaching transfers, painting rims or using stencils. Many of the children had no shoes and some of the women were poorly dressed. Was she expected to work with them? A man pushed past with a barrow loaded with grey unfired plates. In a second building there were several men each throwing pots on a wheel and a group of men bending over dishes with paint brushes. James rose from the group and joined Anne.

'I'll take her now,' said James. 'You've brought your portfolio; good, follow me.' Glancing at some of the pieces as they passed, Anne wondered again if she would be skilled enough.

'Miss Quantrell this is Anne Osebury talented daughter of Sir George and Lady Osebury.'

'Pleased to meet you Anne, let us see some of your work. James can be over enthusiastic sometimes,' said the middle-aged lady, wiping her brush and then her fingers on a piece of rag. The dress that bordered her apron suggested a wealthy background than most of the employees. Anne bobbed and brought the first painting out of her bag.

'Mm,' said Miss Quantrell, 'And the next one. Have you ever had any formal training?'

'No madam.'

'Well obviously you can draw but can you be inventive, can you do the same decoration as accurately on one side of a vase as on the other. Can you be consistent so that every piece in a set, matches perfectly. Will you have an eye for what the public will want to buy next year?'

'I'm sure I can apply myself to learning technique and consistency if you give me the opportunity.'

'But you expect to be more than an apprentice, to earn wages even before you can mix a pot of glaze?'

'James intimated that you would consider it.'

'Well, I doubt that you will have the ability to settle in and apply yourself. Brought up as a lady of leisure is not the foundation to real work as I know too well myself, but much as I consider it a waste of time, I will give you a trial. Come with James tomorrow and you will have two weeks to convince me,' she said before turning back to an elegant vase and dipping her brush again. 'James, tell Bill he has another apprentice.'

Finding her way out of the premises and home again Anne was very thoughtful. She wanted to prove she could settle in and become a real artist whose initials were marked on fine pieces collected by royalty and the rich. Yet the life of a factory? It was such an alien world; did she really want that? Could she stick it out and for years? She shivered and nearly lost her way but as soon as she reached the river, the route home was easy.

CHAPTER 6

In the deep dark of November at 6.20 in the morning, a
knock on her bedroom door gradually awakened her to
the day. Dressed in several layers she joined James for
breakfast. A hot bowl of porridge was set before her.

'Do you always do your own breakfast?' she eventually
said.

'Of course, Elsie can't do everything.'

'Your aunt cannot afford more than one servant?'

'I think she could, but she doesn't want the bother. Bad servants are worse than none. She has a woman who comes and
does some cleaning and another who does heavy kitchen work
but no one else that lives in. Do you want toast and coffee?'

'Yes please.'

'We will need to leave in a few minutes.' Anne glanced at
the clock. When had she last been up so early? Did many people have to work at such an hour?

Outside she expected to find the streets empty, but there
were masses of people, striding along, many bent over in their
haste. In the morning mist there was an urge to be on time, a
rush to earn enough for rent and bread. She found herself hurrying too. At the works she joined a queue of employees. So,
was that what she was, just another artisan? She shivered as
she gave her name to a clerk, James explaining who she was.
Those around her glanced at her. Even in her oldest dress and
coat, the quality of it made her stand out. She was out of place

and the looks and mutterings around her confirmed that she was thought different. What were they thinking of her? Someone they supposed who had fallen on hard times. Galling as it was, she had to admit to herself, that their suppositions were correct. She tried to stand tall and told herself that she could prove that a lady could achieve something. They entered and passed groups of workers, who were putting on aprons and setting work out, before they found Bill.

'Mr Johnson this is our new trainee. Anne, William Johnson.'

'Please to meet you sir.'

'Thankyou. I'm not sure quite what we will do with you, but this morning you can prove to me if you are consistent. Follow me.' At one of the long workbenches, he stopped. A young woman was stirring a pot of glaze.

'Sit here Anne, and Maud will show you how to edge a plate. Maud's in charge of the girls here,' he said his arm sweeping the lines of workers. 'After your lunch break, come and find me and we will test you on something more taxing. Maud, she is in your hands, make sure we don't spoil too many.'

'Yes Mr Johnson.'

'Right girl, just watch me,' said Maud before turning a plate, one finger on the edge, the others holding the brush. An even blue line appeared one inch from the rim. She dipped her brush again and turning the plate, ran it around the rim. Two neat parallel lines. She put the plate further along the bench and picked up another, dipping her brush she began to turn it.

'See the line is even in thickness. Old Bill gets all excited if it's all different. Get sold as seconds them do. You watch me a bit, then see the little pile over there? They ain't no good. You practice on them first and then we'll see if you can try a decent one. What was your name again?'

'Anne.'

'That's it, put that plate on the little wheel. See how to turn it. Practice doing it until you think you can keep the brush even then watch me how I 'old the brush, with me finger on the rim.' Maud turned back to her next plate, a constant flow of lines and perfect plates.

It was a hard lesson and when they stopped at midday for lunch, she felt too tired to eat. As she stretched the stiffness out of her fingers, she stared at the chunks of bread and cheese. After the first few bites, hunger took over and she ate everything that James had brought her. Although some of the other workers had glanced in her direction, Maud had never commented on her background or ability.

'How did you get on?' he said between mouthfuls of apple.

'I think I only ruined about three, but Maud is so quick and accurate, and she accepted me without question or put down. Is there any more tea?'

'No that's it, I'm afraid.'

'Thirsty are you miss, 'ave some ale,' said the girl on the next table, handing across a stone glazed bottle, 'elp yourself.' Anne looked at the open neck that the girl had just drunk from. The owner, whose dress was worn and greasy from age and her shawl holed and scraggly, had the look of extreme poverty. Never had Anne drunk from a bottle, never had she shared a drinking vessel. She looked at the thin face and the simple generous expression. Anne gulped, held the bottle nervously and stared into its mouth.

'Here,' said James taking the bottle, 'pour it into your cup.' As the golden pungent liquid swirled around the tin mug,

Anne smiled.

'Thank you, most kind but don't you want to finish it?'

'Naw, I've 'ad enough. You going to like working 'ere?'

'I think so. Is it a good job?'

'As good as any I reckon. At least it's safe. I worked down a pit for a while. That was wuss. Dirty as a goblin and expecting the roof to cave in on yer any moment.'

'Well, Bill might have you doing something more exciting when we've finished your food.' It was supposed to be a half hour break, but James took her straight to Mr Johnson as soon as they had finished.

'Well Anne, seems you did alright this morning. James is painting roses on these cups and saucers. What I want you to do is watch for a while and then do the underpainting. Practice on an old plate or two, then you do the basic pink petals, stem and leaves but he will highlight them and put the shadows and thorns in. Can you do that?'

'Yes sir.'

'Good, get on with it then and make sure they are all the same size.'

As the foreman walked away, James put a cup on the table before her. 'They'd have never let me start on something so difficult. The problem is that whichever side you look at, the flowers must look equally spaced. You must work it out in your mind. This cup is a second. See if you manage it.' She was furiously concentrating, when there was a clatter on the bench beside her. A man was piling up some half-glazed saucers.

'You done this before.'

'No never.'

'My Betsy, she were 'ere two years before she were let on underpainting.' Anne slightly taken aback to be spoken to, looked up at him. Underneath bushy hair, whitened by deposit of plaster dust, he had an intelligent face.

'Well, I've done lots of other painting.'

'Not the same though, is it? Everyone to their station I suppose but you don't looked dressed to be 'ear. There's lots of folks need a job more than you I reckon.'

'Even I have to earn a living so needs must.'

'You aint got it matched right. See, one of them flowers is lower than the other.'

'Thank you. I can see that now, but this is just a practice piece,' said Anne trying to ignore him. He continued to look down on her as he finished stacking groups of cups and then muttering about aristocratic trainees walked away.

The concentration required left her exhilarated, and in the evening, she enjoyed the conversation with her hosts. She slept so well that she was ready for work the following day. The long hours however began to wear her down, but her interest and curiosity saw her through to Saturday afternoon. On Sunday she rose late but still struggled to stay awake during the morning sermon at the church. In the afternoon she was able to boost her energy levels by doing very little else except to write home. What could she tell them? How could she explain her new address? She hesitated.

Dear Hannah, I think I is better that you do not show mother this letter or my new address, in fact, you mustn't. I really do not know what to say but I am well, safe, and enjoying myself. I have left the Percival's for reasons I do not wish to impart on paper, but I can assure you it was through no fault of my own. Please really believe me. I am now staying with an

*aunt of James Thompson, you remember him, with the greatest
propriety. He is a pleasant boy now I have seen more of him.
She is a delightful old lady, and we enjoy interesting conversations around the fire in the evening. Please don't be shocked
but I am practicing my skill with a brush at a china works. It
is fascinating and while it appears that I am working as an
artisan, I have been treated with the respect due our class,
yet at the same time I have been accepted by ordinary folk.
While for the most part the workers are uneducated, some of
them are extremely skilled and excellent artists. They often
start working when they are eight or nine, so their ability has
time to grow. The best artist is a lady of a genteel background
and while she is a hard taskmaster, she has in her own way
been kind. Because the works already have one painter with
an upper-class background, I appear to have been accepted
by most of the workers as another oddity. While I miss being
waited on and the comfortable life of a lady there is something
dynamic about the town and all that is produced here.*

*Your letters are such a comfort to me, that they are savoured
and reread many times but as I do, I have noted several themes,
one of which causes considerable concern. In your last letter
you mentioned Mr Spenliff nine times. Looking back, I then
observed that in the previous letter it was seven times and in
the one before five. This is a worrying trend. Please do not fall
in love with him. THERE IS NO FUTURE FOR YOU THERE.
He has no money, slim prospects and cannot offer you any sort
of home. You mentioned him dining with you and even playing
chess with father. We have no money either. Don't let your
heart fool you into a disaster!*

*Please continue to persuade Grace to write as it is a good
way for her to improve her English but ensure that neither*

Grace nor mother send to my old address. I am sorry to have to ask you to engage in such subterfuge, but I cannot imagine Mother would understand, nor accept my present situation and would demand my immediate return, nor do I wish her to have further worries. Your loving sister Anne.

In the following weeks as well as a great deal of painting, she was able to enjoy helping them stack the kiln and later the excitement of taking down the bricks to open it. The bricks still too hot to touch yet everyone would be desperate to see if the porcelain they had painted had survived. Her understanding of how the glazes blended, the colours and effects they caused, and her own artistic skill was growing but not fast enough for Miss Quantrell, who offered no wages but did allow an extension of her trial period.

The other workers had gradually accepted her for who she was. They no longer laughed at her ignorance over day-to-day living, nor were they jealous of her not being required to start at the bottom and even accepted that she might just have enough talent to justify her position. The fact that everyone knew she was not being paid, might have helped. Anne continued to think of her role as being an artist but the constant reminder that she was in other ways just a factory worker, was much more difficult for her to admit. To rub shoulders with the lower classes and to be often taken as one of them was galling yet she also learnt that their humanity was the same as hers. Her opinion went from being appalled that her station in life was so ignored, to be being touched by their generous and kindly nature. From being amazed at the ignorance around her yet astounded at their artistry and skills. They might not be able to write their own name, yet they could catch the likeness of some plant or creature in paint.

At Christmas they were given two days off and everybody received a few extra shillings but there were many complaints, as in the previous year they had received more. It was a white Christmas but not the right sort, for it was mainly sleet or snow that quickly turned to slush. A good time to be inside around the fire, rather than in the cold works. Their immediate neighbours were two spinster ladies who joined them for table games and lunch. A gentle, relaxing time but so different to Annes last Christmas where their great house had blazed with candles, servants had scurried around serving a great feast, and Hannah had entertained them on their best pianoforte. The New Year of 1821 was upon them, but would it bring any rising of their fortunes?

On the Friday, a fortnight after Christmas she was feeling particularly tired. After she had eaten her lunch, she sat leaning against the wall. She was jerked awake by Bill leaning over her.

'What's all this? Bit tired are ya, need a little nap? You're 'ere to work. This place is going to the dogs as it is, without little miss stuck up having her beauty sleep 'ere.' And them saucers you done, aint right. 'ave a look see.'

'Sorry Mr Johnson,' she said standing and heading for her bench. Looking around she saw everyone was already back at their places. Only a few minutes after she had started on a fresh saucer, Bill was again looking down on her.

'Did you look at the last one you did? It just won't do.' Putting down her brush she picked it up. At a glance it looked fine yet close up the flowers were uneven.

'Perhaps James can correct it when he puts in the drops of dew and thorns?'

'And is this all you done?' he said gesturing to the line of saucers drying along the bench. 'All morning?'

'Yes, but I'm doing the shadows too.'

'Some of the girls do seventy in a morning and you done -.' He stood counting them. 'Fourteen.' After he had stomped off, James with a glance at his receding back stepped over.

'Don't worry, he's been moaning at everyone today. They look alright to me; in fact, the petals are great. You will speed up with practice.'

'But I'm not earning anything. I've been here six weeks and except for ten shillings at Christmas I've received nothing. I need to contribute to my keep.'

'My aunt has really enjoyed you staying with us. To have another woman to talk to in the evenings has given her great pleasure. She finds my conversation rather limited.'

'Well, not surprised, all you talk about is the works. I must get on or Bill will have more reason for complaint.'

'They are emptying the kiln. I'll see if those pots you threw and painted have survived.' Picking up her next saucer, her forehead furrowed as she put three dabs as centre spots for each flower. Were they equal? Perhaps? Very delicacy, her fine brush wove pink swirls that rapidly became a pretty flower as James walked away. The accuracy needed was a strain. Her own painting had always been free, with movement and expression more important than detail.

More for fun than practice she had turned some bowls and vases on potter's wheel during a quiet moment at the works and was looking forward to seeing them finished. She was very intent on the flow of her brush when James put a bowl down beside her. The simple bright pattern was marred by a long crack and the second item was in two pieces.

'Only one has survived,' he said, as he put down another pile of bits. 'It always happens if you don't get all the air pockets out of the clay.'

'What a shame,' she sighed picking up a broken piece. She glanced down the factory in case the foreman was watching. What would Bill say? Pushing some shards around the bench, she remembered the joy of its creation. The pot evolving through her fingers as she had worked the wheel with her feet and the considerable time spent in its decoration. The colours and simple pictures had been lost in the breakages. Even the complete vase looked amateurish.

'Bill's watching, we need to get on,' she whispered, turning back to her work.

The disappointment remained with her as she walked home alone, the tiredness heavy on her. Reaching the house, she slumped into a chair in the drawing room. She looked at her fingers, red and chapped from working with cold materials, yet she was hot and dirty and for once craved the genteel life of doing little. The maid brought her a letter.

'Can you make some tea Elsie?' said Anne, turning over the letter. It was from Mrs Percival. Hesitatingly she broke the seals.

Dear Miss Osebury,

The children are missing you and I would implore you to return. I have considered the matter and am prepared to increase your salary to £60/year. I would also be happy to oblige you in your request to be treated as part of the family. You will be regarded as a guest and in all respects as per the wishes you expressed so strongly before you left. Please deliberate on the matter and I look to your early reply that I might

give your charges some hope of your resuming your teaching.
Yours sincerely -.

'Huh, not a word of apology and as if it were the money,' she muttered to herself. Rejected out of hand she tossed the letter on the table and composed in her head various scathing replies. She put her feet up on a stool and tried to nap. Eventually, her mind whirling, she read it again. Looking at her hands, dried out from handling the materials, she thought of the parties and gatherings at the great house and realised that sixty pounds was exceptional. She sipped her tea. No doubt the children were being difficult, which was not such a pleasant thought, but visions of dances, wonderful dresses and attentive young men would not go away. She tried to dismiss them with difficult images of James's reaction to her leaving the works. To walk back with head high would be fun, which would make up for the hard work that it would involve, and *"implore,"* that was strongly put. Not an apology but real recognition. Did Mrs Percival know what the word meant? It certainly wasn't part of her normal vocabulary.

She continued to mull over the offer and whether she had the courage to tell James that she might leave the pottery. Not having the energy to make a decision, she picked up the local weekly paper, which she had not had time to read and glanced through it. Usually, she would go and offer to help Elsie in the kitchen. An offer that was not normally accepted other than to put a few things on the table, but she was too exhausted. There was an article about the china works. A director had sold his share and it was intimated that the work force would be reduced. She was normally very interested, but she couldn't concentrate, and picked up the letter again.

'The mistress wants to know why master James is late,'

said Elsie coming in from the other room with some glasses.

'Is he?' said Anne looking up at the grandfather clock. 'I have no idea except the company appears to be struggling but he's not management yet.' After the maid departed her aunt entered.

'James is late. I see you have received a letter. Is it from home?'

'No from my previous employer. She has offered to employ me again and I don't know what to do.'

'Will they treat you better this time?'

'I think so, but I have been happy here. Would you read the letter please, I would value your advice as I am of two minds?'

'Yes, if I can help,' said Mrs Turnbull, sitting and taking out her glasses and leaning forward to illuminate the small page. 'It does look like they are prepared to treat you correctly. Yes, you must go.'

'But James will be upset. He worked hard to find me a place.'

'He may be more upset if you stay.'

'What do you mean?' Anne found herself staring at the old lady whose expression was of concern.

'What do you really think of my nephew?'

'I like him very much. I never had a brother and he's been very kind.'

'But would you marry him?'

'Marry him!' she said sitting up sharply.

'Yes, could you ever think of him that way?'

'He's just a boy.'

'He's the same age as yourself.'

'Is he? I'm really fond of him, but I suppose I think of him as a younger brother.'

140

'But he's falling in love with you. You don't think your view of him could ever change?'

'Oh no, I'm not sure what sort of man I might marry, if I do, but I think they would have to be older and more masterful. James is a joy but not as a husband.' She heard the front open with a crash and he stormed in throwing his top hat onto a chair.

'Stupid clots. Sorry Anne, aunt, but they really are, Mr Tomlins has left the board, Higgins hasn't a clue and Donald Smith is leaving.'

'What will happen?' said Mrs Turnbull.

'They will reduce output, lay off workers, use cheaper glazes, it's investment the factory needs, all the directors can think about is milking the business. Soon there won't be any business left.'

'What will happen to everyone?' said Anne.

'Many are about to lose their position.'

'Is yours safe?'

'For the moment. Do you know they have taken 8% dividend on their investments every year since it started?'

'What would you do if you were in charge?' said Anne.

'Me? Sack Higgins, get Donald back and put him in total control. Up-grade the quality pieces and make the firing more careful, less wasteful, keep up with the fashion and styles of what people want. Perhaps, that's the most important, make what people want today, not what they were buying ten years ago. It should give a good profit every year but in poor years the owners need to tighten their belts like the workers.'

'Well, there might be one saving as I will go back to the Percival's. I'm sorry but the children need me.'

'No Anne, you can't! you mustn't waste your ability. You

are potentially a great artist.'

'I'm not sure I really am. Today wasn't so good.'

'It takes time.'

'I know but I'm not sure it's the life for me.'

'James, her life is with these people, you must let her go,' said Aunt Agnes.

'But she's starting to do very well.'

'Am I, that's not what Bill said today.'

'But I thought they treated you very badly.'

'They did but Mrs Percival has agreed to my requests; please read the letter,' she said handing it across. James, taking it sat down in the nearest chair.

'What does it mean, "your wishes you so strongly expressed before you left?"'

'I had expected to be treated according to my upbringing, but I received no friendship, no kindness, nor recognition of my efforts. I'm afraid I was rather blunt in expressing myself.'

'I can imagine,' he said with a wry smile, 'but you cannot just leave without saying goodbye to everyone.'

'Do you have money for the fare?' said Mrs Turnbull.

'Yes thankyou. I would like to see Miss Quantrell again as she has been so kind and apologise for leaving so suddenly. I will come to see everyone tomorrow and book a coach for the day after.'

Although tired, she couldn't sleep and awoke at four, to lie worrying for an hour over her decision. She didn't hear James leave, nor Elsie prepare breakfast. She was still heavy with sleep when she walked to the factory. The long tables of women workers looked the same when she entered but then a girl, head down and tears streaming, pushed past. Maud stood, hands on hips, her face set in a sad frown.

'That's it for the day, another four girls gone,' she said as Anne approached.

'Sacked?'

'Yes, I don't see why it should be my job. 'Tis the directors who say they must go so it should be them that tells 'em.'

'That's terrible, I'm so sorry. Isn't there anything anyone can do?'

'It's capital we need. Time to redesign, new styles and new moulds. You're a lady, couldn't you invest, Mr Higgins just wants us to make more blue-and-white. Well, you can buy them from any hawker. We can't make them quick enough for the money they gets. Sorry that you are leaving but might be best. Reckon the works be finished within the year.'

'Will you lose your position?'

'I can always get by. Tis the unskilled workers who won't. Some kids will go hungry next week.'

'I was hoping to see Bill and Miss Quantrell.'

'They are all in a meeting with Mr Higgins. You'd best come back later.'

'Thank you, Maud. It was a pleasure to meet with you. Please say goodbye to them. I will miss you all,' said Anne turning, her resolve gone as she took a last look at the busy factory. Everybody fearfully concentrating on their output, with no time for conversation.

'Good luck, your ladyship.'

'Thank you, Maud, goodbye.' After Anne had booked her coach fare with her last sovereign, she wandered down to the river, which was well above its banks, the brown water rushing by. There had been talk of flooding, yet everyone appeared to accept it. Further disaster to come, like much of life. What misfortune was waiting for her at the manor?

The well-worn cab deposited her at the tradesman's entrance of the house. She stretched her tired limbs as the driver lifted out her trunks. She gave him his fare and an inadequate tip, but it still depleted her purse to just two-shillings. Watching him drive away she steeled herself and stepped into the kitchen. Servants turned and stared as she strode through. She found the butler and a footman polishing silver in the Butler's pantry. They looked up but said nothing.

'Mr Johnson, please can you arrange for my trunks to be taken up?'

'Yes miss, when the silver's done.'

'They can't stay outside; it looks like rain.'

'Oh alright; so you've come back, have you?'

'Yes, have the children been behaving themselves?'

'What do you think? But you can't blame them, when there's nobody to keep them in check. They need a good thrashing, they do.'

'Didn't Mrs Percival get any extra help?'

'First there was a man from the village, but they played him up horrible like, he lasted just three days and then a woman who only stayed a fortnight. She was supposed to have good references too. Even had the curate here but he couldn't cope.'

'Where would I find Mrs Percival?'

'In the yellow room.'

'Thank you,' said Anne, departing for the little drawing room, her confidence lifted by the news. The door of the room was closed, and a footman stood outside.

'John. Please announce me,' said Anne. He hesitated but as Anne went to open the door, he quickly stepped forward and opened it. Stepping inside he coughed.

'Er hum, Miss O, Osebury,' he stuttered. Mrs Percival looked up from her embroidery as did her aunt. Otherwise, the L shaped room appeared empty.

'Ladies, I just wanted you to know, I'm back. Please accept my apologies if you haven't received my note but from the tone of your letter, I thought you would appreciate speed rather than notice.' Abigail stepped round the corner, her finger in a book. They all stared.

'Well at least you are here,' said Mrs Percival.

'The children will be pleased to see you,' said Mrs Exton, 'and Abigail will enjoy continuing her French, won't you dear?' Her expression suggesting otherwise, she turned on her heel and disappeared back to her chair out of sight.

'I will go and see them now if you wish, but later may I join you for dinner?' said Anne, her throat dry. The question hung in the air. Should she have dared to ask, or would it have been better to have just turned up? The test of her employers' promise was being measured. A struggle was going on and it showed in Mrs Percival's features.

'We have several guests tonight. I'm not sure we can fit another around the table.'

'Oh, but didn't you say that Sir James has had to cancel,' said Mrs Exton. Mrs Percival turned to look at the old lady. Anne couldn't see her expression, but she imagined it was not one of appreciation.

'I suppose so, but I expect the children to be in bed before you come down.'

'Thank you, I look forward to seeing you later.' With that Anne headed for the stairs which she tried her best to walk up in an elegant way befitting a lady, but towards the top she hitched up her skirt and ran up two steps at a time. Camilla and Alfred were running along the landing towards her. A maid, presumably the informant of Anne's arrival, and the older boys followed. The younger two hugged her as she bent to their level. Edmund and Robert hung back.

'I hope you have lots of good work to show me.'

'There hasn't been anyone to teach us,' said Rob\

'And they didn't know what we'd done,' said Edmund.

'Well, I'm sure you've done something so let's go and see. I have brought you some new books I've borrowed, which we can look at later, including a Latin crammer.' Robert groaned.

'It's lovely to have you back,' said Nanny,

'Been difficult, has it?'

'Yes very.' With a glance at Robert. Anne leafed through the exercise books and copy sheets.

'Is this all you've done?'

'Nobody was interested,' said Edmund, but like Robert, he was looking at the floor.

'Well, you should have been. It's your education not anyone else's. You are learning so you can be sensible, wise and useful adults, not ignorant peasants.'

'We are not peasants.'

'No, exactly, your position in life is to be gentlemen and ladies. As such you should be able to converse and have understanding on many subjects. You are expected to be seen as superior and educated. Members of your class should enjoy learning.' Although as she said it, she thought of the many ignorant gentry she had known.

'Right, you have an hour before supper.'

'But this is play time,' said Alfred.

'Not tonight. Edmund you can copy out this copperplate writing, Robert, I want you to translate this Latin paragraph

146

into English and Alfred can write down a description of what he had for breakfast and lunch. I have to hang up some gowns, but I will be back in a moment, and I don't want to hear a sound.'

CHAPTER 7

Hesitatingly, she entered the dining room, very aware that her evening dress wasn't the latest fashion, nor had its creases from its long sojourn in the trunk disappeared. She was still flushed from the rush of changing her outfit. The table ware and silver sparkled in the candlelight. A cold glance from Mrs Percival, and the butler strode towards Anne, who for a moment felt the interloper, out of place, but this is what she had fought for.

'Please sit here, Miss Osebury,' he said pulling out a chair. Most of the other dozen guests remained standing, milling around at the other end of the table. Should she sit? It was normal to wait for the host to sit first. Mrs Exton arrived at her side and the butler pulled out another chair and she immediately sat. Anne decided to join her. The old lady fiddled with her napkin. No one spoke to them, no introductions, and then people were sitting at the other end. A tall woman sat on Anne's other side.

'Bonjour, I am Countess Alice d'Urbal from the Alsace.'

'Bonjour, comment allez-vous? Je m'appelle Anne Osebury,' said Anne.

'And how do you know the Percivals?' asked the countess. Anne replied in French explaining her role and that her own governess had been from France.

'Is this end of the table only going to speak French?' complained Mrs Exton.

'And my French has become rusty from little use,' said the Rector on the opposite side of the table.

'No of course not, the countess was explaining how her family had come over after Napoleon returned from Elba.'

'He was the scourge of Europe for so long. My husband died at Corunna; that's in Spain you know,' said Mrs Exton with a sigh. The conversation continued to range over the geography of the continent and then to the different habits of the two nations. Mrs Exton was far more knowledgeable than Anne had expected, and it was an interesting discussion, that continued after they retired to let the gentlemen smoke.

'I'm sorry that you ended up at the bottom of the table Aunt,' said Mrs Percival as they walked through to the other room, 'but the duke and his friends like to sit together.'

'Do not be concerned, I'm sure our conversation was more stimulating than any you had with the duke,' said Mrs Exton with a smile at Anne.

When the gentlemen later joined them in the drawing room, Anne was introduced to the duke, a middle-aged man with grey sideburns, and his two friends, a Cecil Morley, and a Robin Huntington, both young men in their early twenties. She curtsied and they bowed. Mr Tiverton and Doctor Hadlow were also of the party.

'I remember you well from when we met at the last shoot. I understand your family has moved to Herefordshire,' said Mr Morley leaning forward.

'Yes, you probably remembered the gunpowder smut on my nose. It's a fine house but society is rather limited in that part of the country.'

'Well, we will have to entertain you, won't we Huntington?' said Morley with a braying laugh, glancing at the other man, who scowled, bowing again in a mocking way.

'Always delighted to amuse the ladies.'

Anne immediately wondered what the tall man's idea of amusement was. He stood with a brooding confidence, his dark hair curling above his collar and his skin tanned. Unlike Morley whose garments appeared the latest fashion and beautifully cut, Huntington's attire had the thrown-on look of one who didn't care, or did he think himself so handsome that he could wear anything? He was looking Anne up and down. An embarrassing, hungry stare. She subconsciously pulled at the top of her dress and stepped away to the nearest chair.

'Come over here and amuse me then,' said Eleanor, tapping the seat beside her with her fan and then drawing it across her face so only her eyes, which gazed on Huntington were visible.

'But we have only just met your governess. She needs to explain why your French accent is so poor,' said Morley.

'Because Miss Osebury has only just returned from making pots,' said Eleanor.

'Pots!'

'Our governess has an artistic streak and thought she might enjoy painting them, but Miss Osebury, the factories were not to your liking?' said Abigail sitting nearby.

Trust them to betray me thought Anne, sitting down beside Mrs Exton. 'No, it was an interesting little holiday. Very illuminating.'

'It's best not to delve too deeply into the lower classes' world, eh what?' said Morley.

'You actually went to work? With the lower classes?' said Huntington, joining Eleanor on her sofa but looking at Anne.

'Well yes, it was quite fascinating, lines of women moulding and finishing basic china pieces, but the best items are hand painted. For that they employ real artists. It was an opening for me to learn from professionals, I've never had the chance before. I think one should take every opportunity to enlarge ones knowledge. Don't you agree Abigail?'

'Gentlemen aren't interested in ladies who paint pretty things, they just want them to be pretty things, to charm them out of their sulky moods,' said Eleanor, who stroked Huntington's arm with her fan.

'But not every lady marries. It is good for her to use her talents,' said Anne.

'I thought that every woman's dream was a rich husband,' said Morley.

'Perhaps, but the leading artist at the works is a spinster of good family and appears to enjoy her life.'

'It is a woman's duty to marry. The joys of motherhood are hers alone,' said the rector who stepped over to stand beside Morley, looking down on Anne. For a lady to sit and the gentleman to remain standing was quite acceptable, but the rector was large, overbearing.

'The foreman in charge of the production was female too.'

'But my dear, that is not a suitable situation for a woman,' said the rector.

'And what is 'suitable'?'

'The home, children, caring for her husband.'

'And if the lady has no children?'

'Well then, the world of the fairer sex, sewing, and embroidery are an appropriate role and of course they can indulge their art at home if they wish.'

'Yes, but even then, it is not taken seriously. Where have you seen a woman's painting given equal standing to a gentleman's?'

'Pretty pictures from pretty ladies are not to be compared to serious art.'

'You don't think a woman can have the same intuition and understanding of her subject? Men say they don't understand a woman, yet they paint their likeness.'

'But the depth and feeling.'

'And I suppose you don't think a lady should manage her own investments?'

'Oh no! No female has the right mentality for such matters.'

'Is that why the law limits ownership, opportunity to borrow money, to run a business?'

'Of course. A lady's mind isn't made that way,' said the rector leaning forward.

'But you have no idea of how a woman's mind works.'

'That's true,' laughed Tiverton, who had joined the group.

'We are to sit with pieces of cloth on our laps, looking attractive and wait on our master's beck and call?'

'Well yes,' said the rector. Anne felt her anger rising.

'Have men been so wonderful with money? My father wasn't.' Conversation was stopping around them. Others were listening. Mr Tiverton was looking intently at her. She felt her colour rising. Should she continue? He was smiling, inwardly laughing at her. Morley and Huntington also amused, looked from the rector's stern face to the young girl and back.

'Is a women's brain smaller? Her ability to think less than a man. Wasn't Elizabeth our greatest monarch?'

'Ah but her advisors, Cecil and Walsingham were exceptional,' said the rector.

'So, it wasn't her choice of men and the way she led them, that made her such a great queen?'

'I think it was the age.'

'Huh, you can do better than that rector.'

'The good book says we all have our station in life, and a woman's is in the home.'

'And where does it limit a woman's role. Where does it say she can't manage a factory or run a business?'

'Proverbs 31 is very explicit on a wife's position; she stays at home and looks after the household.'

'Does it? In the passage you mentioned, the wife is praised for her industry as she buys and sells vineyards, manages her staff, makes and sells garments, negotiates with merchants. She is running a wine producing and clothing business, a major one, while her husband does politics. The bible clearly values a woman as an equal and finally it says, 'Give her the fruit of her hands,' Clearly a woman has the right to her own money. It is not automatically her husband's.' An intake of breath from her listeners who were looking from one duellist to another.

'Would you question my interpretation of the scripture? I, who am the rector of this parish and you but a slip of a girl.' He bent towards her, eyes beneath dense eyebrows glaring at her. She leant back into the chair while he leaned down.

'I thought that is what the reformation meant. That intelligent people can discover the truth for themselves, but you would take us back to the Roman church where the people had to obey ignorant priests who hid the truth.'

'You go too far, miss. Have you become a raving Methodist?'

'No, but I can read.'

'But you have not studied the Hebrew or Greek?'

'I can trust King James's translators,' said Anne glancing

past, for Mrs Percival had come to stand, hovering behind Mr Tiverton, her face dark with anger, 'and I can read the best commentaries.'

'Learning may make a good governess but turn away every eligible bachelor,' said Mrs Percival. 'Men do not want to be told their opinions are wrong, do they Mr Huntington?'

'Er no, terrible thought.'

'And Mr Tiverton, you wouldn't want a wife who would argue the day's events over the breakfast table would you? Or demand to read the paper before you?'

'Not at the breakfast table. Stimulating conversation in the evening might be acceptable but not opinionated debate.'

'You find debate difficult, Mr Tiverton?' said Anne.

'It is generally accepted in society, that there are some subjects that are not to be discussed by gentlemen and that they are certainly not suitable for the fragile minds of maidens, yet you think to break both those taboos in one swoop. It appears you wish to turn society upside down.'

'No, just to be given the same opportunity and choice as a man if circumstances require it,' said Anne, who remained seated, when most other guests were standing in a semi-circle around her. Even Abigail arose to stand on the edge of the intimidating circle but for Anne to stand might suggest retreat. The heightened colour from her annoyance began to recede, to be replaced by embarrassment with everyone looking at her. Some of them not too kindly and she dared not look at her employer.

'You do not have the figure of an Amazon,' said Tiverton, with a smile, 'so I find it difficult to comprehend you in that way.'

'Thank you, I will accept that as a compliment, as I do not

wish to be seen as such,' she said smiling in return.

'My husband used to ask my opinion on the news every day,' said Mrs Exton.

'In France, a lady has few rights, but it is the way of the world,' said the countess. People began to move away until only Tiverton and Morley were left.

'I am afraid Mrs Percival will not look kindly on my entry into your company if I am too outspoken,' said Anne.

'Don't hold back for us,' said Morley, then taking Tiverton's arm. 'When are we to have a last winter shoot on your estate?' They walked away and Anne let out a sigh of relief.

'Whilst gentlemen may admire a lady with wit and sparkling dialogue, they may not to want to live with an argumentative girl,' whispered Mrs Exton. 'She may make for interesting conversation but when a gentleman wishes to settle, he requires a quiet and gentle lady who will run his home in peace and tranquillity.'

'Yes, but a person must be true to their beliefs.'

'A man may enjoy the company of a lively woman, but he marries the quiet one.'

It was a very thoughtful Anne that plodded up the stairs to her rooms. Why had she said so much, especially about her father's finances. A flush of embarrassment rose up through her. Reminding everyone of her poverty had been stupid and Mrs Percival's expression did not bode well for the morrow.

She had left the others in conversation or playing cards, but she knew the children would be up early and demanding her time. A different battle of wits but just as hard. What subjects could she teach them tomorrow?

When she heard the children in the morning, she went into

the school room to find Jenny supervising their dressing with the maids delivering their breakfast. Anne knew at least one of the maids would stay to assist.

'Jenny, I think I will take breakfast with the family this morning if you don't mind,' said Anne before heading for the stairs after rechecking her hair. It was early for the main family to be up, but Anne still hesitated at the door of the main dining room. She swallowed nervously, stepped in, and was relieved to find the room empty. A covered salver held chops and kidneys and another bacon but there was no tea. A maid came in carrying a jug of milk and a dish of hard-boiled eggs.

'Sorry Miss, I wasn't expecting anyone this early.'

'Will there be any tea or coffee?'

'Of course, Miss. I don't normally do it until the guests come down, but what would you like?'

'Coffee please.'

'Yes miss,' said the girl with a little curtsey. It was very pleasant to enjoy a leisurely meal undisturbed by demanding children and to be able to savour the aroma of coffee and bacon in peace. Her feelings of guilt at leaving Jenny were tempered by the knowledge that within a few minutes she would be teaching again. Even when Mrs Percival arrived and sat, Anne remained relaxed, enjoying the quiet efficiency of the service, the debates of the previous evening forgotten. She sipped her coffee as the footman took her hosts' orders and left for the kitchen. Mrs Percival looked at Anne.

'While I have been happy to treat you as part of the family, for you to monopolise the conversation last night with such outrageous views and embarrass my guests is quite unacceptable, and as for upsetting the rector, that is totally unforgivable. If you are to join us, I suggest a demur and quiet disposition would be more suitable, and certainly more appropriate to your position.'

'Yes, I do regret some of my utterances. My apologies, but I think at least some of my opinions were reasonable. When my mother married my father, she had considerable capital of her own, but we lived beyond our means, and he lost it all. If it had remained with her, there would have been money to fall back on.'

'Few women are able to manage money, it is a man's role. Nor is the drawing room the right place to discuss it.'

'Do you really think it's right that a woman has to automatically give all her wealth to her husband?'

'It is the normal arrangement, and it is not for you to question the rules of society and certainly not in my house. For heaven's sake you are just a governess, so learn to live according to your station.'

Later in the morning, Anne was busy teaching when a maid arrived. 'Mrs Exton would like to see you in the main drawing room,'

'Thankyou Ruth, I will be down in a minute; now boys, I expect to see some neat writing when I return.'

In the drawing room she found Mrs Exton, Mrs Percival, and daughters in conversation with a visitor.

'Anne, I believe you know Lady Howle,' said Mrs Exton.

'Yes, how is your Ladyship?' Anne curtsied, 'I hope you are in good health?'

'Yes, thank you, and your parents, I hear that they are living in the depths of Herefordshire?'

'Thank you, they are both well. Is Lord Howle well?' said Anne, sitting in the nearest chair, acutely aware she wasn't dressed to receive visitors. Mrs Exton had been kind to invite her down, but it would have been kinder to have been warned in time to change. Eleanor scowled at Anne.

'Except for a little gout.'

'I'm sorry to hear of it. I hope he will soon recover.'

'You do not follow the new fashion's? Eleanor's dress has such wonderful, puffed sleeves, and the flounces are expertly done. I shall speak to my dressmaker when we return to town.'

'I am afraid I have had little time to arrange my wardrobe recently and I wasn't expecting to be receiving visitors so haven't changed.'

'Who designed your gown?' said her Ladyship returning to Eleanor. As the conversation flowed in a series of compliments and talk of trimmings, styles and lace, Anne's thoughts turned to the schoolroom and what the boys were up to. Had she really missed these morning visits, where ladies sat and talked about fashion and each other. She had to admire the ladies, who could think of enough compliments for each other to fill twenty minutes. It made you feel you were important, but it could be boring. The most entertaining part was running your neighbours down or gossiping about their misdemeanours. Is that what she wanted?

'Well Anne, how are your sisters?'

'Both Hannah and Grace are fine, however it would be to Hannah's advantage if she could visit some of our old friends. That part of Hereford is rather a backwater as far as stimulating society goes.'

'Of course, and she would be such pleasant company,' said Lady Howle.

'I am sure a visit would be mutually pleasurable.'

'Yes, the poor girl, such a wonderful complexion, such genteel manners. She would be a delightful addition to any home.'

'Perhaps you might be kind enough to invite her to stay?'

'It will be my pleasure.'

'That would be very good of you. When might it be convenient?'

'She could come as soon as she likes. I will write to your mother tomorrow. Have either you or your sister been to town recently?' said her ladyship turning back to Eleanor.

'I'm afraid we haven't. There are always so many entertainments here. We have such a constant stream of interesting visitors.' There were further pleasantries and compliments and then Lady Howle rose. Anne went with her to the door where her carriage waited.

'It has been enchanting to meet you again, dear. It must be very pleasant staying with the Percivals, they are such a noble family with such exquisite taste,' said Lady Howle as they descended the steps.

'The pleasure has been all mine to renew your acquaintance, your ladyship. My mother will be very pleased to hear of your visit but of course you are going to write to her yourself.'

'Yes, I will on return. You ought to go in before you catch a chill, and you must arrange to use Eleanor's dress maker.'

'Thank you, again,' said Anne as she stood and watched the coach leave. She waved. Little chance of a new gown but what a chance for Hannah. She shivered and as the coach swung away, she quickly turned to run back up the stairs. A visit to Lady Howle would be a real opportunity. She must write and tell her mother to expect a letter.

In the evening, in the drawing room, she again sat next to Mrs Exton, whom she was beginning to think of as a friend.

She needed to avert the wrath of her employer and sitting beside the old lady, she was on the edge of the conversation but not excluded. Hopefully, she could avoid aggravating Mrs Percival and could observe and be part of society without causing trouble.

Huntington and Morley returned from their smoking and Eleanor was suddenly all coquettish with looks, sighs and mannerisms, leaning forward, with a mass of white bosom showing, and eyelashes fluttering, she patted the seat beside her. Imploring dark eyes looked up at Huntington who after momentary hesitation took the seat. The full allure of her eyes were turned then to Morley who succumbing to their magnetism sat the other side of her.

Mrs Exton her hands active with a piece of embroidering leant close to Anne.

'I'm afraid my niece can be very embarrassing sometimes.'

'Yes, she is very obvious in her conduct.'

Mr Tiverton came and sat opposite, stretching out his long frame on a chair.

'Evening Mrs Exton, Miss Osebury. What are you making?'

'Nothing but opinions over the behaviour of others,' said Anne looking up.

'Ah, and what do you find?'

'That some ladies enjoy flirting to the extreme.'

'A little femininity is perhaps more enjoyable than harsh opinion.'

'True opinion need not be abrasive. Sensible truths shouldn't seem harsh.'

'Your opinion is perfect? You are never wrong?'

'Ha, I am often wrong, and when I am, I hope I have the

courage to say so.'

'Well Mrs Exton, do you ever win an argument with your little friend?'

'No but it makes for interesting conversation.'

'So, besides opinions what are you making here?'

'Just a cushion cover, I always find it relaxing and it is expected for ladies to be busy with something,' said the old lady.

'Why do you think the younger generation seem less inclined to embroider?'

'Poor upbringing. I have always believed it is good training for managing a home.'

'You do not sew Miss Osebury?'

'Only when I have to. Now, why should ladies busy themselves while gentlemen don't?'

'What should a gentleman do, clean his guns?'

'Perhaps that might not be suitable.' She smiled, 'An accidental discharge of gunpowder in the drawing room might cause a check in conversation.'

'Ah, so what do you expect us to do; repair our socks?'

'You are teasing me. My argument is, not that men should be busy, but that ladies do not need to be.'

'My husband learnt to repair his uniform after his valet was killed,' said Mrs Exton.

'Would you know one end of a needle from another?' said Anne.

He smiled. 'The cotton goes in the blunt end, I believe.'

'Your knowledge amazes me. I presume that is from observation rather than experience? My issue is not so much with our class, where generally we are people of equal leisure, it is in the lower classes where women have greater burdens than the men. Nor am I saying that women shouldn't spend their

161

time with the sewing needle if they wish, but she should have the freedom to choose her occupation.'

'Are you concerned for the working classes?'

'I learnt from my time in Ironbridge that they are often decent and generous, that they are people like us.'

'Many of the gentry give no thought to the lower classes from one year to another.'

'Come, Tiverton, will you join us for a round of whist?' said Morley coming to join them. 'Ladies, please forgive me for dragging him away.'

'And I must leave you too, Mrs Exton, as I must complete my preparations for tomorrow's lesson,' said Anne, rising.

'You are very conscientious, my dear.'

'Not really, it is for my own benefit. If the lessons are interesting, I will have less trouble with my scholars. I must wish you goodnight.'

On the next evening Mr Morley had arrived at the table before her and was sitting beside Mrs Exton with Doctor Hadlow on the other side of her. Mrs Exton was laughing at something Morley had said.

'May I join you,' said Anne, as a footman pulled out her chair.

'That would be delightful. A lovely lady on either side, what more could a man require from life,' said Morley.

'A good income and a good dinner,' said the doctor.

'True, but if you have the income, you should get the dinner,' replied Morley.

'It may also bring admiring ladies,' added Mrs Exton.

'But it is easy to see when the cooking is right, ladies are more difficult to fathom,' said Morley with a sigh.

'Do you find us so incomprehensible?' said Anne.

'You appear delicate, yet sometimes you ladies can be so demanding. One moment full of kind commendation and then the next day, difficult about every little thing, and without any logical reason for the change,' said Morley.

'Is this your aunt?'

'Well yes, she can be like that, but it's Eleanor, she was very affable yesterday, yet today isn't speaking to me and refusing to tell me why. Says I should know.'

'What have you done, Mr Morley? What terrible sin?'

'I have no idea; that is the problem and she won't say.'

'Did you compliment her on her hair?'

'Her hair?'

'Yes, it's different today.'

'Just a little I suppose. More curls.'

'When did you notice?'

'After breakfast.'

'And you said nothing! A capital offence. Eleanor thrives on approval and yours especially.'

'Is that all. It really isn't so different,' he said gazing down the table at Eleanor, who was chatting happily to those around her. Mr Tiverton was two places away on the other side, partially hidden by a silver table piece of two bears. A slight smile suggested he was listening, but he had remained silent.

'And Mr Tiverton did you notice, and did you praise?' said Anne.

'I was careful to say something. I am aware that ladies thrive on such tribute.'

'Gentlemen can be equally vain.'

'Oh no, we do not acknowledge that. It is a lady's weakness to require such accolades,' said Morley.

'We are weak, are we?'

'It is accepted that ladies are fragile and delicate in mind and body,' said Morley.

'You say women are the weaker sex, but I observe that bearing babies takes great fortitude and endurance.'

'That is also not a suitable subject for the drawing room,' said Morley.

'But it is an essential part of life. Without it humanity ceases.'

'Of course, but it remains polite not to discuss it.'

'Why not? Although it must be the greatest joy to give life, many women fear the danger and pain that goes with it. Discussion might alleviate some of their anxiety.'

'Where did you discover all these opinions in just eighteen years?' said Morley.

'I suppose my governess, and my parents would have been an influence, but it is mainly my own observations and reading.'

'Had your governess come straight from the barricades of revolutionary France?' said Tiverton leaning sideways to look around the table piece.

'No, her views were very balanced. Have you read Wakeford's "Reflections of the present condition of the female sex"?'

'Doesn't sound my sort of book.'

'Perhaps you should try it.'

'You sound like you belong to the Radical party,' said Tiverton.

'No, I don't think so, although I probably side with them on the repeal of the corn laws. Probably more Whig, than Tory but I am not sure any party represents my views.'

'Do you imagine you understand everyone's policies?'

'I believe the newspapers must give a reasonable account of the issues. The massacre at Peterloo was terrible.'

'Would you side with the mob?' said Morley.

'No, but I would agree with many of their concerns and the treatment of the crowd was heavy handed and you call it a mob but surely it was just people concerned for their future.'

'Without order the country will slide into rebellion.'

'When a man's children go hungry it is apt to bring extreme reaction. If more effort was put into finding work for the men, there would be less danger.'

'But a man must be responsible for his own family. He cannot expect society to take on his responsibilities.'

'Generally, no, but we should help our fellow man when we can. The Hampden club in Birmingham is I believe, made up of respectable people who believe in peaceful improvement by petition and argument.'

'Where do you obtain these ideas?' said Morley who had been looking from one to the other.

'I cannot believe Miss Osebury, that these sentiments are yours alone,' said Tiverton.

'I assure you they are.'

'Impossible.'

'Why do you so wish to provoke me Mr Tiverton?'

'I do not know. Perhaps it amuses me. A lady so full of her own opinions.'

'So, when you are not chasing foxes or shooting birds, I am to be your sport?'

He smiled. 'And considerably more challenging, foxes and pheasants do not argue back.'

'But you don't enter the debate. Others discuss, you just

look on and grin.'

'Perhaps it is refreshing to escape the empty compliments and self-flattery of so many of the fairer sex.'

'It is not just the ladies who flatter.'

'No, I acknowledge that.'

'All is vanity.'

'We can agree on that point.'

'I think I see. Is it that because you recognise the truth of my arguments, that you look on but do not put your own view?'

'I see the point of some of what you say, however outlandish, but these matters are so ingrained in society that it will not change. You ride full tilt at impossible fences. I admire you, in that when you fall, you so quickly recover. What I do find odd is that all you then do, is rush again at the same fence, which you cannot overcome and fall again.'

Finally, the days were getting longer and for Anne, not totally happy but settled, the constant battle to keep the children's interest tempered by a little society most days. Still an outsider, allowed but not welcomed by her host, she spent an hour or two each evening after dinner meeting guests and family alike but then would leave them early to their cards or recitals. Visitors came and went, but the three younger bachelors, were regular and particularly welcomed.

She was reading the newspaper, with an occasional comment on its contents to Mrs Exton when Mr Percival and Mr Huntington entered.

'Sugar offers the best returns. We had record production in our plantations last year,' Huntington was saying.

'But what of the human misery. Everywhere, they speak against slavery,' said Percival.

'Beasts are suited to their burdens. Would their lives be any better in Africa, where the tribes are ever in conflict? Slavery was just a by-product of the tribal wars, and now it is against the law to bring in fresh stock, the plantations have to breed their own replacements, so the value of slaves has risen.'

'What would happen if slavery were to be abolished, wouldn't the plantations lose most of their value?'

'Every investment has risks, and it won't happen. Too many men would lose money.'

'No risk with government bonds. 5 ½. percent is good enough for most of us and no man need be enslaved,' said Tiverton, from where he had been sitting with Eleanor.

'Only for men with your capital; most of us need more,' said Huntington. 'The plantations topped twenty percent last year and government rates will drop if we have no more wars to pay for.'

'Yes, but it is a cruel business.'

'Do you really live off the backs of slaves, Mr Huntington?' said Anne.

'My family's estates are well run; they are treated like children in a happy family.'

'I am afraid I don't believe you. Children grow up and leave. If your slaves run away, what is their punishment?'

'This is not the place to discuss this,' said Tiverton.

'Why not? It is a reasonable question.'

'Yes, we will continue at another time,' said Percival walking away. Huntington with a glance at Anne said nothing and then followed.

'Do you think Mr Tiverton, that women should not know where some gentry receive their income?'

'It is better to talk of more pleasant matters,' he said rising.

167

'Don't leave me,' said Eleanor reaching for his arm but he pulled away and drew up a chair opposite Anne.

'The world is full of suffering that we have no control over. If we think over every tragedy or the hardship of those that build our world, we would be constantly downcast. Let us thank God that some of us can live above the sordid world of gain.'

'But should we not try to improve their lives?'

'Of course, and I have argued long with many of my father's friends on the topic and have even listened to Mr Wilberforce, but I fear the true end of slavery will be some time coming.'

'You think it will end?'

'Assuredly, but whether ten years or fifty I cannot say and when they end one form of slavery, they will invent another. Let us talk of other matters. Eleanor says they are to have an ensemble here tomorrow for dancing. Will you give me the third and fourth?

'Just the third and fourth? I will remember but is eight percent a high return on an investment?' said Anne with a glance up at the butler who was serving drinks.

'Madeira madam?'

'Yes please – thank you,' she said taking the glass which sparkled in the candlelight.

'I'll have a top up later Johnson,' said Tiverton. Swilling the port around in his glass, he waited until the butler was out of earshot before leaning forward. 'Why does a girl like you take an interest in such matters? It all depends on the risk. It is a good rate but with what security?' Huntington had returned and was glancing from Anne to Tiverton.

'And will you give me the first two dances then Miss Osebury?' said Huntington.

'If you wish,' said Anne trying to disguise her dislike and turning her head away from him.

'Chasing higher returns in a business you don't know, can lead to hardship as your father discovered,' said Huntington. Why had she agreed to dance with him? She didn't need to be reminded about her father's losses.

'But it's not some far off investment, it's a china works in Ironbridge that produces beautiful things and gives employment to many. People who otherwise might go hungry?'

'If it is well run, it would not be short of investors. Is that where you were enhancing your painting skills?' said Tiverton, sipping his port.

'Yes, I stayed with a most respectable lady, a Mrs Turnbull, and her nephew who was also an artistic apprentice and who was concerned for the business. I'm sure it has great potential, but they were laying off workers, rather than improving the business. It was said that the directors have taken eight percent every year, without giving much guidance.'

'I am sure there are many men who would invest. The Midlands is an area of rising middle classes, merchants, and manufacturers, all out to make money and raise themselves. Real gentlemen do not concern themselves with mercantile matters, unless it is their own agricultural estates,' said Tiverton leaning back in his chair.

'I know but wouldn't it be a wonderful business to assist? Surely you know someone who would be able to inject some capital.'

'Why would you, the daughter of a gentleman, take an interest in a china factory?'

'Don't the gentry have an obligation to help? I think it

would be very satisfying to see a good manager appointed to improve the business, to see new lines introduced, and to see the workers' jobs secure.'

'My dear girl, you mustn't try to follow in your father's footsteps,' he said rising. 'Enjoy Eleanor's ball instead and leave the financial world to men.'

Mrs Exton leaned over as Tiverton walked away. 'If you try to be clever or instruct the gentlemen, your chances of matrimony will be worse than if you had smallpox.'

She could hear the music as she came down the stairs. Her first dance in the house and the first chance to wear her ball gown, but it was high waisted with narrow sleeves which marked it as old fashioned, so whatever the quality of the silk, she would look out of place. Hopefully not all the older ladies would be wearing the latest style. She made a last effort to tuck in a wisp of hair. Without a personal maid it had been difficult to make herself presentable. Stepping through the doors she looked around for Mrs Exton. At least the old lady would be pleased to see her. One or two guests glanced in her direction but then looked away.

A dance had already started.

'Miss Osebury,' said Huntington striding across the floor. 'You promised me the first.'

'I did Mr Huntington, I did, but it will have to be the next one.' She gave a little curtsey.

'Well let us hope it is at least a quadrille, I cannot abide these slow promenades.'

'It has a certain elegance, where everyone can be seen at their best.'

'Yes. That is all that they are, a fashion parade.' For a moment they stood and watched, the graceful slow swirl of dresses, the elegant bows and gestures. A stately display of adornment and the tailors art.

'Do you not aspire to the styles of the day, Mr Huntington?'

'Your beauty can be seen without the need to flaunt it.'

'I thank you for your compliment and I see that you have given more thought to your cravat than normal.'

'Huh, I can't be bothered most of the time,' he said touching the multiple folds of his neckerchief. 'My valet despairs of my dress. You have never seen a Scottish reel?'

'No, are they not like our county dances?'

'Yes, but at three times the speed; whirling around the floor. Much more to my liking.'

'What of a waltz?' Why did she say that? She was pleased that Huntington had noticed her and not left her standing in solitary pose leaning against a wall, but she didn't want to dance with him, especially in the intimacy of a waltz?

'Ahh yes, I would claim you for the first waltz.'

'Are you not dancing with Eleanor?'

'Oh, I will dance with all the girls here and even a few old maids. Mrs Percival will scold me if I don't but when there is a waltz, I will claim you for myself.'

'I will try to remember,' she said, but thinking how she could best avoid him. 'Do you know if there will actually be waltzing?'

'Bound to be. The Percivals always want the latest thing. I think we ought to follow the Vienna tradition where you ladies have a card with all the dances recorded. Here you can never tell what comes next.' The set was ending, and couples were joining or leaving.

'Miss Osebury, good evening, I hope you are not letting

171

Huntington monopolise you tonight,' said Mr Morley, stepping towards them with Abigail on his arm. His little bow was restricted by his partners severe posture.

'Good evening, Mr Morley, Abigail, you danced very well.'

'Thankyou. It is good of you to join us,' said Abigail.

Perhaps I would have come before, if I had been invited, was the reply that hovered on Anne's lips. Or should it have been? Why do you say that, when it is the last thing you want, but instead Anne did a little bob and said, 'My pleasure, but Mr Huntington, we ought to join the set.'

'Then I will have to have the next,' said Morley as they walked past onto the centre of the floor.

'She is also engaged for her second,' said Huntington over his shoulder as he escorted Anne to the end of the set. It was a quadrille but a slow one. When another couple barged into each other, Huntington winked at her. There was something roguish about her partner that both frightened and thrilled her. He was also an accomplished dancer, effortless and easy in his movements. It felt very pleasant to be wanted, to feel the swirl of her dress, the exhilaration of the music. She must be careful not to drink too much wine or she would do something silly. A second dance, where Huntington's masculine strong arms and graceful movements became a delight. Laughter from a group at one end of the room, and a rising buzz of conversation showed that everyone was enjoying themselves.

The dance ended and she looked around for Mr Tiverton, but he was nowhere to be seen. Mr Morley was suddenly at her side, bowed and took her hand raising it high in an elegant pose and led her towards the dance floor.

'Are you enjoying yourself Miss Osebury?'

'Yes, thank you,' She was tempted to say more but she

wished to avoid gushing flattery. But for her to be dancing with someone like Morley whose beautifully cut jacket, waist coat and cravat were of the finest quality and the latest fashion, was wonderful. He confidentially turned and paraded with the grace and confidence of his class. She sighed with satisfaction to be with such man of charm and pleasant humour.

'And my friend Huntington didn't tire you?'

'Oh no sir.'

'Such a pleasant occupation dancing, and with such lovely partners. You have added greatly to the charm of the evenings here, but you always leave us so early,' he said turning away in the first move of the dance. As they passed again, Anne replied.

'You forget I have responsibilities and need to be up early to set the children their lessons.'

'Of course, but you will not desert us this evening?'

'Oh no, but you must understand before I can teach a subject, I must learn it,' she said as they passed back, to back.

'Is that what you used to do sitting in the corner of the hall each evening?'

'You noticed?'

'Yes, but Mrs Percival told us not to bother you,' he said as they parted, and each went down outside a different side of the set. They met again at the bottom.

'I was bought up to enjoy the pleasures of drawing room conversation, but now my role is a lonely one. I love my pupils, but they are not my friends, and the servants are of a different class.'

'Well, you will find many friends at Mrs Percival's parties.'

'I'm sure.' But she knew he was wrong. The men might flirt with her but with no real intention of deepening the relationship, while the younger women saw her as a competitor and the older ladies looked down at her. When the dance ended, they danced a second and then she danced with Doctor Hadlow who told her that he would introduce her to his wife, but he never did. She danced with Morley again and then a waltz was announced, and Huntington was at her side.

'Miss Osebury the dance we have been waiting for,' he said taking her hand. No request, no enquiry just assumption. He danced well, the strength in his arms supporting her in a delightful way as he whisked her around.

They went straight on to a second dance and then a third but then he excused himself. 'My apologies that I must leave you, but I promised Abigail a waltz and then I must dance with Mary Hooper.' He bowed and then whispered, 'I'd prefer to dance with you anytime. Ah I think Mr Percival wishes to take my place.' Anne looked around seeking a way of escape, but he was standing in front of her, beaming. He was the last person she wished to dance with. The shock of his approach brought the memory flooding back. Cornered alone in a dark room with her grabbing for her.

'Miss Osebury, will you give me the pleasure?' he said holding out his hand.

'I think I need to sit this one out sir.' she said walking away from him towards a chair.

'Please, it will help me make amends for my boorish behaviour.'

'I have been dancing all evening sir and would appreciate a rest.' And it was much more than boorish behaviour, she thought. She looked around hoping someone might join them and prevent further private conversation.

'I had hoped my foolishness had been long forgotten. I really was in love with you.'

'Mr Percival!' She turned and found herself glaring. 'It is not so easy to forget and although forgiven, I'm not yet ready to dance.'

'Oh alright, here's Tiverton, he can be your next.'

'Evening Percival, Miss Osebury, my apologies for being late but are you free now?' He had the aroma of horse and was dressed for riding.

'Yes, thank you, and I was free earlier too.'

'I'm sure the gentlemen didn't leave you on the side-lines.'

'No, I have danced all evening.'

'I am glad you are enjoying yourself?' he said leading her on to the floor. He appeared unsure as to the hold as they stood ready for the music to begin.

'Yes, it's been delightful. Do you enjoy the waltz?'

'I have never danced it before so please be patient.'

'It is the gentleman's responsibility to lead.'

'That could be a problem,' he said looking at his feet.

'I could attempt to lead you.'

'You'd better not, I will try, I am aware of the basics.' They didn't speak as the band began to play, Anne being acutely aware that he was concentrating on the steps. They did several circuits of the floor and gradually his confidence and ability increased.

'Ouch,' Anne exclaimed as he trod on her foot.

'Sorry, are you alright,' he said as they stopped in the middle of the floor.

'I will be, carry on,' she said breathing out her pain. 'Riding boots are perhaps unsuitable for dancing.'

'My sincere apologies, my haste has only made matters worse.' Cautiously he led her on again and then it ended. 'We must find you a seat. I'm really sorry.' He supported her as she limped to the nearest chairs.

'What have you been doing to our governess,' said Morley, stopping in front of them, with Eleanor on his arm.

'Mr Tiverton, you had promised me the first two. I was left distraught and all alone, my heart damaged beyond repair,' said Eleanor.

'Is this true Miss Osebury, was Eleanor all alone or was she frolicking around the room?'

'We all felt bereft, but Mr Morley happily rose to the occasion. What delayed you?'

'I have been to our estate. The Rector is ill, and I thought it my duty to attend on him. He has held the living for many years and has been a great support to the family. It was difficult to get away.'

'You had better dance with Eleanor while I sit for a while.' She bent and rubbed her foot.

'Are you sure?'

'You can tell me of your estate when you return. I know nothing of your family.' He rose and went off and danced a waltz with Eleanor and then Abigail. It was pleasant to watch for a while.

'How is your foot,' said Mr Huntington, coming and smiling down at her. 'Are you feeling able to dance again?' He stood, holding his hand out.' Anne glanced at the clock. It was nearly twelve thirty. Soon the music would end.

'Yes let's.' She rose, and he led her out onto the floor. They twirled around and past the others. He was a such a good dancer. Her foot continued to hurt but it didn't seem to matter in the excitement. They danced another. There were fewer couples waltzing, only the keen dancers taking a last opportunity. Most guests were watching as they crowded to the door or collected their coats in the hall. A hubbub of goodbyes but Huntington danced on. Anne was tiring and finally the band stopped. The pain in her foot returned, and she wished she had a fan to cool herself. She worried that she was flushed red from the exertion.

'Would you like a little walk outside to cool off?' said Huntington, taking her arm.

'Oh no, it's so late.'

'Well, if we can't have a walk now, what about a ride tomorrow? Have you seen my new gig? Perhaps we can enjoy a drive out?' said Huntington.

'That would be very pleasant, but I am only free on Saturday afternoons. Would Mrs Exton be invited along?'

'Mrs Exton! Why would she join us?'

'She might enjoy an outing. Who had you in mind as a companion?'

'Do you mean chaperone?'

'Well, yes. One must be seen to act with decorum.'

'Don't you trust me?'

'Not entirely.'

'Huh, ha,' he laughed, 'I'll not seduce you Anne, may I call you Anne? You would be very safe with me, and it only has space for two.'

'Perhaps we could borrow one of the Percival's carriages instead.'

'You have no parents here, to watch your every move. You speak about ladies having the freedom to make their own way in life; well, this is your opportunity to show your independence.'

'It is not quite the same,' she said, her brow furrowed.

'Why?'

'I'm not sure, and you know it isn't, moreover part of winning any argument on a woman's role, is showing that we can be prudent and act wisely with our liberty. Also, I think Mrs Exton would make an excellent companion and enjoy an afternoon out, but I must go to bed, thank you for some wonderful dancing.' She curtsied and he reluctantly let go of her arm, took her hand, and kissed it. She looked around in concern that this had been noticed. Only Tiverton who was in deep conversation with Mr Percival was looking, he nodded at her and mouthed, sorry.

'Mr Huntington, a companion for our drive out?' she prompted.

'Hmmm, I'll consider it.' But if he did, he soon forgot.

March came, bringing the first signs of an early spring, with the ploughmen, turning the new weeds glistening with the sparkle of morning dew into long brown furrows, the crows and gulls squawking and fighting in the air behind as they dived for the fresh worms. In the hedgerows, thrushes and robins sang their melodies as they marked out their territories for their coming broods. At dinner, Morley leaned across the table.

'Miss Osebury, I don't know if you are aware, but we were planning a coach outing tomorrow and Miss Hooper who was due to join us has a chill, so we wondered if you would like to make up the party? Eleanor and Abigail are coming.'

'I'm not sure my employer would approve.'

'Ah but Tiverton has thought of that. All I had in mind was a general jolly, but he said there is some battlefield near here. Never heard of it myself but if you brought the older boys, it

178

could be educational.'

'Well in that case, yes, if Eleanor can confirm her mother is happy, but what of the weather?'

'My groom swears it will be fine but wrap up well. Eleven tomorrow at the front. We'll get Eleanor to fix her mater.'

When Anne arrived on time at the front door, she found she was alone with the two boys. Had Mr Morley really organised a trip? Nobody else had mentioned it but then she had hardly seen anyone. Anne had breakfasted too early to meet any guests. The boys would be disappointed if it wasn't happening. Was Morley a man for organising such events? Had he really meant it? All she knew about the visitors were from what Jenny discovered from the servants which wasn't much as they didn't talk to her.

'I'll go round to the stables shall I,' said Robert hurrying away. Edmund went to follow.

'No, stay here Edmund in case any of the gentlemen come this way as arranged. Let's go inside the hall until someone comes.'

Although the sun occasionally appeared between the clouds, there was a sprinkling of frost on the grass making the landscape look cold. She wrapped her coat around her. In the hall, a maid passed and then the butler. Should she go to the drawing room? Then she heard a whinny and the crunch of wheels on the shingle. Outside the landau was drawing up, Robert jumped out as the coachman brought the horses to a halt.

'Is Mr Morley coming,' said Anne as she tripped down the steps.

'I was just told like, to have the coach here by eleven,' said the coachman.

'With the hood down?'

'Yes Miss.' Shivering she pulled her coat around her even tighter and looked inside.

'Is there any heating?'

'No Miss, nobody said nowt about bottles or such.'

'Good morning, Miss Osebury, boys,' said Morley coming out of the front door. 'Decidedly nippy.'

'Hello Morley, Miss Osebury, boys, all ready for your trip?' said Tiverton coming to stand beside him. 'I suppose the girls are late.'

'I spoke to Eleanor's maid about five minutes ago and she assured me she was ready,' said Morley, 'and here she is. I hope you are wearing your thickest petticoats?'

'Mr Morley my petticoats are not your concern,' she said but giggled. She was dressed for the cold, with a fur trimmed hat and silver fox coat, but Abigail who followed just had a shawl, although no doubt she wore layers of underclothes and her velvet dress looked thick and warm. Her hands were hidden in a fur muff.

'Have you no coat Abigail?' said Tiverton.

'No Mr Tiverton I will be fine.'

'Do we have any rugs Maison?' said Tiverton.

'I'll get some sir,' said the coachman jumping down and swiftly walking to the stables.

'Right in you get.'

'Tell us about the battlefield?' said Anne.

'Well boys do you know your Shakespeare?' said Tiverton.

'A little,' said Robert.

'And you, Morley?'

'It was all a mystery, "Into the breach dear friends" and all that, eh what.'

'That's in Henry the Fifth but at the battle of Shrewsbury he was just there as a young prince. It was his father who fought the rebels under Henry Percy better known as Hotspur. A major battle in the wars of the roses, and both sides had many archers. Prince Henry must have seen how deadly the long bow had become as he was to make great use of it later at Agincourt.'

'Is there much to see?' asked Anne.

'Probably not, so we will have to use our imagination.'

The rugs were brought, legs were covered, and Tiverton sat facing forward, with the Percival girls either side and Morley, Anne, and the boys with their backs to the driver. Edmund had to sit on Robert's lap. The crack of a whip and they moved off, the great horses setting a good pace on the smooth road, their breath, puffs of mist in the still cold air.

'Are we related to Hotspur,' said Edmund?'

'Probably but I don't think there's a proven link,' said Abigail.

'I'll be Hotspur then,' said Robert, 'What happened to him?'

'He opened his visor at the wrong moment and received an arrow in his eye,' said Anne.

'Oh.'

'Where is Mr Huntington today?'

'He went down to his club in London the day before yesterday. He spends too much time worrying about his investments,' said Tiverton.

'Or playing cards with his friends,' said Morley.

'It is very naughty of him deserting us,' said Eleanor pulling her silver fox around her. It was a beautiful coat, to which

Anne's didn't compare. In fact, hers was a hand-me-down from her mother. Abigail pulled her shawl tighter. They were all going to be cold by the end of the ride, even perhaps Eleanor, whose warmth from her coat was wasted as she let it fall open, revealing her low-cut dress and ample bosom which moulded around Tiverton's arm. The coach slowed as they turned onto a muddy lane and rolled its way through the potholes. Anne banged against Morley. 'That's all you gentlemen think about; your London clubs.'

'Some chance,' said Morley, 'my aunt insists I stay up here. I haven't been on a jaunt for ages.'

'You are very considerate of your aunt?' said Anne.'

'He has to be, Lady Emily controls the purse strings,' said Tiverton.

'Ha, only part of my income is from her allowance, but it is as well to keep the old lady sweet. I am her only beneficiary, but I still consider it wise to give her my attention.' So, it was true that his wealth depended on this rich relative.

'How come you live with her?' asked Anne.

'I was brought up by various aunts. My mater died at my birth and then my father from wounds after Trafalgar, so I hardly knew him.'

'Can you remember him at all?'

'Yes, long curly side-burns; suddenly home and swinging me about as if I was some monkey, and then later, returning as an invalid suffering from his injuries, with the house having to be silent which was quite an ordeal for a seven-year-old.'

With a clatter of wings and panicked cry, a startled pheasant rose from the verge. They all jumped.

'Father says we're to have the last shoot of the season next week,' said Robert.

'I'm old enough to have a gun now. Robert has one,' said Edmund.

'You will have to speak to your father,' said Anne. Tiverton turned to Robert and asked about his gun which brought an enthusiastic explanation. Tiverton continued his interest and they talked of guns and hunting. Morley and the sisters were chatting too, so Anne sat back, remembering another coach trip with a young man. She bumped against Morley again. 'Sorry.'

Had Geoffrey gone back to sea, and had he regretted his treatment of her?

'Terrible choice of roads Tiverton,' said Morley.

'I'm sure he chose them deliberately. If the puddles become any deeper, I will be on your lap Mr Tiverton, ' said Eleanor.

'A charming thought.'

'Perhaps if you put your arm round me, I'd not fall about so much.'

'You can hang onto that strap.'

'I prefer holding on to a handsome man.'

'You are embarrassing us, Eleanor. Your young brothers aren't used to seeing your outrageous flirting,' said Abigail.

'At least I'm not too puffed up to have some fun.'

'Now ladies, let us see what Tiverton knows about this battle,' said Morley.

'The battle of Shrewsbury in 1403. Just imagine that you have joined fourteen thousand other young men, all itching to show how brave they are. Marching along with a sharp sword in your belt and holding a long spear, you feel invincible with such a crowd but, look.' He waved his arm in a wide arc. 'There is another vast army approaching, the thunder of great horses, hundreds and hundreds of them, and archers, each with a quiver full of arrows, ready to darken the sky with a rain of death -.'

As Tiverton enthralled the boys, awakening their imagination, Anne looked at him and Morley. To be out with such entertaining men was a delight. Morley, pleasant, and kind, a foppish gentleman to his fingertips, laughing at his friend's serious demeanour as he sought to describe the horrible battle. The boys' eyes glowing in excitement. Tiverton, more difficult to understand, often laughing at her, other times serious, and questioning everything. It was challenging to know where you were with him, and then the missing, handsome Huntington, with his piratical air and animal magnetism. Three sophisticated men, that could give a rich home but what chance did she have? Could she love them if she had the opportunity? Geoffrey, she had liked for his open boyishness, but these were real men of the world. Even the easy-going Morley, in his smart fashions and under the wing of his aunt had a maturity missing in Geoffrey.

Mary Hooper, the girl she had replaced, was said to have an income of £2,000 a year and although her nose was overlarge, and she had too many teeth, her complexion was excellent, and she had a fine figure. She also had the bearing and confidence of someone with a secure income and had danced with a practiced elegance. Abigail and Eleanor would also come into considerable wealth on their parents' demise, besides good marriage settlements. Even without the shame of her family, Anne knew she couldn't compete. Why would any man of property consider her when other ladies, equally pretty, held such wealth? The stigma of her father's failings only added to her unsuitability for marriage. It should have been Hannah sitting in the coach, not Anne, then there might have been at least a chance for her and for all the family.

'And your family, Miss Osebury, do you have brothers or sisters?' said Morley. For a moment Anne hesitated. Tiverton's battle description was ending. She waited. This was perhaps her chance.

'I have two sisters, a wild, younger one of ten, who climbs trees, even better than I could when I was her age and Hannah who is nineteen, the most beautiful woman I know. She is tall with fair golden hair. Every man she meets falls in love with her and she is so elegant and kind. Never a cross word. I used to try to walk like her but I never managed it. She, sort of, glides across the ground.'

'She sounds too much of an angel to be real,' said Tiverton, 'and could sisters be so unalike?'

'Mr Tiverton!' said Anne in a mock severity.

'Miss Osebury is mocking you. I'm sure that such a creature doesn't exist,' said Abigail.

'Do not judge her by myself. Where I am impatient, she is patient where I am cross, she is calm. Probably having to deal with me brought out the best in her.'

'I could understand she would have to be tolerant,' said Tiverton a smile briefly playing on his lips.

'Well, I'm not always difficult but, if something's important, then it's, well, important.'

'So, what is important beside giving ladies the right to their own money?'

'Many things.'

'A warm coat,' said Morley with a shiver, 'that's important.'

'Yes, and how do the poor earn enough to own a coat?' said Anne looking out over the cold fields.

'The labouring classes can look after their own, and they are not a suitable theme for discussion,' said Abigail turning away to gaze at the landscape.

'Ah, here we are I think,' said Tiverton. The coach pulled in at the side of the lane.

'That be the church, sir,' said the coachman leaning back and pointing with his whip.

'Come on boys, said Tiverton opening the carriage door. The boys and Morley alighted. Anne glanced at the sisters who looked over the bleak open fields with their silver dusting of frost and then at each other. Anne decided not to wait and followed the gentlemen. She caught up with them at the door of the church. They turned the heavy handle and swung the oak door open. A musty aroma suggested it was rarely used.

'Good morning,' said an old lady from where she sat in one of the pews.

'Can you tell us where the battle took place?' asked Tiverton.

'Well, it be difficult to tell exactly like, but it was all about ere. In the churchyard and under this floor is a great grave where many of the poor lads were buried. They say on a full moon, you can hear the clump of marching men and the swish of flying arrows.' Anne shivered, unsure whether from the cold and damp of the building or the thought of a ghostly army.

'If you follow the path that goes around the fields you are in the battlefield. The king's army was to the south and Hotspurs to the north, but some think the battle ranged all round.'

After they had wandered around the building, looking at the plaques and a notice describing the history of the battle and the church, the boys were becoming fidgety, so they went outside and began to walk along a worn path. The boys ran ahead, reliving medieval conflict in pretend attacks on each other. Morley pulled a couple of sticks out of a cut hedge and broke off the twigs.

'Here you are, some swords but don't poke your eyes out,' The sisters had joined them, and Eleanor put her arm through Tiverton's.

'It's rather muddy,' she complained. Abigail took Morley's arm and, with Anne ahead trying to keep up with the boys, they continued. The open landscape gave no suggestion as to the death and drama that had played out centuries before. Looking back, she saw that the two couples were happily chatting as they walked arm in arm. Would this excursion lead to commitment and to marriage? Had she been brought as an amenable chaperone, one who would not prevent the cementing of their relationships? Was she to be the spinster, looking on, but never having the chance of marital happiness herself? A governess for the rest of life with a series of families, loving other people's children, never her own, always on the edge, never appreciated. The thought was as depressing as the winter fields under the greying winter sky. A whack from Robert's stick on her leg brought her back to the present and she chased him along the path.

'A sneaky attack, I'll get you Robert,' but he quickly ran away. When she gave up, Edmund came bounding up, to hand her a second stick he had found. After that, she and the boys played a series of running sword fights. It wasn't easy, keeping her dress out of the mud and defending herself, but it was fun and the exercise warming.

'I'm glad to see fencing is part of the curriculum,' shouted Morley. Tiverton just grinned.

'It's very demeaning. Is that what you do in Hereford? said

Eleanor.

'Only with my younger sister, but if I'm to teach boys, per-haps it should be part of their education. Do you fence Mr Morley?'

'I did as a boy, but you still do, don't you Tiverton?'

'Yes, but only at a club when I'm in London. I could bring some foils to the house and give some instruction if you would like.'

'Yes please,' cried Robert and Edmund together.

'How much further are we going to walk. It is just empty fields,' said Abigail.

'Come on Abigail, Miss Osebury wishes to explore the whole site.'

'But my petticoats are becoming filthy, and my shoes have never been so soiled.'

'Alright then, back to the coach,' said Tiverton.

They were still some distance from the church, when they saw another coach draw up and Jenny wave from within. When they reached her, they were greeted by the younger chil-dren and a second coachman. Two bottles of wine and pewter mugs had been laid out on the coach floor with two bundles of cloths. The children had milk and Jenny unwrapped the first bundle to hand out pasties that were still warm.

The girls at first declined them but as the savoury aromas spread through the cold air, they eventually gingerly took one each. China plates were provided for the adults.

'To spring,' said Morley raising his mug.

'To sunshine,' said Anne clinking hers with his.

'To the ladies,' said Tiverton bowing to the sisters, 'and to many more picnics.'

'And to proper picnics with chairs, hampers and champagne, not a ploughman's pasty standing in the mud,' said Abigail.

Eleanor, glanced at Anne. 'Is this what you ate at the pottery?' she said, gesturing disdainfully with her half-eaten pasty, 'with all the workers.'

'Sometimes.' How could she explain that she had enjoyed being with the labouring class without being considered as connected to the lower classes herself? Wanting to be rich and secure was one thing, ignoring the lower classes was another. 'Some of the men heated up their lunch on the kiln when it was lit.' said Anne turning over her plate. 'This was made in Ironbridge at our pottery, but it's only been done with a transfer. Not one of our best.'

'You must be so glad to escape such a place,' said Morley.

'And such food,' said Eleanor tossing the remains of her lunch on the grass. Her white gloves were stained.

'Did you found it a diverting adventure Miss Osebury, something to tell your children in later life,' said Tiverton, 'or somewhere you were desperate to get away from?'

'Both, I think, but mainly an opportunity to learn. Satisfying one's curiosity is always pleasing.'

'Miss Osebury is a great one for learning, she is often hidden in the library with a pile of dusty books,' said Abigail.

'You have some very interesting volumes, although there are some strange ones too. I love browsing through them.'

'But there's nothing readable or modern.'

'I thought women preferred embroidery to old books?' said Morley.

'Not this one.'

'Miss Osebury doesn't sew at all?' asked Tiverton.

'That's not true, I can darn a stocking, and when I was

smaller, I did the usual samplers.'

They journeyed on, passing through several small hamlets in a circular journey back. Anne wondered if she could tackle Shakespeare with Robert. Among the books in the house were several of his plays, including Henry V. It was difficult teaching children of such different ages, for it would be beyond Edmund.

CHAPTER 8

Initially, Anne had sent a letter home every week, so she was concerned to find that she had not written for over three weeks. On her first evening, on returning to Arleston Manor, she had sent a quick note updating Hannah on her renewed employment but not since then. Feeling guilty she picked up her pen.

Dear Hannah, please, forgive my lack of correspondence, I have been busy with my early evenings, enjoying good company around the dinner table with the family and their many guests. Mrs Percival makes it plain I am only there on sufferance and some of the guests show a similar attitude, but the men treat me well. Three weeks ago, it was requested that I come to the drawing room as Lady Howle had called. It was pleasant to renew her acquaintance and she spoke of you with many kind remarks. She said she would be delighted if you would go and stay with her and that she would write to mother immediately and suggest it. I presume that she has done so and that plans are already in fruition. You might even be in town by now for all I know! Perhaps your letter is in the post, and you are now enjoying society again. I look forward to hearing of your stay. We had an informal ball recently. It really was a pleasant evening and while my dress may look unfashionable, I danced all night. Some of the gentlemen are quite attentive but one soon realises that you are not the main attraction.

Eleonor is a dreadful flirt, outrageously so, but the men don't seem to realise how hypocritical she is. In fact, they buzz about her like wasps around a summer picnic. She makes love to them with her eyes, using flattery and coquettish expressions, taking every opportunity to hang on to an arm or sit close, yet behind their backs she rudely describes their imagined faults. Abigail is filling out a little and is becoming more attractive but as cold as a fish. There are three regular and very eligible bachelors who frequently visit, often staying for many days, if not weeks at a time, they are all wealthy if the gossips are to be believed. Mr Morley is very fashionable, amusing, and genteel. You should see his cravats and waistcoats. Mr Tiverton, is older, more serious with a character difficult to understand and Mr Huntington, more worldly than the other two. It is he, I must admit, that excites me, very handsome yet I think he has a dark side. Mr Morley charms me and Mr Tiverton often annoys me and probably looks down on me but at least I am mixing with proper gentlemen. I am as wary of Mr Huntington as you must be wary of Mr Spenliff but for very different reasons. Mr Spenliff is good and penniless, Mr Huntington rich and probably bad.

The unfairness of life continues to be revealed to me. Wouldn't it be wonderful to have a fairy godmother to wave a magic wand and make the deserving poor, rich and the wicked rich, poor? But I suppose everyone to their station in life.

If your stay with her ladyship doesn't last or doesn't introduce you to suitable society, you'd be better coming here. Tomorrow night there will be another dance. It is a great pity you cannot be here in my place, for I feel sure someone would fall in love with you and offer you his hand. If I pretend to be ill and say that I must go home, you could take my place.

The children are becoming more obedient so if you were strict from the first day you should be able to control them. Perhaps I could take to my bed here, spread dots of paint on my face and ask Mrs Percival to send for you.

If you approve of my devious plan, I will start looking in the medical books for some strange illness to fool the doctor. Although you may think I write in jest, I really do think we ought to try to bring you here. What are your neighbours doing? Has Mr Rawlins repaired the roof yet? I look forward to hearing of your time with Lady Howle.

The following evening, Anne arrived late at the ballroom as the children had to have their stories and Jenny always struggled in assisting Anne with her dress. Huntington had returned in time for dinner and while she hadn't spoken to him, she expected to have the pleasure of dancing with him later. When the meal was over, she stepped into the ballroom and looked around. Two older ladies at the other end of the room looked her up and down in disdain and turned away. Anne steeled herself for further reproach but told herself to ignore it for nothing was going to stop her enjoying herself. It was the dancing that mattered.

'You are looking delightful Miss Osebury,' said Morley rising from a chair and bowing. 'Will you give me the pleasure of the next.'

'Thank you,' she said, continuing to take in the scene as he came to stand beside her. Huntington was dancing with Abigail and Doctor Hadlow with Eleanor. There were about fifteen couples on the floor. Mr Tiverton was talking with Miss Hooper at the other end of the room. Her new gown looked extravagant. Anne wanted to have a closer look so that when she next wrote home, she could continue to update Hannah on the changing fashions. The dance was a genteel parade where everyone had plenty of time to talk, yet the colourful swish of silk dresses and the superbly cut coats of tall gentlemen spoke of easy wealth and style. Some of the gentlemen's waistcoats were as vivid as the ball gowns and their cravats as many layered as the petticoats.

'A large party again tonight,' said Morley.

'Yes, a delightful scene.' This was the life she wanted, she felt proud to be part of it, and considered it her right, even if many didn't welcome her. Everyone to their station in life and this was hers if she could hang on to it. The dance was ending and with a flourish of elegant fingers her partner ushered her on to the floor. She danced again with Morley and then with the doctor and finally two quadrilles with Tiverton. After supper, the waltzing began, and Huntington was at her side.

'I thought you had forgotten me,' she said.

'How could I? Your hand.' He led her out on to the floor and they stayed there for three dances.

'You must be thirsty Miss Osebury, allow me to obtain you some refreshment but you must promise not to dance with anyone else.' He bought her a large glass of champagne. She wanted to drink it slowly, but she was too thirsty. 'Drink up, the music is calling.' They continued on, with Anne having to concentrate as the alcohol appeared to have gone both to her feet and head. After the next one, she said.

'You must dance with someone else. Five in a row will have everyone talking.'

'I'll get you another drink and we can sit out for a moment.' He brought a second glass of champagne.

'No, tea please.'

'A second glass won't hurt.'

'If I can't stand, we can't dance.'

'If I hold you close, your feet needn't touch the ground.'

'You might just have the strength, but I prefer to be conscious.' A tea arrived and after a quick sip they were off again.'

'Have you seen the enormous moon tonight, Miss Osebury, or can I call you Anne? After all we have known each other for several months now,' he said as the dance ended.

'Some fresh air would be pleasant, but we were only introduced when I returned from Ironbridge.'

'True, but I admired you from afar before then. Come, let us gaze at the heavens, it is not so cold.' He took her arm in his and they walked to the door.

'I have seen the moon before you know.'

'Perhaps, but not with me.'

'Do you paint it a different colour or change its position?' They stepped out onto the front steps and stood to one side of the door in a small area where in the summer sat a large potplant. He was very close to her.

'Isn't it magnificent,' he said as they stared up at the great orb. Further away from its brightness, stars twinkled. 'Really full, and it's giving shadows too.'

Around the edge of the drive were parked, a line of miscellaneous carriages. The horses stood, but were not still, a constant rattling of traces, shaking of heads and snuffling of nostrils. Most of them rested a leg by standing on only three, alternating which one was off the ground. There were no coachmen to be seen but not all could be keeping warm in the servant's quarters. From the blackness of the carriages, surely someone was watching.

She shivered. 'Actually, it's very cold.'

'We will not stay long, come close and I will keep you

warm,' he said encircling her with his arms. He kissed her forehead.

'Mr Huntington!' Further comment was lost as his lips found hers. He was squashing all breath out of her, and for a moment, she enjoyed the experience. So, this was love, and she felt desire rising up within her. This handsome man wanted her. A horse whinnied and its carriage wheels grated as, although braked, it was dragged forward a few inches. They would be seen. What was she doing? Shame! She struggled and twisted. 'Please no.'

'I am sorry, but I have wanted to kiss you from the moment I saw you, and please call me Robin.'

'This isn't the place or time.' Her head back, away from his lips, gave no release from the enfolding arms. 'Please let me go.'

'Don't you love me,' he said releasing the tightness of his hold, but it remained around her, imprisoning her. Her back was against the stone façade. 'If this is not the place; where? Perhaps you could come to my room later.'

'Mr Huntington, what are your intentions?'

'To hold you, to kiss you, to love you. Do you not feel the same? You have been in my arms all evening; it is where you belong.'

She gulped, she felt she was slipping into a dream. His hold tightened, pushing her against the wall, his lips on hers and then his hand was on her breast. For a moment she exhilarated in the sensation and then she was struggling again, pushing away from the wall, fighting for air.

'Oh Robin, I don't know. What are you saying?'

'I want to love you.'

'What do you mean?

'Isn't my affection enough?'

'Of course, when love is giving up on all others and cemented into commitment.'

'I have never wanted to love a woman more. I delight in you, in being with you, holding you in my arms.' He snuggled his nose into her neck. The warmth of his breath and skin brought a glow within her. A shiver ran up through her body.

'Oh Robin, do you really mean it? - But exactly what do you intend? A girl has to know,' she whispered, her voice husky.

'Of course. Yes, I will marry you if that is what you mean?'

'Oh Robin, yes.' The door opened beside them, and an elderly couple went down the steps without seeing the lovers. A coachman miraculously appeared, and a coach began to pull out of line.

'We must go back inside. I cannot feel my feet.' Using all her strength she pushed past, and he let her, but held her hand until they were inside. Guests were mingling in the hall, a footman and maids finding coats. Several glances were made in their direction. Anne blushed, her body frozen, yet hot, her spirit singing, her mind anxious, yet dulled, she stumbled but Huntington caught her. She found her way to a chair. The band was still playing.

'Ah, there you are. You promised me a dance,' said Mr Tiverton standing before her. A questioning glance at Huntington. 'Are you well?'

'Miss Osebury was noticeably hot from dancing, but the night air was rather extreme,' said Huntington. Anne looked up from one gentleman to the another. Wasn't Robin going to say something? What was she supposed to do?

'I'm fine now,' she said, smiling at Huntington, her eyes

seeking his, willing him to speak.'

'Then a dance,' said Tiverton leaning forward and extending his arm.

Morley came up behind him. 'What are you all doing here? Gentlemen, a last chance to waltz, Eleanor will be seeking one of us.'

'Miss Osebury's engaged,' said Tiverton taking her hand. She looked over her shoulder at Huntington, expecting him to protest, as she was led away. Huntington just smiled and winked.

'Later,' he mouthed.

Was she engaged? Did Robin mean it? Should she say something? A proposal was a very serious matter. Alright he was a risk, but he was so handsome, she could help him, love him and be rich. Mr Tiverton was concentrating on the steps. His dancing was better, not the effortless glide of Robin but smooth enough. They had circled the room twice before he spoke.

'You are very silent Miss Osebury. What has been your opinion of the evening?'

'Delightful,' she said, 'really delightful.'

'You dance very well.'

'Thank you and you're better now.'

'But not up to Huntington standards?'

'No, I am afraid not, but keep practicing.'

'I am happy to, in fact at these affairs it is difficult not to. The moment I find myself standing at the edge, Mrs Percival is glaring at me.'

'If she sees you dancing with me overmuch, her glare will be exceedingly intense.'

'Huntington's monopoly of you made that difficult. Be a

little wary of that gentleman.'

'I thought he was your friend.'

'Just as Eleanor is yours.'

'Hmm, if by lucky chance, I am considered in competition with Eleanor for the hand of the gentlemen here, in what way are you in competition with Mr Huntington?'

'That is not quite what I meant. You can meet and know people well, discussing interesting topics with them but remain aware that there are parts of their outlook on life you can never share.'

'So, you look down on him.'

'No, you misunderstand me. There are just sides to his character I do not admire. I have seen more of life than yourself and some of his are not to be approved.'

'I thank you for your concern, but I am well able to protect myself.' The music was coming to an end and the dancers were walking off the floor. 'Thank you for the dance.' He bowed and walked towards Mr Percival. Suddenly she felt tired. Looking at the clock she saw it was nearly one. Huntington was crossing the floor towards her, his hands out as if to grasp hers but changing his mind he swiftly put them behind his back.

'I'm in the fourth bedroom,' he whispered. 'The one with the sculpture of Achilles beside the door. We can talk more there.'

'Mr Huntington! My father's address is Clifton Hall, Hereford.'

'Why would I require it?'

'To write to my father. I am only eighteen as you know.'

'Ahh, yes of course, Clifton Hall, right.'

'Goodnight. I will see you tomorrow.' She began to walk

away. He made no attempt to take her hand but appeared thoughtful. What was she to make of him? What did she really know of him? Halfway up the stairs, she stopped, and stood, watching the last guests leave, some passing on the stairs going to their beds, some going outside to their carriages. A few would be in the library enjoying a last drink. Servants continued to scurry backwards and forwards, the butler irritable and demanding. They would all be tired tomorrow. Mr Huntington slowly walked upstairs, talking to Morley.

'Goodnight, Miss Osebury,' said Morley with a flourishing bow. She smiled. Huntington said nothing but again as he passed, mouthed, 'later.' She continued to watch and then she saw the housekeeper.

'Mrs Carpenter, a word please.' Anne hurried down the stairs.

'What is it? There's a lot to do before some of us see our beds.'

'You were brought up in this part of the country Mrs. Carpenter, can you tell me about Mr Huntington?'

'Tell you? As you appear to be part of the gentry now, I reckon you should tell us, and anyhow I haven't time for gossiping now.'

'It's important, please.'

'Well, he's known as a gentleman who likes the girls. Bad as the master he is for getting the maids in trouble. They say 'is family has great property holdings, and that many of the mines in Yorkshire are theirs. They also say that the rent 'ardly covers his losses at the green tables. Mind you 'e must win sometime. That flash gig came from some wager he won. Bit of a bad un but the rich can do what they like and he's so good looking, I reckon you could forgive him most. Now I've got ta get on.'

Walking up the stairs, her steps slowed by her troubled thinking, she mulled over the housekeeper's comments. This wasn't what she had wanted to hear, the idea of marrying someone whom she might not be able to trust but then she thought of Hannah stuck in the cold empty house with few visitors, and of Grace growing up with no prospects. Could she reform him, would their love be strong enough to keep him close?

Yes, she could, surely a wife can keep a man in check but then she thought of the Percivals. However, she would ensure her affection was stronger than her employers and if she could take on a job in a factory, if she could become a governess against her parent's wishes, then she could reform Robin.

The clock in her room reminded her of the hour, she quickly washed and made ready for bed. As she turned the covers back, she thought of the bolt on her sitting room door. On her immediate return to the manor, she had locked it every time, but she hadn't bothered with it on the last few nights. She went and pushed it home. Sleep was slow in coming, the excitement of weddings, and anxieties about Huntington's intentions unsettled her, until she imagined herself in Robins arms and then a happy dreamlike slumber came.

The scratching at the door gradually entered the depths of her sleep and then it became an urgent knocking. She stumbled out of bed, her brain a fog. Hardly awake, she banged into her sitting room table, the sound crashing through the silence. She stopped at the door her hand on the bolt.

'Let me in, it's Robin,' came a whisper.

'Go back to bed,' she said and turned, stumbled through the rooms, and fell onto her bed ignoring further knocking.

Getting though the day was difficult. Her disturbed night had left her drained. She was out of her depth. Should she have let him in? She knew her own desires would have become difficult to control if she had, but how could she avoid upsetting him? As a gentleman he would be bound to honour any outcome of such love, but it was always the woman who received the blame in a scandal. For once she wanted to talk to her mother. She was short with the children, even telling Jenny off at one point. At dinner, it was a relief to see Mrs Exton already sitting at the table but as she walked towards the seat, Huntington was there before her, sitting down next to the old lady and gesturing Anne to sit the other side of him.

'You are a tease,' he whispered, 'Why didn't you let me in?' The rector was sitting down opposite.

'Good evening rector,' said Anne. 'Did you write?' she added in a whisper to Huntington.

'To your father?'

'Yes.'

'Not yet but I will.'

'Please. I am very appreciative of your offer, but we must have his approval.'

'We must keep it a secret for a while,' he said.

'Why? It is not fair to keep Eleanor and your other admirers in the dark.'

'I need to talk to my father first.'

'Do you need his permission?

'No, my fortune is my own, although on some of it I only receive the income.'

'Will you write tonight?'

'Please do not make demands of me, all in good time. Tonight, we can discuss it.'

'In the drawing room?'

'No, we cannot talk there.'

'What are you doing, whispering at that end of the table Huntington? Come up here and talk to me,' said Eleanor patting the empty chair beside her. There were few visitors and the servants had not reduced the number of chairs.

'Tonight,' he whispered before leaving her. She poked at her food; even the cook appeared to be out of sorts. The meat was oozing blood and the vegetables were dried up.

'Mrs Exton, I do not like to hear scandal but tell me all you know about Mr Huntington.'

'Come now Anne, you like gossip just as much as the rest of us. Well, there is plenty about that gentleman, but I am not sure whether it's true. Just be careful.'

'Everyone tells me to be careful, but no one tells me why. You know my family has no money. If I were to receive any sort of offer, I must take it, regardless of my preferences. I cannot afford to wait for the perfect love.'

'Do you think he might propose to you?'

'I think he has, but he wants to keep it a secret.'

'Hmm, what does that mean and what else does he want?'

'Um, well.' what could she say?

'Some-times, men are much keener on physical affection than the legal arrangements,' said Mrs Exton.,

'Very diplomatically put.'

'Keep him waiting.'

'He is very exciting.'

'Oh yes, he is very handsome and charming and could easily sweep a girl off her feet, but he is very financially aware. Write him a note and ask for a reply. What-ever you do, don't ever allow yourself to be alone with him. I repeat, do not be alone with him, ever!'

'That's telling me, thank you.' After dinner she ran upstairs and found some paper. Later sitting in the corner of the drawing room, carefully shielding the page, she judiciously wrote.

Dear Robin,

Thank you for the wonderful expression of your love last night and your proposal of marriage. I am deeply indebted to your kind offer and clarifications of your intentions. I would encourage you to write to my father to confirm his permission which I feel sure will not be refused. To dance with you and be held in your arms last night was a delight and I look forward to a lifetime with your arms around me. May the warmth of our affection, bring everlasting love to us both. I look forward to hearing from you. All my love, Anne xxx

She folded it and waited. Guilt at being so manipulating, of mistrusting him, of not giving in to his simple demands of love, hung heavily. Would it do any harm to grant him his desires and yes, her own too? Would she destroy her best chance?

He came in with the rest of the others, the waft of tobacco preceding them. Huntington gave a slight smile in her direction, but it could have been to anyone. The men continued to talk as a group. Tiverton and Morley eventually came over.

'Mrs Exton, Miss Osebury, I hope you enjoyed your dinner,' said Morley.

'I think the cook's exertions yesterday, were too much for her,' said Mrs Exton.

'Have you recovered from dancing all evening?' said Tiverton turning to Anne.

'Yes, thankyou. I think I could have danced all night, but the children would have suffered this morning if I had,' said

Anne.

'Will you join us for whist Mrs Exton?' said Morley.

'My pleasure,' said the old lady rising.

'Well,' said Tiverton sitting beside Anne, 'What have you taught the boys today?'

'That late-nights don't suit me, and the Romans were both exceedingly clever and cruel.'

'You appear to enjoy history.'

'It's fascinating to know how people lived, the life they chose and difficulties they had to overcome. And looking back at other people's problems is sometimes easier than working out your own.'

'And what problems does a governess have in a rich household like this?'

'Four children and their mother for one.'

'That's five.'

'So, your tutor taught you arithmetic,' she said with a smile. 'And how is Penny?'

'She gives a wonderful ride.'

'Perhaps we may see you on Friday if you are on the hunt, Robert is riding, and I will take the children in my governess cart to follow where we can.'

'I will look out for you.'

'You always arrive on horseback when you come, you wouldn't prefer a gig like Mr Huntington?'

'We have no steward, so I mainly manage the estate and its tenants myself. A horse is easier for some of the lanes and tracks.'

'Have you many tenants?'

'A few. My father is very keen that we are responsible landowners and that we improve the land.' Much as she enjoyed talking to Tiverton, she wished he would leave so that she could secretly pass her note to Robin. The conversation dragged on, Abigail came and joined them. Anne was aware of her own tiredness and that the children would be as demanding as ever in the morning. As the other two conversed, she leaned back. Huntington walking passed, leant to put his empty glass on the low table beside Anne and whispered.

'Tonight.' Had any one seen? His message given, he walked on, to stand talking at the other end of the room with Mr. Percival. There was no way she could give it to him there. She rose, gave her excuses, and started for the stairs. On the first floor she looked around, waiting till there was no servant near and swiftly walked down the corridor. Stopping at the Achilles statue, she slipped the note under the bedroom door. She straightened and saw Mrs Percival's personal maid had stepped out of a bedroom and was standing looking at her. Not knowing what to say Anne walked past the servant, trying to pretend posting letters to a guest was normal. Aware her pretence was so false; she blushed deeply, the guilt etching her face as suddenly her dress felt too warm and her petticoats too numerus.

She prepared the following days lesson and was in bed by eleven. Sleep was slow in coming and just as she was beginning to doze the familiar scratching began. She sighed and went to the door.

'Robin, please, don't cause a scandal. We mustn't meet like this.'

'But my love, let me in, please, only to talk.'

'Jenny is next door, and she is a light sleeper.' This was a lie as she slept like a log. 'I'll see you tomorrow. Drop in when the children are having lunch. Then we can talk here.'

'Please just for a moment.'

'I would be sacked.'

'Please.'

'I have to go back to bed, Goodnight.'

Sleeping was impossible. How she longed for his company, to lie with him, to be held in his arms. She ignored the continual knocking and finally fell asleep. She awoke in the dark at about four am. full of worry. Partially regretting her decision, she told herself to be strong and tried to sleep again but it did not come easily.

She was late rising, had a rushed breakfast, and trouble teaching so by the time she arrived for dinner that evening her mind was full of the day's cares. Robin had not visited during lunch which was probably the right decision as Camilla had been very difficult and there had been no maid to help nanny. As Anne sat down at the table, she continued to think of how to improve her teaching of Latin to Robert. As he progressed, her lack of knowledge of the subject was becoming difficult to overcome.

Looking up, she searched for Huntington. Everyone was sitting down; a mumbled grace was given by Mr Percival and the first course started to be served. She was sitting between Doctor Hadlow and the Rector, but Mr Morley was opposite.

'Do you know why Mr Huntington is late this evening?' said Anne.

'Back to town,' said Morley.

'What, London? When will he be back?'

'He never goes for less than a week. It's too far.'

How could he go off just like that? Perhaps to see his father.

'Is his father in town?'

'No why would he be, he hardly leaves the estate.' She had

received no note, heard nothing since the knocking on her door. Would he have left her a letter in the hall? She excused herself and went to check. There were no letters. Suddenly she felt sick. He had run away like Geoffrey. Cowards all of them. The bitterness rose up in her, and she wanted to lash out at something. A large vase tempted her but, with difficulty, she overcame the temptation. She knew how much work went into them, and it was particularly fine.

She clenched her fists, her hunger gone. She paced up and down, telling herself that there might be a reason, an excuse, but she knew there wasn't. If she had let him in, would her affection have clarified his marriage desires? Did he think her cold and unloving? Had she ruined her best chance, or had she saved herself from ruin? By the time she returned to the table, the first course had finished but it was of no concern as she had lost her appetite. She sat rigid and only answered Mrs Exton's enquiries with a monosyllabic yes or no. As soon as the meal was finished, she brushed aside the old lady's enquiries and stormed up the stairs to fall upon her bed in tears of anger and regret. Eventually after she had sobbed out her frustration, she thought of Mrs Exton's sympathetic concerns. She had to go back and make her excuses.

She found her sitting alone in the corner. 'Please except my apologies earlier but something had upset me.'

'That's alright. Is there anything I can do, or do you want to tell me about it?'

'I'd better not as it involves another that you know well. Your embroidery is coming on beautifully.'

'Thankyou dear,' said the old lady holding up the piece for Anne's scrutiny. As they continued to chat, they watched Miss Hooper and Eleanor laughing and flirting with two of the men.

'Why doesn't Mrs Percival censure her daughter?' whispered Anne.

'She was quite a flirt in her youth herself. Perhaps she is reliving it through her daughter,' said Mrs Exton.

'That's terrible.'

'A little flirtation can be very effective.'

'I think it is very degrading.'

Mrs Exton leaned across. 'In my observation, men like to talk to strong characters, but they are frightened to marry them. My husband was a brave soldier, but could he find the courage to propose. I had a difficult time encouraging him to speak to me. You must flirt and be just a little coy. Mr Tiverton prefers you to all the others, but he bathes in their attention and remember you have no fortune. He may not know his own heart. Eleanor's arts are to be observed.'

'I couldn't, it is so dishonest. I wouldn't lower myself.'

'Treat it as fun, discuss the world's problems one minute, but flirt the next, laugh at his anecdotes, respect him, he is the best of suitors. You are a pretty young woman, enjoy teasing the men.'

'But Eleanor is your niece!'

'I confess she is but on the other hand I like Mr Tiverton.'

'I like Mr Tiverton too, in an annoying sort of way, but I am never sure whether he is laughing at me or not. I don't know if I could fall in love with him. As I am always rude to him, I doubt he really likes me.'

'Do you prefer Mr Morley? He too looks for femininity in a woman.'

'I think I love both gentlemen a little, although I thought I loved another, but do you really think Mr Tiverton likes me?' What was she saying? A moment ago, she was heart-broken

over Robin, now she was thinking of others. Was she so shal-
low? Was love such a fickle thing or was she the fickle one?
Hannah would have been very critical of her inconsistency
and where was her sister when she needed her? Anne craved
her advice, love and even censor. Always, they had discussed
their feelings and thoughts. Now she needed to mould her
own character and opinions alone, without her saintly sister
to guide and nag her, to make the right decisions and to be a
better person.

'I think they all enjoy your company,' said Mrs Exton gently breaking into Anne's reflections.

'I must not let my feelings grow as it is so unlikely that any
gentleman would marry me in my present situation. I have
already experienced growing friendships end because of my
penniless state. It has been very painful.'

'Of course, but it is a risk you have to take. Flirt a little, be
feminine, be coy.'

'I prefer integrity. Flattery is very dishonest.'

'It need not be. You are looking for the good in someone,
showing you appreciate their qualities.'

'Most of the time you are not, you are just inflating their
egos, often for your own advancement,' said Anne.

'I do like Mr Morley, he has such good manners, but it is
not flattery. You can always rely on him for a kind word, gentle humour or easy conversation,' said Mrs Exton.

'Very true, even if nothing of consequence is said. I saw his
aunt at the dance, she looked very fierce.'

'She is but she dotes on him and would wish for his true
happiness. I doubt Eleanor would be a good match. On his
arm you would be welcome in any society and there would
be few cross words between you.' He appeared to have said

something amusing as the far group burst into laughter and then the group were dispersing.

'If you bring humour and happiness to your friends, then you will always find satisfaction in life.'

She brooded over Huntington for three days, being neither a good companion to Mrs Exton, nor a kind teacher to the children. Her sleep was disturbed with personal recriminations and regrets but through it all she knew she was probably better off without him. On the third evening after dinner, Anne returned to her sitting room early. She had never been much of a believer, even after having gone to church every Sunday but there came a desire to meditate, to think through life, her own and those around her. She had a New Testament, the pages of which she had hardly opened, and she read various passages. There was no sudden inspiration just a strengthened desire to accept her situation and not let the pain of rejection overcome her.

The following morning, Robert brought her a letter he had seen on the hall table. 'For you miss.'

'Thankyou Robert, it's from my sister.' she said turning it over. She would have to ask Mrs Percival for some of her wages before she wrote again. When the children were eating lunch, she managed to find a moment to open it.

Dear Anne, Mother was surprised to read of your meeting with Lady Howle and particularly to your mention of her intending to write. We have received no letter from her since Christmas. When mother wrote to her in late November, mother mentioned, much to my embarrassment, that it would be pleasant for me to visit. Our last letter from Lady Howle was her seasonal letter but there was no invite for me to stay. It is a great pity because I think mother had set high hopes on a visit and is now disheartened, because one more dream has been dashed. Let us however think the best of it and that her ladyship has simply forgotten or is waiting for a more suitable time.

I wouldn't dream of taking your place even if it was done in an honest way. Mother needs me and I could not keep your children in check for a minute. We have had few visitors --.
How strange, thought Anne, her Ladyship had shown real enthusiasm for a visit, yet no invitation had been sent. Was Lady Howle just being polite? Surely not, but it was difficult to think otherwise. She read on but there was nothing important except kind wishes and sisterly love which, pleasant as it was, did not solve their predicament.

Her choice to be a governess had been all about escape. She had never thought of it as a position for life, simply as a step back into society, but society didn't think of it as such. It was clearly a very specific station that was impossible improve on. She had hoped it could have led to better things but clearly once a governess, always a governess. An uneducated girl might start as a maid and over the years rise to be a housekeeper, but Anne's role appeared to be a trap for a lifetime. She sighed, but the meal was over, and the boys were fighting. Back to work!

'Leave him alone Robert!' she shouted.

The horse was being backed into the shafts of the governess's gig, when she arrived at the stables with the children. As Robert was riding in the hunt there would be enough space in the little vehicle. Once they had settled in, and the traces tightened, she sat back to balance the weight on the shafts of the two wheeled cart. She let off the brake.

'Now remember to stay in the same place so the balance is right for the horse. Walk on.' Steering the gig between the busy activity of saddling up in the yard, she entered the park and on to the nearest field which was crowded with gentry on large hunters. Anne kept to one side enjoying the colourful scene as they watched the riders assemble. The hunt master blew a cornet and the hounds streamed out into the next field, the mounted riders following.

'Which is your favourite horse?' said Anne.

'I like the greys,' said Edmund.

'That brown and white piebald,' said Alfred.

'I like the little pony Robert is riding,' said Camilla. 'I want one like that.'

'Yes, I think your father will soon have to buy him a bigger one. What about the chestnut that Mr Tiverton is riding?'

'The one skipping about?' said Edmund. 'Why's it doing that?'

'Because she's excited and loves to run.'

The hounds were milling around the nearest covert and then the hunt moved on to the next small wood. Suddenly, the hounds let up a howl, as with a flash of brown, a fox fled before them. A blast of the horn and everyone was off, the thunder of heavy hooves rumbled across the ground.

'There goes Robert,' cried Edmund.

'Let's hope we can keep up.' As soon as the big horses had left, she flicked the reins and they followed through a gate and along a lane and then across a field to another gate. The main riders were drawing away but not quickly. The next field had recently been ploughed so she turned to an entrance on one side that led into a lane.

'Edmund, can you open it?' she said. He jumped out but a farm hand was coming up the lane.

'Oi'll open it,' the man shouted. He swung the gate back and she eased the horse through. They made good time up the lane, which passed through woodland. There was a cross-roads, and she turned left in the direction she hoped the hunt was going. As the road passed fields again, Edmund stood up.

'Careful.'

'I can see them. They are going across to the heath.' He sat down suddenly as the gig jerked. She flicked the reins and set the pony into a trot, rattling the cart up the stony track. At the next junction she turned right. A short way down the road, a gate suggested there was a way back through the fields.

'Shall we try it? Jump out and open the gate, Edmund.' She followed the signs of cart tracks across the pasture until they came to the other side. They could hear the hunt but couldn't see it and there was no gate. A labourer, relaying the hedge, waved, and pointed to the corner of the field. She drove over and discovered it dipped sharply and there was a gate beyond, that they hadn't been able to see.

'Steady,' she called as the cart angled steeply down. They all leaned back. A group of cows around the gate moved away. Edmund jumped out without being told but he couldn't open it. Applying the brake, she climbed down. She had to lift the gate to allow it to swing. Where the cows had trampled the damp ground, it had become a quagmire. Before she climbed back into the cart, she endeavoured to wipe her boots on the wheel rim, but it was only partially successful. Her petticoats picked up the dirt from her boots and what Edmund had brought in.

Over the next field they went, and along a grassy lane where they spied the hunt on the other side of a field on their left. It was milling around a small wood where they presumed the fox had gone to ground. They drove into the field. The hunt master was calling the hounds off, and the hunt streamed past on its way back to the lane. Great horses practically rubbed the little carriage's side.

'Hello children, you've kept up well,' said Tiverton, reining up beside them. Penny's chestnut coat gleamed in the clear air.

'She looks well,' said Anne.

'I note a little envy.'

'I acknowledge it.'

'Another time perhaps.'

What chance she thought, of that ever happening. 'Perhaps we could swap now, and you could return in the cart.'

He laughed. 'I don't think I could fit, and it is not a lady's saddle.'

'I think both would be manageable if you really wished it. I have ridden astride before.' He just smiled and moved on.

'Morning Miss Osebury,' said Morley, coming up, 'fine day for a ride. You look concerned.'

'No, it is nothing, except I have learned you can be happy with your lot one moment, and then envy sweeps it away in a second.'

'It is early in the day for philosophy.'

'Do you think you will find a second chase?'

'We hope so, but I'm saddle sore already. Will you continue to follow?'

'No, I think I will drive on to the village and see if we can buy some liquorice.'

'Hurray,' cried Alfred,

Anne had persuaded a valet to clean her boots, but she laboured over the petticoats herself, yet managed to be at dinner before the others. The day's activities had made her hungry.

'Did you enjoy today's adventure, Miss Osebury?' said Morley as he sat down opposite her.

'I did, it was great fun, except I would have preferred to be riding with you, rather than trailing you in a cart.'

'And the children?'

'They loved it but trying to get Robert to bed after all the excitement won't be easy. Fortunately, it's nanny's role.'

'So, you would like your own hunter,' said Mr Tiverton, sitting down next to Morley. The gentlemen were going to be in trouble with Mrs Percival if they kept sitting at the bottom of the table near her, she thought.

'Rather beyond my financial reach.'

'You will need to find a rich husband,' said Mrs Exton. Anne liked Mrs Exton but sometimes she lacked diplomacy.

'But every woman's ambition is a rich husband,' said Morley.

'And what do the gentlemen want. A pretty face and a fine figure I suppose,' said Anne.

'Yes, but a spouse must also be easy to live with.'

'Of course, but typically, men always want beauty which is so hard on a plain woman.'

'A comely face, not outstandingly beautiful but a warm smile, revealing a softness, and a kindness in the eyes with an honest and a courageous character would be quite acceptable,' said Morley.

'Quite a list, but what about the shapely figure!' said Anne.

'Oh yes. To us bachelors, the femininity of a lady is a mystery to worship,' said Morley.

'Would you want us to exaggerate femininity, to the extreme of some ladies we could think of?' said Anne.

'There are some young women who may not be as beautiful as they think, but even as I recognise the falseness of their flirtatious ways, I confess I am flattered by them and yes even charmed by them,' whispered Morley, with a glance to the end of the table.

'But Morley, could you accept the cheeky, teasing look of Miss Osebury instead of the kind eyes you desire?' said Tiverton.

'We know Miss Osebury is always provocative, but she has a pretty smile too.'

'But is her provocation feminine and appealing or is it an outrageous attack on the world of men?' said Tiverton.

'I never feel attacked by Miss Osebury, confused, and questioned perhaps, but not attacked.'

'Never intimidated?'

'Are you trying to provoke me Mr Tiverton? Do you know Mrs Exton, I offered to allow Mr Tiverton to try my conveyance in exchange for his horse and he neither offered nor even replied?'

'It was an amusing exchange but as I didn't wish to be the laughing-stock of the hunt, with my legs hanging over the side of your cart I presumed it was not a serious suggestion.'

'You see Mrs Exton, one moment it is considered that I am too serious, the next that my words are only for amusement. Whatever I say is never correct. I can never please Mr Tiverton.'

The gentleman drifted away to a card table to wait for Percival. Morley whispered, 'Delightful creature really.'

'So, you are smitten; enchanted by those sparkling eyes,' said Tiverton.

'Oh yes she's very captivating but much as you might admire a tiger, you wouldn't wish to live with one.'

'Ha, ha,' laughed Tiverton. 'But otherwise, you would really consider her? Marry her?'

'Yes, I know she has no money, and my aunt would have a fit but if she was more amenable.' He stopped and turned aware of the those around them. He leaned closer, 'You find that so surprising?'

'That Cupids arrows find their mark in my friend Morley, yes, I do. You would really consider her.'

'Is that so strange?'

'Well certainly surprising. A governess!' He shook his head.

After she had breakfasted the following morning she hastened to the school rooms, trying to remember what her teaching plans were going to be for the day. She was surprised to find that the children's breakfast had not been cleared away. Jenny was standing, hands on hips. An embarrassed maid hovered by the window.

'Here's your governess now. Will you finish your breakfast so we can clear it away?'

'No, I wanted sausages, not yellow egg,' demanded Edmund.

'You like omelettes.'

'No, I don't; I don't have to eat it if I don't want to.'

'If Nanny says you haven't eaten enough, you eat it. Come on Edmund, Nanny's right, you normally love a good omelette. Cook has made it especially for you,' said Anne.

'I won't! Servants can't make me eat it.'

'This is Nanny telling you.'

'She's just a servant like you. Silly old women without money.' Anne's slap took everyone by surprise including herself. Edmund white with shock, was working his mouth, he wanted to cry but he was well used to his brother's blows. His pride however was hurt enough to finally squeeze out some tears. The maid was trying not to smile.

'You don't talk to Nanny like that. She works hard to look after you; you ungrateful boy.'

'I'll tell mother and then you will be sacked.'

'Not until you have apologised.' He started to rise but Anne was making sure she was between him and the door. 'Say sorry.'

'Won't.'

'What would your father say? To be so rude, so very ill-mannered. Say sorry and then eat at least half of your egg and the bread otherwise you will be doing your lessons late tonight.' He looked at her, at Nanny and the tears began to flow.

'Sorry,' he mumbled. He picked at his food for several minutes.

After he had eaten some of it, Anne said, 'Oh take it away, we can't wait for you all day. You will be hungry later, now Robert let me see your Latin crammer.' It was a difficult day, so she was relieved when the lessons were over, and she could leave them to their nanny. It wasn't helped by her own guilt and annoyance at losing her temper or by the boys continuing their lack of respect for Jenny who loved and cared for them. She was just changing for dinner when a maid knocked on her door.

'Mrs Percival wishes to see you,' she announced.

'What, now?'

'I believe so.' The maid's expression and that she continued to stand at the door, suggested that Mrs Percival was not expected to be kept waiting.

'Please tell her I will be down shortly.' Now what could all this be about? Any ordinary issues could be brought up at dinner which was only twenty minutes away. She shrugged but worry began to creep into her thoughts. Surely it wasn't about her hitting Edmund. There had been no contact between mother and son as far as Anne was aware.

She found her employer in the drawing room; Mrs Exton was with her and looking embarrassed.

'Ahh Anne, I have received reports that you hit Edmund; is this true?' demanded Mrs Percival.

'It is, but he was very rude.'

'How dare you! This is my son. We made it abundantly clear that Mr Percival and I do not believe in corporal punishment. Your superior attitude does not bode well for your future. Monopolising the conversations, flirting with our guests, and carrying on like you are the mistress of this house, rather than an impoverished governess is not to be borne. Do I have to constantly remind you of your station? You will lose your position in this house if you act like this, and I will ensure that no other genteel family will ever employ you.'

'Would you have your son brought up without censure, to insult those who care for him. Jenny loves and serves your children day and night. No child should abuse his nanny.' She stopped, pursed her lips, holding back the words that threatened to rush out, the accusation of failed motherhood, the delegation of day-to-day responsibility of her children and that Jenny had taken on the role of mother. Mrs Percival sat stony faced as Anne breathed deeply. Had she said too much already, had she just lost her job, would she be going back to the china works?

'It was only a slap. Your children have ceased to be controllable. Do you want them to grow up offensive and mean to those around them or do you want them to learn respect and concern for others?'

'You speak of respect, yet you do not respect your superiors, nor your place. Perhaps I shall have to find a replacement capable of obeying their superiors'

'I am sure Anne would not have hit Edmund unless he deserved it,' said Mrs Exton.

'My place in this house has been to educate and assist in bringing up your children to be true ladies and gentlemen. They were out of control and behind with their lessons, this I have diligently strived to change. Your sons need discipline.'

'It is not for you to decide what they need but to carry out my orders. This is your last chance! One more disobeying of the rules of this house and you will be on your way home. Just see that you apologise to Edmund and that it never happens again!' Anne curtsied but said nothing. She dared not speak, for if she did, the words threatened to run away. Strong words that would lose her, her position. As for apologising, that wasn't going to happen, but she wouldn't acquaint her employer with that fact. Where was the handsome Huntington to whisk her away from this life?

At dinner, a rebelliousness swept over her, she smiled sweetly with her head on one side, and put her hand on Mr Morley's arm while complimenting him on his cravat, just as Eleanor would have done. It appeared to have even more layers of ivory silk than normal. She then smiled at Mr Tiverton, in what she felt was a coquettish manner. He looked slightly taken aback.

'Are you flirting with me, Miss Osebury?'

'You appear to enjoy it so much I thought I ought to try. When we danced the other evening, I thought what strong arms you have and how safe I felt within them.'

'You did not. I trod on your foot. Eleanor may have mastered the art, but it does not become you. You have nothing to prove.'

A stare from Mrs Percival was enough to remind herself of her danger. She was also so embarrassed by her own behaviour that when the meal ended, instead of retiring to the drawing room, she made her excuses to Mrs Exton, and collected her drawing equipment from the school room. She then retreated to the entrance hall. For some time, she had been meaning to copy a statue there and make some preparatory sketches of a Dutch sea scene that hung in the corridor. After a frustrating start, she settled down, forgot the difficulties of her employment, and began to feel she had caught a good likeness. Footsteps made her look up. Mr Morley was looking on.

'I had always wanted to see what you could really do. Hey Tiverton, come and see our little artist at work.' As the other gentleman approached, she turned the pad, so her efforts were hidden.

'Well, let us see,' he said.

'It's very impressive. Really looks like marble,' said Morley.

'I haven't finished it yet.'

'I am sure we can make allowances. Now don't be shy, it can't be so bad,' said Tiverton. She turned it round. He took a corner to angle it, to catch the candlelight.

'Mm, I must confess it is very good. Nearly as well as a man could do!'

'Mr Tiverton! I challenge any man in this house to do better.'

'While you might win, constantly challenging the menfolk is never wise.'

'And I wouldn't win in the outside world, because my art would not be judged on merit, but on my sex.'

'Yes, I admit you are probably right, perhaps you would therefore be better to concentrate on the abilities that are acceptable for you ladies?'

'If God gives a woman talent, should she not use what she has been given? In the Bible, the man that hid his talent was punished yet men deny women the rights to use their skills.'

'Embroidery can be very artistic, and no man would wish to compete.'

'Mr Tiverton why do you love to vex me?'

'Because it amuses me to see the fire in your eyes and I suspect some of the time you are amused by your own opinions. Now, can you do portraits of real people?'

'Certainly, unless they are particularly annoying.'

He laughed. 'So, you might find me difficult?'

'If I look at the cartoons in Punch, I might find the inspiration. There is a similarity in your nose, to the one portrayed of the Duke of Wellington.'

'I am glad to find that you consider my visage equal to a duke.' Mrs Exton came up behind the men.

'Mrs Percival is asking after you gentlemen. I am afraid Anne is in her bad books so it would be wise to leave her to her sketching.'

'Well Miss Osebury, it appears we must leave you to your

cold friend,' said Morley patting the statue and giving a little bow. Tiverton just smiled and winked. She returned to her drawing, making several quick sketches which she hoped would prompt inspiration in the children the next morning.

When Anne arrived for dinner the following evening, she found that neither Tiverton, nor Huntington were there. There were other guests, including a very noisy gentleman and his wife, whose loud conversation and even louder laughter echoed around the dining room. The lady's outpourings were particularly high pitched. Mr Morley sat at that end of the table with them but after dinner, when the gentlemen returned from having their smoke, he came straight over to Anne and Mrs Exton.

'How are you ladies?' he said and then whispered, 'is this going to be the quieter end of the room tonight?'

'Really Mr Morley, I heard you making as much noise as the others at dinner,' said Anne.

'Well, I had to, to make myself heard.'

'And where are your two friends tonight,' said Mrs Exton.

'I've no idea as to what Huntington is getting up to; some card game somewhere I'll be bound. Tiverton's gone to his home I believe.'

'But none of his family are in residence or are they?' said Mrs Exton.

'No but he is still fussing over his tenants. I think the estate deteriorated with his father in London so much. Tiverton has been busy with drainage and suchlike, trying to improve the land and the farmers' income and eventually I suppose increase their rent to pay for it.'

With two of the gentlemen away over the next few days,

Anne found herself sitting next to Miss Hooper, in her beautiful evening dress. It was unfortunate as it made Anne's look shabby in comparison. The young woman was inclined to ignore Anne at first but was gradually drawn into conversation by Mrs Exton.

'So,' she said, eventually turning to Anne, 'what is it like managing four children and of such different ages?'

'Difficult, for Robert would be better at school.'

'Why don't you suggest it?'

'I have several times.'

'I couldn't think of anything more disagreeable.'

'It was a shock, having to study, trying to understand subjects I had no knowledge of, and learn the art of discipline.'

'Boys too. I'm not sure I like small boys; they are very problematic.'

'Most males are problematic.'

Miss Hooper laughed. 'Very true. Talking of challenging men, I understand Mr Huntington will return tomorrow.'

'That is excellent as Mrs Percival said there is to be another dance next week and Mr Huntington dances so well.'

'Yes, it was observed that you enjoyed dancing with the gentleman last time and that you were holding his hand even after the dance had ended. Are we to hear of an announcement?'

'No, Mr Huntington is a great flirt and likes the ladies but there is nothing of consequence between us.'

'That wasn't the impression given.'

'In the excitement of dancing so pleasantly, we forgot ourselves. At least he didn't tread on my foot like Mr Tiverton, who came in his riding boots.'

'Ah Tiverton, he's a real gentleman although not so handsome as Huntington,' said Miss Hooper looking around as if she feared being overheard, and then whispered, 'Eleanor is very fond of Mr T, but she will be disappointed.' It was just loud enough for Mrs Exton to hear, particularly as she was leaning towards them.

'What have you heard?' she asked.

'Only that I am particularly looking forward to his return,' said Miss Hooper, with a "pleased with herself" smile. 'My personal maid heard him and Morley discussing whether an antique ring belonging to his grandmother would be acceptable for an engagement or whether he should buy something more modern.'

'And who might be the fortunate lady?' said Mrs Exton.

'I couldn't say but as I am the only lady here who can offer a suitable marriage settlement besides the Percival girls you must make your own conclusions. He is always so full of compliments, and we danced with such assurance. I hope you will not mention this to anyone.'

'A marriage settlement is not always essential,' said Mrs Exton.

'Oh, I think it is. Why would a man accept any woman without capital or income?' Why indeed, thought Anne and why mention it in my hearing?

'Mr Morley,' called Mrs Exton, for he was a little way down the table. 'Miss Hooper insists that no man would consider a young woman, unless there was a suitable settlement and income from the lady, yet I understand you believe true love is stronger than material influences,'

'Of course, love overcomes all thought of financial gain, however money might I suppose make a pretty girl appear even prettier, adding to her general desirability.'

CHAPTER 9

On returning from breakfast the following morning a maid passing on the stairs, said, -

'A letter for you Miss, in the hall,'

'Thank-you,' Another letter, no doubt from Hannah who had been so reliable with her correspondence but when she picked it up, she saw it wasn't from her sister; it was her mother's writing. She often added post-scripts to Hannah's epistles but had never written direct. Worried, Anne tore it open.

Dear Anne, I really don't know what to do. I need your help as Hannah has become infatuated by that curate Spenliff. He is equally obsessed. I fear they will elope to Scotland. Surely not? Hannah would never disobey their parents. *Mr Spenliff received an inheritance from some distant aunt of one hundred pounds and thinks it is a fortune and enough to marry on. Please can you either arrange for Hannah to stay with you or for you to come home immediately and help me avert this disaster. Lady Howle hasn't written or replied to my last letter so there is no hope there. I have enclosed five pounds for your travel. You must come. Please don't fail me, or your sister will be living in a hovel with a dozen children.* Really mother you must be mistaken, and curates don't elope. He might lose his position. *Your father is no help and I think it will be the last straw for him if they do. Only you can talk her out of it and give some hope to your father. Don't delay, Mother.*

She remained standing beside the hall table, depression

bringing indecision. She would have to go, and just when she felt reasonably settled. It was so unfair, and Mrs Percival was upset enough with her as it was. And if she did have to go would her employer allow her to return? She straightened her back and walked towards the drawing room. What excuse could she give? She couldn't admit that her sister might elope. What could she say, without a direct lie?

'Mrs Percival, may I have a word,' said Anne looking around the room, which except for her friend Mrs Exton was otherwise empty. 'My mother has requested my urgent assistance at home for a few days.'

'That certainly isn't possible.'

'I wouldn't ask if it wasn't important. To quote my mother.' She looked down at the scrap of paper. '*I need your help. Don't fail me. Only you can give some hope to your father.*' I would remind you that I have worked hard to bring the children's work up to standard.'

'It's just not convenient.'

'But I must, I'm afraid,' said Anne the continuing to hold the letter in clear view but in a way that it couldn't be read.

'And if it was allowed, how long would you be away?'

'I hope, only about a week.'

'A week! We can't spare you for that long.'

'I'm sure the boys will be alright, and I will set them some work.' No drawing room conversation for her tonight. 'Jenny is better at keeping them in order now.'

Mrs Percival frowned, 'It's ridiculous, as a governess you place is with your pupils.' Anne didn't reply but stood stiff and resolute. 'Oh alright, but make sure it is not one day longer.'

'Thank you, I shall be as quick as I can, and I promise to keep it to a week.'

'Edward can take you to Shrewsbury in the landau tomorrow. Will you be taking your luggage?'

'Oh no, just enough for a few days. Thank you again.'

Sitting alone in the smart coach, leaning back in the aroma of the fine leather cushioning, and looking out on the countryside, she thought of the other journeys she had made. Of squashed post coaches, overloaded gigs or unhappy leavings. Yes, times had been difficult, yet somehow, she'd survived, and she had learnt to deal with the aches of her heart. What could she say to Hannah? How could she persuade her that there was life beyond the narrow boundary of Clifton Hall and a poverty ridden curate?

She was bone weary when she stood again in the old hall, the rattle of the receding cab, which was little more than a farmers cart, the only sound as it trundled away. There was no one there to greet her, had no one heard? She wanted to wash, yet she knew she had to speak to Hannah without delay. A clatter from the stairs above and a hoop came bouncing down. Grace!

'Anne,' shouted the miscreant leaning over the bannisters and then leaping down the stairs two at a time.

'Careful, I've not come back to see my sister breaking her head on the flagstones.' But the girl, in a flurry of dirty skirts, expertly judged each flying step, until she had thrown herself into Anne's arms.

'Are you back to stay?'

'No just a quick visit.'

'Is it because of Mr Spenliff? He is really nice.'

'He may be, but people have to live and for that you need income. His is negligible. Where might I find her?'

'In her room unless she is taking one of her long walks, however I think mother banned her from leaving the house.'

'Thank you, if you see mother tell her I am back and gone to find your sister.'

Quietly opening the door, she saw Hannah, sitting by the window with her back to her, staring out over the grounds. Somehow, even from behind she appeared unhappy, Was it the slump of her shoulders, the set of her head? Anne wasn't sure but she sensed her sorrow.

'Hello Hannah, I'm back.'

She turned, pale and drawn and regarded Anne with the slightest of smiles. 'Mother shouldn't have concerned you. I'm not going to run away or anything.'

'Tell me about it and then we can discuss what we can do.'

'There is nothing to discuss. We are in love and will eventually marry. If I'm not allowed, we will have to wait until I am twenty-one. It is only nineteen months and then there is nothing mother can do.'

'But it would still be going against their wishes.'

'Yes, but you cannot ignore love.'

'You are ignoring love, your mother's, and mine too. I know Mr Spenliff is nice enough but without capital, he cannot provide you a home.'

'We can rent a little cottage and when I am twenty-five, I will receive a small income.'

'What one hundred and fifty pounds a year? That won't go far! You have to live, dresses, reasonable food to put on the table, a maid, even a cook, a pony and trap to get around in, and not only for yourself but for your children when they arrive.'

'We don't need to be rich.'

'We are not talking about riches but survival. What happens if one of the children is ill or your curate catches some disease from his parishioners, will you have money for a doctor, for medicines? Be practical Hannah, there are good men out there, who are rich as well as charming.'

'I don't want a rich man, just Archibald.'

'Archibald! And you would be called Mrs Spenliff, what sort of name will that be?'

'I thought you would have some sympathy, Anne; you are as bad as mother. You, who are just a governess, and your letters do not disguise your loneliness or the burden of your position.'

'Oh, Hannah, I know. If only you could meet some of Mrs Percival's guests, there are charming men amongst them. If we could just arrange for you to socialise among them.'

'Do you appear to have an opportunity there?'

'No Hannah, there are four reasons why not. One, I am not elegantly beautiful like you. Two, not charming and kind and three, my opinions and rebellious streak attracts no man. Lastly our poverty remains, but with you, your beauty would compensate. On three out of four of the for mentioned reasons, you would be a success.'

'I cannot be so mercenary.'

'But you are the only capital we have. Grace and I were relying on you lifting our family. If you brought us a good connection, we might rise with you. Without, we are penny-less spinsters.'

'But Anne you are pretty, I'm sure some man might love you.'

'Wait for the ball at the Denfords. I'm sure there will be eligible bachelors there. Whatever you do, do not commit yourself to Mr Spenliff.'

Hannah didn't reply but looked at the threadbare carpet. Finally, she turned and looked out of the window again.

Anne sat back, the melancholy of her mood pressing down on her. She ought to light a lamp, for while it was only 4.00pm, the overcast March sky was as dark as her temper. She looked across at Hannah, sitting upright in her stubborn resolve and her mother weeping gently into an embroidered handkerchief. Sir George stared into his glass, only Grace who sat on the floor doing a jigsaw was unaffected by the sombre atmosphere. Anne had been home for five days and all her arguments had been in vain, in fact, they appeared to have simply stiffened Hannah's resolve. Anne had to go back, but she couldn't leave her mother.

'There is a gentleman at the door asking to be shown in. He has instructed Dickens to stable their horses,' said Jane coming into the room. She looked around at the family scene, and at Lady Osebury's red eyes. 'Shall I tell him to wait?' Was their maid ashamed of her employers? No one spoke. Jane looked from one to another.

'Light the lamp,' said Anne eventually.

'Perhaps we could light some candles,' sniffed her ladyship with a glance at her husband to check if the expense could be justified. 'Is it one of our neighbours? Did he give his name; a card?'

'No madam I didn't catch it, but he doesn't look the sort of person to be kept waiting. He has a valet with him, who is assisting Dickens.'

'You should have taken his name, but you'd better show him in, then,' said Anne. 'Grace can light the chandelier.'

'Who can it be, that would call at this God-forsaken place. I thought we had escaped our creditors?' said Sir George, sitting up. There was a general straightening of attire and smoothing of hair as Grace jumped on to a chair with a taper and began to light the candles.

'Careful Grace, … Mr Tiverton!' exclaimed Anne as he entered.

He tossed his cloak on to an empty chair before Jane could take it. 'Sir Osebury, Lady Osebury,' he bowed. 'Anne, please will you introduce me to your parents?' No one moved or spoke, even Grace hesitated, the taper in her hand threatening to burn her fingers. The light of several candles, as the flames took hold, appeared to puncture the gloom.

'Eh - my Parents, Sir George and Lady Osebury, my sisters Hannah and Grace, Mr Tiverton from Shropshire.' She hesitatingly stood as did her mother eventually.

'Delighted to meet you sir, madam,' said Mr Tiverton with another bow, 'and to see this fine old house. May I warm myself by your fire.' Without waiting for a reply, he walked over to it and crouched for a minute, his hands held out. 'Decidedly cold for March; ice on the road, thought my horse would have me in a ditch more than once.' He turned and stood before it, smiling at Anne.

'What has brought you so far from your estates?' she managed to say.

'Ah yes, why travel so far? What would bring me to take a journey? Perhaps the Percival's abode lost its charm. No one to start the debate, no one to puncture the hypocrisy, no one to tease the bachelors. Follow the star as the wisemen did.' The family sat, mouths slightly open, looking from Anne to the confident stranger in their midst.

Anne coloured, but joy was replacing shock, pleasure replacing embarrassment. 'Mr Tiverton you amaze me, and flatter me, it is out of character, it is not your way, I do not comprehend you.'

'You are correct, my character has been upended or perhaps you are only just seeing it as it is.'

'Well, however confusing, my apologies that you find us in this old house.'

'We are forgetting our hospitality,' said Sir George, to everyone's surprise, 'A glass of wine or if you prefer, we can call on the kitchen to make a hot punch. We do not dine till six.'

'Your luggage. What room would be usable, which would be best,' said Lady Osebury as if to herself sitting back down.

'Thank you, a glass of wine will suffice. I did travel on a whim, so I have little baggage, but I would not put you out.' Sir George rose and collected a glass from the sideboard which he filled to the top, emptying his bottle. He stepped to the fire and held it out to their guest. Sir George had become miserly with his wine, a hoarder, normally only offering derisory glasses to others but for once he appeared happy to share.

'Hannah, go to the kitchen and see Mrs Perkins about which bedrooms can be aired and made ready,' said Lady Osebury. Hannah left, with a last questioning glance at their visitor who remained standing, leaning on the mantle shelf as if he owned the house.

'So, you came on a whim?' said Anne eventually.

'Yes, I wanted to see if your sister was as beautiful as you said, and indeed, I must confess she is,' he said, sipping his wine.

'Does she put Eleanor and me in the shade?'

'Eleanor yes, but nothing would put you in the shade or if she did, she certainly couldn't keep you there.'

'More compliments Mr Tiverton. I see the journey has addled your brain or did you slip on the ice after all and bump your head? Perhaps you have forgotten.'

'Anne!' exclaimed Lady Osebury.

'Do not be concerned madam, I am well used to such treatment. Are you not pleased to see me Anne?'

'Yes of course,' she said, a wide smile growing and for a moment she felt her eyes prick. That would never do. A wave of affection suddenly overflowed her; a depth of feeling that surprised her. She mustn't let her emotions be seen but the smile wouldn't go. 'And did you come on Penny?'

'I did, and now are you going to tell me you are more excited at seeing the horse than its rider?'

'Penny was never rude to me, but it is good to see you too.'

'Your home is in Shropshire?' said Sir George.

'Yes sir, not quite as large as this, but large enough and part is an ancient hall so excellent for balls and such like when the family is in residence. My father is an MP and resides in London whenever parliament is sitting. In reality, my parents only come up for the summer and the shooting season. The house is normally empty which is why I have been enjoying the hospitality of friends like the Percivals who delight in balls and constant parties.'

'Anne has mentioned the parties.'

'Yes, the Percivals, are never content unless there are at least twenty sitting down for dinner. I miss my younger brother who is an officer in faraway India, so I take particular pleasure in a busy household.'

'Does your father not entertain?'

'Indeed, he does, but they are mainly serious old men discussing the affairs of state. Fascinating debate, in which they rarely give me any opportunity to contribute, especially when I disagree. I hope in time to gain their acceptance as my skills improve. In the last few years, my time has been spent in dealing with our agricultural estates.'

Hannah returned and explained the lodging arrangements and suggested where Mr Tiverton could wash and change if he wished. He bowed and followed her out. Anne rose to accompany them.

'Just a moment young woman,' whispered her father. 'Who is this gentleman?'

'You denied any romantic attachments, yet a man, obviously a gentleman of standing, has ridden seventy miles to see you,' said her mother.

'I am as surprised as you, although however partial I might be, as a penniless governess I had never expected or even hoped that his interest was other than the general amusement of the local society. We often engaged in banter although we did have some serious conversations too.'

'Is he rich?'

'Mother is that your first thought? But yes, he is, I believe, seriously wealthy; Eleanor will be very annoyed that he is visiting me. Can I go and see that everything is being done for his comfort?'

'I'm sure Hannah can cope. It will be good for her to meet a real gentleman. He may fall for her and then we can say goodbye to Mr "very poor" Spenliff.'

'Mother!' Yet her mother was right. The pangs of jealousy welled up in her, Mr Tiverton had become her friend and much as she wanted to help Hannah, it was too much of a sacrifice. Had he really come with romantic intentions or on impulse as he said for a change of scene? Even on the spur of the moment it was strange. Or had he heard her sing Hannah's praises so often, that he wanted to meet her? Anne stood and strode out of the door. Mr Tiverton was coming down the stairs, chatting amiably to her sister. They looked perfect together, both tall and well suited. The clouds had briefly parted, and the low setting sun threw a last ray through the long window on the stairs. It glinted gold on Hannah's hair. Anne wanted to cry out in rage and pain. Mr Tiverton saw the sun's rays too.

'Come Anne, show me a little of the grounds while it is still light. My apologies to your parents, and Hannah, I will see you later.' Anne stormed ahead.

'There isn't much to see, as there is so little maintenance; it all grows wild.'

'Have I offended you by coming unannounced,' he said, catching up.

It wasn't his fault; he was just a man, easily turned by feminine beauty. Her self-loathing of being shorter, and of not realising the danger of her sister to her own happiness, of being the unloved middle child, all swept over her. She dared not look at him in case he saw her mood.

'It's a fine prospect, the winter sun setting behind the mountains is splendid,' he said tucking her arm in his. 'Does this view of blue, Welsh peaks, not give you daily pleasure?'

'It is a fine prospect and one day I hope to ride over them.' Yes, if Hannah went off to be married, leaving her to look after her parents, she might find some satisfaction in exploring the wild places of the Welsh border, but it would be no compensation. 'So far I haven't been more than half-way; I need a better horse.' They looked up at the yellow sky with fleeting clouds.

'Let us be serious for a moment Anne,' he said turning and looking closely at her. He bent down on to one knee. 'When you left, the household became staid, with its light extinguished.' What was he doing? 'Absence makes the heart sorrowful. Will you do me the honour of becoming my wife.'

'Mr Tiverton, Clive,' she said, using his Christian name. It came naturally without thought, yet she had never used it or even thought of it before. 'Really! You really want to marry me?'

'Of course, are you so surprised?'

'A little, greatly. Stand up now, your breeches will become damp and even in this lonely place someone will see us.'

'And your answer?' he said as he stood.

'Oh yes, with the greatest of pleasure.' He stood up and looked down on her, with a smile hovering and eyes soft. One of his hands enclosed one of hers.

'Aren't you going to kiss me?' she said eyes twinkling.

His smile widened as he cupped her chin in his hand and leaned forward to kiss her gently on the lips. Her arms folded round him and when his lips retreated, she leant closer and kissed him back. He enfolded her in his arms. They stood solitary, in the middle of the overgrown garden, in a long embrace, Anne, the happy knowledge sweeping over her that she had found her real love, and, in a man, she could totally commit to; and Tiverton that having finally made up his mind and overcoming his uncertainty, it was a right and wonderful decision. He fumbled in his pocket and withdrew a ring.

'Perhaps you would like to try this on. We could buy something more modern if you preferred.' She slipped it on, twisting it around. A circle of small pearls around a large emerald on a gold band. A ring, on her ring finger!

'It's lovely, your grandmother's,' I presume?'

'How did you guess?'

'Maids have ears and Miss Hooper had hope.'

He laughed. 'Can one have no secrets? Does it fit?'

'Yes, a little snuggly. I'm not sure I can get it off.'

'It would be better not to wear it until after I have spoken to your father.'

'But it won't come off.'

'Now Anne, don't tease. You can wear it later.'

'You try then? It needs soap.' She held up her hand and he wriggled the ring but without any force and appeared more interested in the small hand with its elegant long fingers.

'Alright but don't let your parents see it yet.' He pulled the hand to his lips and kissed it.

Grace creeping back through the kitchen came across Mr Rawlins.

'They are kissing. It's disgusting, I must tell mother.'

'She will find out soon enough, but I dare says it's good news so perhaps you should go and confess to your spying.'

The happy couple eventually broke apart and, holding hands, walked to the house until they reached the door to the drawing room, where Clive tried to disengage his hand, but Anne hung on.

'I need to talk to your father.'

'Go on then,' she said letting go as they entered. Her parents suddenly drew apart as if caught in some underhand conspiracy. Grace as proud informant was standing beside them.

'Sir Osebury, I wonder if you would be able to give me a moment of your time in private.'

'If it is to ask a certain question regarding my daughters hand you have my blessing and our congratulations,' he said.

The informality of her father's reply, and the ignoring of usual conventions was a surprise to Anne, until she remembered the scattered papers and empty bottles in her father's library. To dispense with private discussions might avoid embarrassing questions over money too.

'Thankyou sir, that is very kind of you.' He bowed. Anne for a moment caught Clive's hand and briefly squeezed it before crossing the room and embracing her father. She had forgotten her father's smile. It had been lost for many months.

'If it would suit you, it would be convenient to have an early wedding as I recently purchased a particular investment which I suspect will need a little of my time, especially at the beginning, and Anne's too. Would that be possible?'

'Mine!'

'Yes, a certain china works. Your young friend showed me around. He is relying on your passing on ideas of "present-day" fashions in porcelain.'

'You have bought a share in the company?'

'Yes 51%, so I own it, or we do. A fitting wedding present?'

'Mr Tiverton, Clive, you don't buy a great company on a whim.'

'No, but knowing your concern, the idea of taking an interest had been there for some time. A profitable investment that brings good to the poor of our society is worthy of consideration. I had made no serious application or pursuit when I stumbled on the opportunity and ended up owning it.'

'Really,' said Anne, looking back on their many conversations. Had he really been considering it for some time?

'I would also like to introduce you to my family and spend some time with them in the London House. My mother entertains regularly so a good place for research. While a grand wedding from my home or in London might be preferred, we could have something simple here and then call on them as man and wife. I believe parliament is sitting and of course my father may be involved in planning the coronation, so it is unlikely for my parents to feel able to visit.'

'I don't know,' said Anne, watching her mother's embarrassment. How could they afford a wedding there?

'Mr Spenliff would be happy to do the ceremony,' said Hannah.

'And we could certainly have the wedding breakfast here. I can hire in staff from around the county,' said Mr Rawlins who had come into the room unnoticed. 'And any other items you need can soon be purchased, even in Hereford.'

As it all appeared a dream, Anne was happy to go with the flow. To be settled, with a loving husband and soon. Clive was a man she knew she could completely love and be loved by, with no fear of rejection, someone she could trust and respect.

'There is an excellent seamstress in Hereford whom I would recommend for your dress and the bridesmaids,' continued Mr Rawlins, with a sweep of his hand, encompassing Grace whose eyes were sparkling with excitement and Hannah who had just entered the room. 'It would be wonderful to brighten up the old house.'

Lady Osebury, Mr Rawlins and Clive sat around in a circle, planning it all with the occasional request to the future bride and father of the bride on certain issues. Anne was surprised to find she was happy to concede to their suggestions. Six weeks-time, in six weeks-time, she would be married! The big question was not how many people, should they invite but how many of those sent an invitation would brave the roads in

April, and actually come so far.

'Perhaps we should suggest Mrs Percival sends one of her children to be a page boy,' said Tiverton.

Anne laughed. 'She will be upset enough without that. I presume she thought you were destined for Eleanor. What will I say when I return?'

'You cannot return just before your marriage,' exclaimed Lady Osebury, her face white and strained with shock at such an idea.

'I think I must, I promised her that I would not be away for more than a week. I cannot break my word.'

'But this is different, your wedding supersedes other responsibilities.'

'It will be inconvenient but if I go, I can give her a month to find a replacement.'

'No, I will write and explain,' said Lady Osebury, 'You cannot possibly go back.'

'Clive, do you not agree it is my duty?'

'It raises many difficulties but if you have promised, you must. We could postpone I suppose. I'm not sure how they will greet you however.'

'Cast me onto the drive with ashes on my head, I suspect.'

CHAPTER 10

The time had come to leave the hall and go back to Arleston Manor. The Osebury coach had been temporarily mended, enabling Dickens to drive them to Hereford with Clive's valet riding behind with his hunter on a loose rein. It was great pleasure to sit together in the old coach, but their imminent separation hung heavily on them, and they said little but remained content in each-others company. When they arrived, Dickens had immediately turned back for the hall complaining that he didn't trust the repair. It was busy at the Inn, but there was a small saloon, set aside for the gentry where they could sit and enjoy a cup of chocolate together. Clive's mare would be in the stable for an hour's rest and feed before he rode on.

'Well Anne, I feel guilty leaving you here, letting you travel all the way back to the Percivals alone, but it will be the last time by public coach I assure you,' he said taking her hand.

'Do not be concerned, I am well used to such adventures. Perhaps I may find travelling in the Tiverton's private coach so boring that I introduce you to the joys of squeezing in amongst the unwashed population of post travellers.'

'I hope not. But when I come to collect you from the Percivals, I will ensure our coach is looking at its best. Will you want me to provide a maid or travelling companion?'

'I would like to invite Mrs Exton to travel with me.'

'An excellent idea.'

'You have not told me about the Severn Pottery and your visit.'

'Well, all I knew was the company name and that of Mrs Turnbull, but I had to be in Ironbridge for another reason, so I went along to your china works, and asked to meet the leading artist, whom I understood was a genteel lady. Obviously, it was an unusual request, but I stood there confidently and the little man at the door eventually said follow me. It is certainly a busy place, although I could instantly tell from the empty benches that the factory was below capacity. I stopped him, and asked after each process I saw, and I spoke to some of the workers. The poor man became quite agitated as if I was some spy from a competitor.'

'Did you meet Mrs Quantrell?'

'Yes, a lady of good breeding.'

'And what did she say of her absconded pupil?'

'That you had shown great promise, but you didn't like hard work.'

'That's not true!' she said, but with a smile as he was grinning. 'It was, I admit, a terrible shock. Teaching children didn't appear so hard afterwards, but how did you go from an unplanned visit, to buying it?'

'After I had discussed it with the lady and seen what they did, it confirmed all you said about the business needing direction and investment. There was to be a director's meeting the following day. Two of them were staying at the Tontine so I had dinner with them that evening. Basically, four directors were keen to carry the business forward but another five wanted out. After some hard negotiations I came away owning the greater part. Not all is complete but legally it is ours.'

'Goodness, really, and did you see James Turnbull?'

244

'I was sipping my coffee with these older men when your young friend burst in. Suddenly all apologies and tongue tied when he saw who I was with, but we found him a chair, and we encouraged his views which he shared with enthusiasm. In ten years-time he could be running it. In the meantime, the directors will bring someone called Donald Smith back to run it. I met him at the works the following day and had a second look round.'

'That's wonderful. I look forward to meeting them all again.'

'Yes, but they will be expecting my new wife to give them some ideas.'

'Well, you will have to take me around the best London shops! Then I can see what the competitors are doing. Mrs Percival has a rather elegantly shaped tea set, yet it has old-fashioned decoration. I think we could do a better version but it's innovative pieces, unusual teapots, sculptures, and models that might command better prices.'

He took her hand and ran a finger over his grandmothers old ring. 'I hope they don't give you a hard time when you return.'

'Well, you won't be there to tease me anyway. Now tell me, when did I become the centre of your affections?'

'I don't know really, somehow you grew on me, got under my skin,'

'What, as an irritant?' she said, grinning.

'I thought you were an annoying but amusing child, yet one I rather liked against my better judgement.'

'Well, when I first met you, it was in the library, and you were just one of the old gentlemen.'

'And you were quite polite that evening.'

'I'm always polite but one's judgments are important. How did you go from considering me, not as an amusing child, but as a future wife?' she said raising one eyebrow.

'You politeness is in dispute; however, it wasn't until I saw you and Huntington floating around the dance floor that a sudden stab of jealousy made me think seriously. I discovered I was not thinking of you as an amusing child anymore but as a desirable woman.' He pulled her hand to his lips and kissed it. 'I realised just how special you were to me and then your going home spurred me to act.'

'My outspoken opinions didn't put you off?'

'No, not like poor Morley. I think he was quite taken by you but feared your confrontational character. The fact that he considered you romantically and had great affection for you, also helped me to make up my mind and even hearing of your adventures at painting china made me appreciate your character. Imagine Eleanor having to earn her own living.'

'You weren't concerned about a little confrontation?'

'I think I can keep you in order.'

'You probably won't have to try too hard,' she said squeezing his hand.

'Will you wear the ring at the hall? Morley has seen it and may recognise it.'

'I'll take it off when I arrive but not before,' she said taking her hand back.

'And when did you realise your own affection?'

'Well, I think you had always intrigued me from the first day I saw you bathed in cigar smoke in Mr Percivals library, but I have learnt in the last few months to restrict the feelings of my heart. I think I always liked you even when you were at your most annoying.'

'Just liked!'

'Yes, but that was then. My feelings have grown a little since. Love came on me rather suddenly.'

'And when was that?'

'Recently,' she said looking at the floor. Some of the floorboards needed replacing.

'How recently?'

'Well -,' She toyed with her gloves, twisting them around.

'When?'

'When you asked me if I was pleased to see you,' she looked up, her eyes twinkling mischievously.

'What! Just two days ago!'

'I'm sure it was already growing but it wasn't until you stood there leaning against our mantelshelf, asking me if I was pleased to see you, that it came home to me, just how wonderfully delighted I was. I will also be thrilled when I've served my notice and we can be together again, but now you must be upon your way; you have a long ride ahead.'

They stood, he kissed her and holding hands they walked outside where his valet waited patiently with the horses.

'Are you sure you will be alright?'

'Yes go, I'll be fine,' she said giving him a little push. His valet brought their horses over and they mounted up and with a last blown kiss, Clive rode out, leaving Anne a forlorn figure standing outside the inn. She had been used to the adventure of travelling alone but had never felt lonely before. She told herself it wasn't for long and went back inside, her mind already a jumble of wedding thoughts, scary visions of her employers expression and ideas of porcelain designs. She must do some sketches.

When Anne dismounted from the cab and entered Arleston Manor, she expected stares, questions or at least some curiosity but the servants she passed, took neither special notice or interest. So, no one had heard of her engagement. Normally gossip travelled quickly between the leisured classes. The fact that it hadn't, just showed how disconnected the society in Hereford was from the rest of England. She went straight up to the schoolroom in her coat. As she approached, while still on the landing, she heard a commotion and glimpsed the back of Mrs Percival entering the room. Putting her bag down outside her own room, she hurried on.

'What is going on?' shouted Mrs Percival. 'I can hear you in the drawing room.' Anne stopped at the doorway.

'Robert twisted my arm,' cried Edmund. Looking passed her employer, Anne could see tear-stained cheeks.

'He called me a liar,' said Robert.

'You said Miss Anne wasn't coming back.'

'Whether she is or not, we'll have no name calling. And you, Nanny, will keep order here,' said Mrs Percival but when she saw the way that the cringing subject was staring past her, she turned.

'Yes Edmund, I have returned,' said Anne as Alfred and Camilla rushed to clasp at her legs.

'And about time too. You promised a week and it is nine days,' said Mrs Percival her face red and glaring.

'My apologies but I am here now and can take charge. However later I will need to have a private word, if I may.'

'It is just not good enough, your position is to be in the school room. That is what you are paid for!'

'I appreciate that but let me see what the children have been doing while I have been away.'

'Mm, well, I will see you later, it's most unsatisfactory, quite unacceptable.'

It was going to be another interesting interview thought Anne. With the children comforted and back to work, she headed for the drawing room wanting to get it over with. She found Mrs Percival and Mrs Exton, but the Rector was also with them.

'Good afternoon rector, I hope you are well. My apologies for disturbing you and I can come back later,' said Anne with a little bow.

'Pray don't mind me as I am just leaving,' said the gentleman rising. 'I hope you are not imparting radical opinions on any young minds.'

'No sir but I do hope to teach them how to discover knowledge and true opinion for themselves.'

'Hmmm. Well, I will bid you good afternoon.'

'Yes Anne, and now you have driven the Rector away, how can I assist you or have you come to apologise for the tardiness of your return.'

'I regret that I have to give one months-notice.'

For once Mrs Percival was speechless. Her mouth appeared to be working but no sound emerged. 'This is ridiculous, absolutely ridiculous, you have only just returned,' she finally stuttered, her face reddening. 'What is your excuse for the inexcusable?'

'I will be married in six weeks' time.'

'Congratulations,' whispered Mrs Exton.

'So, you went home to meet with some previous attachment. You lied! For you told me your father needed to see you.'

'He did. It was totally unexpected. In fact, I had no idea that the gentleman had any true affection for me.'

'It was disgraceful of you to take a position if you were anticipating a proposal.'

'I can assure you none was expected.'

'Four weeks is not long enough. How can I find a suitable replacement in that time?' Look what happened last time you deserted me.'

'Robert needs to go to school. No governess should be expected to manage a boy of his age.' If only Hannah would be persuaded to come in her place but all efforts in that direction had failed.

'If this is a man from your own circle in Herefordshire, he can wait. He is, I presume?'

'He is a gentleman of standing so I cannot delay his request for an early wedding,' said Anne hoping that her employer would not enquire further. It would all come out soon enough, but not today if she could avoid it.

'It has been a great deal of trouble meeting your requirements, and now you are going. It is not to be borne,' she sighed - 'But I suppose I will have to accept it. Please make sure you have a comprehensive list of everything they have done and should be doing; not like last time.'

'I will endeavour to do so and of course, if my replacement arrives before I leave, I will be happy to spend time with her. I'd best go back to see how the boys are doing,' said Anne, turning on her heel.

'Just a minute. Who is the gentleman -?' But Anne was already through the door and had no intention of answering. 'The next governess will be of a mature age, not a silly girl.'

'I think Anne has done well with the children,' said Mrs

Exton after she had left.

'I acknowledge that, I suppose, when she is here! But at least if she goes, she will not be a competitor for our girls. It will be a relief not to have her monopolising the gentlemen.' Mrs Exton remained silent.

Anne was nearly late for dinner. The only place left was between Abigail and Mrs Exton. She sat down and mouthed her apologies to Mrs Percival.

'I thought Mr Tiverton was meant to be sitting there,' said Abigail.

'Is he here?' said Anne, looking around anxiously, a blush rising up her neck. Surely her secret must be written for all to see. She calmed herself by the reassurance that her fiancé wouldn't have changed his plans so quickly. Although his sudden arrival at her home, meant that he was capable of doing just that.

'I don't think he has returned,' said Mrs Exton. Anne stopped herself from asking further of him and fiddled with her serviette. When Abigail turned to converse with the lady on her other side, Mrs Exton leaned close to Anne.

'Do you know when he will come?' she whispered. In the buzz of conversation, the question went unheard except by Anne. She just looked into the old lady's twinkling eyes. 'It will come out soon enough,' added Mrs Exton.

'Please don't say anything.'

'Your secret is safe with me but congratulations again.'

'Thankyou. How did you guess?'

'A certain gentleman needed your address near Wales.'

'Would you like to come to the wedding,' whispered Anne.

'How would I travel there?'

'Perhaps with me in his coach.'

'Then I'd be delighted. It will be quite an adventure; it's many years since I have been further than Shrewsbury.'

Two weeks passed slowly and except for two short but affectionate letters from Clive, nothing had changed. She had written only once to his London address as she needed to take it to the post herself to avoid gossip. She mentioned that their secret remained. He was known, at first, to be in London but there had only been speculation about his whereabouts since. In his letters he had said that he would arrive in a few days but hadn't said which day. Fortunately, his handwriting was not recognised, and their secret was safe.

It was Friday evening; Anne was tired and arrived just as everyone was sitting down for dinner. A footman directed her to a chair.

'I thought Tiverton was coming tonight,' said Morley from further down the table.

'He's just arrived and is changing,' said Mr Percival.

'Excuse me,' said Anne rising, aware of the panic in her voice, 'I've forgotten something.' She ran up to the second floor and waited in the corridor where the main bedrooms were. Somebody was coming down the stairs from the third floor. It was Clive.

'There you are, I thought you might still be in the school room,' he said, rushing to her and clasping both her hands in his. He glanced around but fortunately all the servants were busy elsewhere. 'I've missed you.' He gave her a quick kiss.

'And me you, but it's been so difficult. Everybody keeps asking me whom I'm going to marry.'

'Well, we won't be able to keep it a secret now I'm here.

Someone will guess every-time I look at you.'

'Are you going to tell them tonight?'

'Yes, but I'll tell the chaps when they are having a smoke and then Percival can announce it when we re-join you.'

'That's a good plan, if we can manage dinner.'

'Have they started?'

'Yes, I'd better go in now and you can come down in a minute,' She gave him another kiss and stepped on to the stairs. Looking up she saw that Jenny was leaning on the top rail watching. Anne waved, and she waved back but as if in a trance of astonishment. Anne skipped down the stairs, grinned at the footman on the door and scurried to her seat. A bowl of soup had been served.

'I thought you would want the soup,' said Mrs Exton who was sitting opposite.

'Very thoughtful of you.'

'Is everything alright my dear.'

'Yes, thank you.'

'I thought it might be, as you are positively glowing.'

'Miss Osebury, you look remarkedly well this evening,' said Morley from further down the table. 'When are we going to meet your secret lover?'

'I don't believe she has one Morley, it's just her way of teasing us,' said Huntington.

Tiverton walked in and at Mrs Percival's instruction the butler pulled out a chair between her and Eleanor. Conversation slowed. With the faintest glance at Anne he sat, and the buzz of chatter resumed. She found it difficult to eat and couldn't help regular glances in his direction. He seemed to be busy talking to those around him but kept looking in her direction and appeared annoyed at Eleanor who was trying to interrupt his conversations, even grasping his arm to obtain his attention. Why did he keep looking at her? Would they last the meal? Should she excuse herself, claiming a headache or something? She refused a sweet and just sat, willing the meal to come to an end. Finally, the ladies rose and left the dining room. Anne found a seat in a corner of the drawing room where Mrs Exton joined her.

'It always surprises me how unobservant our fellow creatures can be,' she said.

'Sometimes it can be very convenient,' said Anne looking around with a frown of concern, fearing they might be heard.

'Yes, but even the blind eventually sees the obvious,' whispered Mrs Exton.

'Can we talk of other matters.'

'Of course, I hear that Mrs Percival has had the first reply to her advert for your position.'

'I am pleased.'

'I recommended that you assist at any interview.'

'That would be interesting.'

'Now, tell me, how are you going to have your dress made in time? And are you not missing out on all the preparations?'

'I will have two weeks and my family appear to have it all in hand.' They continued to chat quietly in the corner until Mrs Percival came over.

'Anne, would you like to read this.' The neat well written letter and testimonial suggested a competent applicant.

'The lady appears very suitable,' said Anne.

'My opinion too, however, she cannot come for another two weeks.'

The door opened and the gentlemen filed in. There was a general looking around, a searching for something, until all male eyes were on her. She slid down on her chair but then seeing Clive smile at her she tried to sit up straight; the moment had come.

'Ladies, I hope you are enjoying your coffee, please carry on,' announced Mr Percival coming to stand behind his wife. 'Tiverton here, has been withholding on us and has confessed of a clandestine involvement with our own governess. Yes, it is he who will marry our little mouse. My congratulations to you both. I hope you will both be very happy.' Every lady turned, a footman pouring coffee started to spill it and stopped, jug frozen in mid-air. Silence followed by the sounds of breath held outflowing.

Anne, now bright red, sat still and tried not to look at her employer or her daughters. Eleanor half rose and then sat abruptly. There was a sudden flow of exclamation.

'Well done, Anne,' said Mrs Exton and then much louder above the sudden buzz, 'My congratulations Mr Tiverton.' There was a general murmur of felicitations and Clive walked over to Anne, who rose, as did Mrs Exton.

'Please have my seat,' she said.

'Anne, do you wish to escape?' he said.

'Perhaps, when you have received your coffee, we could go and sit in the hall.'

'My hand Miss Anne and Tiverton you old dog, well done,' said Morley, coming over as did everyone, one by one. Strangers and so-called friends. Huntington insisted on a kiss from the future bride. Mrs Percival could be seen hovering, indecisive but she just could not do it. No happy felicitations were possible from her and with anger etching her face, she stormed out of the room's far door. Eleanor followed with a last hateful look.

Weddings can all be very similar but as most people do it only once, that's how they wanted it. Mr Rawlins came up trumps in all sorts of ways, some slightly bizarre. Roast mutton, mutton pies, mutton stew and of course venison. Anne and Clive taught everybody the waltz, Sir George kept off the wine until the speeches were over and the happy couple never argued once, but Anne had several arguments with her mother. Clive gave an amusing speech and Morley an even funnier one. Grace behaved like a lady until she went outside during the reception, tore her dress and fell in the mud. Mr Spenliff was very confident and gave a good address, but he only looked at Hannah, not at the bride and groom. Mrs Exton told everyone about the officers giving her an archway of sabres to walk under at her wedding and many more locals turned up to the wedding breakfast than had been invited. Their wedding night was at the hall, and they rose late. Coming downstairs arm in arm, Anne decided to raise a subject that she had been hoping would complete her happiness.

'I understand your rector is retiring and the living might be available?'

'Yes, he has been quite unwell, but he is nearly seventy,' said Clive.

'Would you feel free to bestow it on Mr Spenliff?'

'Why should I give him such a valuable living?'

'You know why, and well, my sister as you know isn't like me. She is graceful and charming and would make a delightful neighbour. My only concern is that you will constantly see what a poor bargain you made when you married me.'

'She is certainly your opposite?'

'Exactly. But they will be a benefit to the local society and

Mr Spenliff is a very hardworking pastor.'

'Oh yes, I'm sure, but so would be other more experienced men.'

'What like the rector near the Percival's? You should give my future brother-in-law the living because he is an excellent man. His Christianity is genuine. Isn't that enough? But if it isn't, he will marry my sister, whatever we do to try to change her mind and they will need a home.'

'Of course, and I have already talked to him.'

'Why didn't you say?'

'I wanted to see how long it took for you to suggest it.'

'Tease,' she said squeezing his arm.

'Mr and Mrs Tiverton,' announced Mrs Carpenter as they entered Arleston Manor again. Had the housekeeper come especially from her usual responsibilities to say those few words. It wasn't her normal role. She smiled at the happy couple as they went through the door. A smile of congratulations but also one of triumph, as if Anne's elevation was something for all to share in. She was pleased that her marriage was not a cause for jealousy. Mrs Exton who had returned in the coach with them, stayed in the doorway watching.

'Mr Tiverton you are very welcome,' said Mrs Percival rising, but her eyes said otherwise and through gritted teeth added, 'and Anne, delighted.' Eleanor remained seated until her mother turned with a look of reproach. Languidly she stood. Abigail however stepped forward and shook Anne's hand.

'Anne, I hope you will be very happy,'

'Thank you, I believe we will.' They all sat, and various pleasantries of no import were exchanged on fashion, weather, and travel. For one moment Anne had the wicked thought of asking the name of Eleanor's dressmaker now that she could afford it but left it as a thought to keep her amused during the small talk. After ten minutes of this, Anne was about to ask to see the children when they burst in. The younger two rushed to sit at her feet, Edmund drew up a chair and enquired after her health. An older lady and Jenny had also entered. Anne rose.

'Edmund, perhaps you could introduce me to your governess.'

He stood. 'Miss, I mean Mrs Tiverton this is our new governess Mrs Emerson, Mrs Emerson, Mrs Tiverton.' He bowed to both and sat down again.

'Very glad to meet you Mrs Emerson, I hope the children are behaving themselves?'

'They normally do,' said their governess with a worried glance at Mrs Percival.'

'Has Robert gone to a school?' said Anne.

'Yes, in Shrewsbury but he comes home every weekend,' said Edmund.

'It appears to be working well,' said Mrs Percival.

'Perhaps I may be allowed to see what the children have been doing,' said Anne rising. 'Would you be so good as to lead the way, Mrs Emerson.' With a further worried glance at her employer, she started for the door. 'As we have taken so much of your time, we shall say goodbye now Mrs Percival, and thank you for your hospitality. It really has been a pleasure.' It was the triumph that Anne had dreamed of, but she had been surprised to find that such satisfaction was not important; her own happiness had dissolved all resentment. As they climbed the stairs Anne said, 'well Mrs Emerson, I hope you are settling in, and that the family are treating you properly.'

'It's a grand house and the foundations of your teaching were very helpful.'

'Remember to stand your ground, both with the children but especially with their mother.'

After they had looked at all the children's work and Anne had shared some of the issues of teaching with her replacement, they walked out into the extensive park, hand in hand with Camilla.

Finally, they turned and looked back at the great house. 'Well Anne, time to say goodbye as we need to be on our way to the Tontine for tonight.'

'Clive, would you mind if I wrote and offered for Abigail to come and stay,' she said.

'Of course not. I agree it would be good for her to escape her mother for a while but later, we have a busy day at the works tomorrow and then to my home, or should I say ours.'

Printed in Great Britain
by Amazon

39167552R00145